# THE
# CUCKOO'S
# NEST

# THE CUCKOO'S NEST

## JAGDISH JOSHI

PARTRIDGE
A Penguin Company

**Partridge books may be ordered through booksellers or by contacting:**

Partridge India
Penguin Books India Pvt.Ltd
11, Community Centre, Panchsheel Park, New Delhi 110017
India
www.partridgepublishing.com
Phone: 000.800.10062.62

# GUWAHATI

The blast almost blew the Mitsubishi Pajero off the road. Gurung managed to bring the skidding vehicle to a stop just a few feet from the burning police Gypsy jeep. Two police officers or what remained of them were silhouette shapes in the flaming inferno of the vehicle. Peter jumped out to assist a victim who had his severed arm hanging from a mass of mangled flesh. His face was covered with blood and burned flesh hung from his torso. Peter was not sure if the person was still alive. He lifted him with Gurungs assistance and laid him on the rear seat of the Pajero. As he turned around to reach for other victims, there was another blast which flung him on to the gutter which ran alongside the road. The explosion shattered the windscreen and left a gaping hole, the size of a cricket ball on the driver's side of the Pajero. Gurung had been hit by shrapnel which left him bleeding in the upper arm. Peter pushed him into the vehicle beside the other casualty and got behind the wheel. He could barely make out the way through the crushed opaque windscreen. There were body parts all over the road and the market yard, indistinguishable from torn metal and other debris left by the blasts. It was a terrible sight and the survivors were too shocked and numb to come to the rescue of the victims. The scene of the blasts which had frozen for some moments like a picture on a hung computer monitor was slowly thawing and some activity had commenced. There were people running about and shouting all seemingly looking for someone to start the process of picking the injured and the dead. It was a terrible sight and made Peter very angry. The National Democratic Liberation Front (NDLF) terrorists had slaughtered more than a hundred innocents in the Assam valley in the last two years. This blast was definitely an act of revenge for their cadres killed by security forces in an encounter in Upper Assam recently.

Peter drove at a furious pace to the Civil Hospital which he found chaotic as usual. There was a large crowd of bystanders who had rushed here along with the relatives of the victims. With some difficulty he managed to get hold of a ward boy and secured a stretcher to carry the victim from the Pajero to the casualty ward. The ward was overflowing with the wounded and many lay bleeding on the bare floor for want of beds. The local police had occupied the Medical Officers room and were busy doing their paper work. Peter went and spoke to the officers about Gurung and the victim he had brought in. They recorded his statement and informed him that he would be summoned later to the Police Headquarters for the enquiry into the blast. Outside Peter ran into Gurung whose shrapnel wound had been stitched and dressed. He looked a bit tired and smiled weakly when Peter asked him,

"Gurung tum kaisa ho, sab theek hai na?"

Gurung had spent fifteen years in the army and had opted for retirement some years ago to look after his aging mother and his small farm in the foothills of Sikkim. But soon he had to move out and seek work as his pension was not enough. He was lucky; his army background helped him secure a drivers job with the Majuli Oil Corporation.

The salary and perks were good and he had also got a small house to stay in the campus.

Peter Collins spoke good Hindi and Assamese, having spent his childhood in Golaghat in Upper Assam where his father had been a manager in a tea estate. The family had returned to England in 1952 when he was six.

Peter, a hydro carbon specialist, had joined Majuli Oil Corporation just two years ago. He had been happy to come to Assam; Majuli was peaceful when compared to the troubled Assam Valley. The project was an important one and he had a good team of professionals to work with. The drilling operations were in progress and they had already capped five wells. The oil was ready to flow but five kilometers of pipeline had yet to be laid on the bed of the River Brahmaputra. The mighty river had posed many challenges and the task was being handled by the Gulf Oil special team from Qatar.

Peter worked and lived on the riverine island of Majuli. His own work comprised of drilling and setting up processing platforms for evacuation of gas and crude oil from the oil wells on the Island. Majuli was the home to eight hundred engineers and oil drilling specialists drawn from three continents. It was the biggest oil project in the country and was of great strategic importance to its economy. For the government it was high priority and funds flowed in effortlessly.

Gurung helped Peter to remove the shattered windscreen and clean the shards of glass from the seats and the footboards. They drove back to Majuli, with the wind blowing in their faces. Fortunately there was no rain and they reached home around midnight tired and hungry and emotionally drained out.

# PATTIYA

Anand Mehta, the Chief General Manager Majuli Oil Corporation had moved reluctantly to his new assignment in Guwahati. The Brahmaputra valley had been a scene of insurgencies through the last decade. Kidnappings, murders, extortions, bomb blasts had become the order of the day. There had been political assassinations, bank robberies, mining of highways and even an attempt at high jacking a domestic airlines flight. Peace had been restored partially with most of the ethnic groups accepting political settlement. However there were a few groups still active seeking political recognition and a homeland for their people. Presently it was the National Democratic Liberation Front (NDLF) up in arms against the state. All the insurgencies had been actively supported by militant elements in the neighboring countries which were themselves facing conflict. Gunrunning had always been a profitable trade in the region, only the clients kept changing.

Anand moved around his project sites under heavy escort of professional security guards which his company had to recruit after losing three senior managers to the NDLF violence. Brigadier Vivek Sondhi, a retired paratrooper had restored confidence in the company's staff and officers. The project work at Majuli had picked pace remarkably during the last three years; and this year the company had announced special bonus for its entire staff. The senior managers and executives had the choice of taking a holiday overseas in lieu of cash; Anand opted for a vacation to Thailand. He loved the country with its beautiful golf courses and resorts in Phuket, Pattiya and Koh Samoi. He was looking forward to getting away from Guwahati after the hectic twelve months since he joined Majuli Oil. Guwahati was boring to the extreme-with no decent clubs, hotels or cinemas. Dish TV was the only entertainment for Anand. And Sundays he would drive up to Shillong for a game of tennis with some friends.

Guwahati for Anand meant getting away from Mumbai and Asha; away from a part of his life he wished to forget. A failed marriage, separation and eventual divorcé that he was not quite reconciled with. He had discovered Thailand that year. A week's holiday in Phuket then had healed some wounds and helped him forget the bitterness of parting. And now almost one year on he was getting to like the work he was doing for Majuli Oil.

The company's main operations were in Majuli, under the supervision of Peter. Anand's job was to coordinate activities of the various projects which were connected with Majuli Oil. There were the joint ventures with Russian oil major, Petrogaaz Corporation for developing the network of pipelines and the refinery project with the Indian company, Sayadhari Oils and Gas in upper Assam. There was another refinery being built by a public sector company, Assam-Bengal Oil in the Twenty-Four Parganas district of West Bengal. The gas and oil pipelines were to traverse through Bangla Desh and the route alignments were still being negotiated between the two countries. Anand had to travel the entire region to ensure that all stake holders in the Majuli Oil were on course and there were no delays.

The consortium of companies involved had chartered two helicopters and Anand had a hectic schedule which had him hopping between Majuli, Jorhat, Kolkata and Shillong where the foreign collaborators had set up their offices for the comfort of their expat executives and technical experts.

It had been a grueling year and for Anand this vacation was a welcome break. He looked forward to a week of relaxation and some quality golf.

A sense of excitement and exhilaration overtook him as he landed at Pattiya after a brief stop-over at Bangkok. The Thai Air flight from Kolkata had been comfortable and the elegant hostess had vetted his appetite for food and flesh. He liked the country, its food, the golf courses, its pristine bays and the gentle girls in the massage parlours.

The girl at the front desk of the resort was expecting him and greeted him with a winsome smile.

"Good morning Mr. Anand, welcome to Pattiya. Your room overlooks the bay and your golf has been arranged for three p.m. Have a good holiday Mr. Anand."

Somehow the Thais related well to Indians with their mannerisms and Sanskrit names. Anand was a common name in Thailand-although it had its variations-Chayananda, Tulsananda, and Bhoominanda. The country's early history like of neighboring Cambodia and Indonesia was heavily influenced by the culture and religions of India. Hindu influence had prevailed for centauries until it gave way to Buddhism, which was introduced in the region by the decedents of Emperor Asoka and his followers. Anand was most impressed by the Thai version of the salutation *namaskar* which he discovered during his first visit. Boarding the Thai Air flight he had been greeted by the charming and very elegantly attired air hostess's 'Sawasdee khrap', hands pressed together, fingertips pointing upwards touching the face, head bowed. Later Anand thought that though it had been so similar to the way we wished our seniors back home, it was far more graceful and sincere in its welcome.

Anand called room service and ordered a beer. He was not hungry as the lunch on the flight had been substantial. He just wanted to catch some sleep before he went for his round of golf. A tankard of the wonderfully chilled liquid soothed him. He kicked off his shoes and sank deep into the cushioned rattan chair. Within minutes he was fast asleep.

# NEW DELHI

Venkat Subramanian was just six months away from retirement. As a Civil Servant with an outstanding record, he had been posted as the Union Home Secretary eighteen months ago. This was the most important assignment any civil servant could aspire for and a crucial one for him. The internal security of the country was his responsibility. He coordinated the work of all the security services and intelligence networks in the country. The Intelligence Bureau was the primary agency gathering information on political and anti-national events happening in the country. The IB was well provided with the scientific tools of investigations. They were the snoops and had their own air wing with a fleet of executive jets and a dozen helicopters which could operate from the Himalayan peaks to the islands in the Bay of Bengal and those in the Indian Ocean and the Arabian Sea. Their wireless network covered the entire country and they had the capacity to intercept communications in the neighboring countries too. Venkat also coordinated the activities of the external intelligence agency, the Research and Analysis Wing (R&AW) which was responsible for providing intelligence inputs from overseas sources and had its undercover officers in diplomatic assignments in Embassies around the world.

It had been a seven day a week and eighteen hours a day job for Venkat. His physical being had become part of the majestic Burma teak paneled walls of his spacious room, the teak desk and the somewhat rickety swill chair that he sat on. That chair had sat more than a dozen of his illustrious predecessors who had seen history being made in the sub-continent.

Venkat peered out of the window of the Cessna 525 as it winged over Ashoka Hotel and straightened up for its approach to land at Safdarjung airfield. For some unknown reason the Palam ATC Control had diverted his flight to this small airfield in the center of Lutyens New Delhi, which was largely used by the Delhi Flying Club for training pilots. The pilot had no choice and had complied with the instructions; whatever the reason for the diversion, it seemed pre-arranged. Safdarjung Airport, rarely operational after sunset, was a picture of activity. The runway lights were on and the control tower manned guiding his aircraft to land. There were a number of vehicles waiting on the tarmac, their red lights flashing.

The pilot taxied towards the terminal. Venkat's car was on the tarmac and so was his assistant Beni Babu, tightly clutching the blue leather courier bag to his chest as if fending of the cold December wind, as it swept across the asphalt tarmac.

"Good evening Sir, some important messages," he said handing over the courier bag.

"The PMO had called, Sir. The Prime Minister desires a meeting with you and Secretary R&AW urgently. I was advised to tell you to drive over to the South Block as soon as you arrive. Secretary R&AW has sent you the papers in the courier bag with an executive summary for the meeting. He will meet you at the PM's office."

Venkat glanced at the clock on the dashboard. It was 9.50 pm. He would again be very late for dinner; Chitra he knew would understand. Thirty years of married life had made her extremely tolerant of his irregular hours. She had found solace in the performing arts. A student of Guru Mohapatra in her school days she had taken up dancing again after her graduation and marriage and was now a recognised exponent of Kuchipudi. With Venkat's help she had travelled far and wide to the Americas, Europe and the Far East with the cultural troupes of the ICCR (Indian Council for Cultural Relations). She had had the singular honour of dancing before a session of the UN General Assembly. They'd had their share of difficult times. But the birth of their daughter almost ten years into marriage had delighted them no end. Suhasni was a lovely child with Chitra's doe like eyes, deep black hair and a radiant smile. She had been a bright student and like Venkat a record holder in History. She had won the Commonwealth Scholarship and had left for Cambridge last fall.

Venkat reached for his mobile and rang home. Chitra was not in; she was away at her guruji's place in Bharati Nagar choreographing her new dance drama. She had been requested by the Ministry of Culture to produce the inaugural programs for the cultural week organised for the Golden Jubilee of India's Republic Day. The Queen of England and the President of South Africa were to be the principal guests on the occasion. For Chitra this assignment was most challenging of all and she had been working night and day on the script and the musical score. The entire production involved a bevy of, musicians, dress designers and recording technicians. The event was barely a month away and the work seemed never ending. The dress designers had done an appalling job and the costumes had to be redesigned. The sound recordists were a bunch of young lads with over developed libidos, constantly chasing the attractive girls of the Kathak troupe from Ahmadabad. Chitra had quite a time getting things in place. Of one thing she was sure; the musical score would be brilliant, produced as it was by the famous *Vadya Vrinda* orchestra of the All India Radio.

The Executive Summary of the document "Majuli Dossier" in the courier case was alarming and sent Venkat's blood pressure racing. The NDLF in Assam had established new links with the Pakistani Inter-Services Intelligence (ISI). The R&AW agent in Chiang Mai had confirmed contacts of the NDLF cadres with the ISI agents in Myanmar and Bangladesh. This was going to be tricky—the ISI had already played havoc in Punjab, Rajasthan and Mumbai. Now it was getting into the northeast in an attempt to poison its fragile political and economic system. Its contact with the NDLF could jeopardise oil-drilling and processing operations in Majuli, besides aggravating the insurgency. Majuli had been in the news ever since Schulmberger's confirmed large reserves of oil and gas, much larger than all the existing ones in the country put together, perhaps the largest discovered in recent times anywhere around the world.

The river Brahmaputra, the life line of the Assam valley, had ravaged the region for hundreds of years. Mammoth floods each year wiped acres of crops besides destroying homes and taking its toll of lives. But the river was also the life of the people and the region. Civilizations had inhabited its shores and it had been the land and later the kingdom of the Ahoms for centuries. The region had evolved its own culture and tradition and was known as the land of the beautiful people. Now with the recent discovery of hydrocarbons below its basins the Brahmaputra seemed to have blessed the people with oil, promising jobs and prosperity. The government had accorded the project high priority and committed large resources for its development.

Venkat called Saxena on his mobile. He had great respect for the R&AW chief and valued his advice and views. He was the archetypal IPS officer and had made his way to the top by pleasing his political masters. However, in the matter of organizational abilities for gathering intelligence and processing it, Saxena had few peers. He had done his rounds of assignments and postings in Geneva and Paris. But it was the assignments in Myanmar and Islamabad in the mid eighties that put him on the trail of the ISI's nefarious plans for the country. The ISI had devised plans for the North East states too and had trained its agents in Bangladesh to disrupt their fragile economy and frustrate the efforts of the Central Government to introduce democratic institutions among the local tribal groups. Saxena had found his life's mission in the challenge posed by the ISI. He had succeeded in wiping out sixteen ISI inspired spy outfits in Jammu and Kashmir and Rajasthan and had personally apprehended four ISI agents in Mumbai in 1994 and secured their prosecution in the famous RDX smuggling case. He had also vetted and authenticated the Majuli document that Venkat had received in the courier case at the airport.

Saxena had his best officers assigned to the Asian region as India was surrounded by trouble spots on all its borders. Besides the training camps of the ISI sponsored Jihadis across the Western borders in Jammu and Kashmir, Punjab and Rajasthan, there were the Tamil Tigers waging a civil war in the Northern Provinces of Sri Lanka and its agents roamed freely in the southern state of Tamil Nadu gathering funds and sympathy for its movement. Then there were the Karen and other ethnic rebel groups in Myanmar literally administering the northern half of that country bordering the north eastern states of India. These rebels had provided logistic support to drug smugglers in the Golden Triangle region of Myanmar, Thailand and Cambodia in the past and were now into smuggling armaments for the Tamil Tigers in Sri Lanka and the rebel groups in the Assam Valley. The hill tribes in the Chittagong region of Bangladesh were another unruly lot; brutalized by the local administration and their farms destroyed, they had taken up smuggling of drugs and arms for survival. They were the group now identified in the Majuli dossier as providing shelter and logistic support to the NDLF foot soldiers and the Naga rebels. The Maoists movement in Nepal was of recent origin and there were indications that they were providing weapons to the radical Naxal and Maoist outfits in West Bengal, Bihar and Orissa.

Saxena had been waiting for Venkat's call. They exchanged notes on the Majuli document and talked for long on other connected issues that the PM would definitely raise during their meeting. There had been some ugly incidents in the Kashmir valley, and Human Rights Groups were pointing their fingers at the army and the border security force. There had been major demonstrations in Jammu, New Delhi, Mumbai and Shimla and effigies of the Pakistani PM had been torched at these places. Pressure was building up on the PM to do something. The policy of the Government had been termed as cowardly. The Pakistanis were not making his task any easier in managing the difficult problems facing the country. They seemed determined to carry on the proxy war through their agents and provoke India to attack. The attacks on the Hindu pilgrims on visit to the Lord Shiva's shrine of Amarnath had become an annual feature. There had been terror strikes on temples in Jammu, Punjab and Gujarat. The hit and run tactics of the ISI sponsored terror outfits had no other objective but to provoke a war. All attempts by the PM to engage their leaders in a dialogue had been unsuccessful so far.

The PM was waiting for them in his South Block office. He was his usual relaxed self but the tension was palpable and the burden of pressure came through as he spoke.

"This Majuli matter is serious. We have to nip it in the bud. The NDLF should not fall into the trap of the ISI. We will have no choice but to go to war if Majuli is sabotaged. We need not think of military solutions only to wean away the NDLF. We should seriously consider opening a political dialogue. I know," he added nodding at Venkat, who wanted to speak, "that our Assam Chief Minister Hemu Gogoi would oppose it tooth and nail. He has his political compulsions. But so do I. My compulsions are those of the nations. I want to end the campaigns of the last of the fragmented ethnic groups seeking political solutions to their problems. We cannot encourage these groups to further subdivide the people. We have in the past accepted language as the basis for state-hood. We cannot accept any other criterion now. It will open a Pandora's Box. Gogoi did not handle the NDLF adequately when they started their students' agitation. He could have given three or four seats to them in the last State Assembly elections. But he was adamant. I told him-'A*arre baba*' include them in your government. Make their leader Purkait a minister of state in the cabinet and the whole movement

14

will collapse. He will disappear into his district after the swearing in ceremony, driving around in the official car with the red-beacon flashing. The District Superintendent of Police will call on him at the State Guest House, and Purkait will get bowled over by the salute he gets. The police security and pilot jeep will further add to his status and satiate his political ego and pride. But Hemu did not listen, and look what has happened. He has driven the NDLF into the open arms of the enemy."

"Sir, I agree that we may try the political route. I will tackle Mr. Gogoi. We have enough material on him. He too has been running a profitable business of smuggling drugs out of Myanmar. The US Federal Drug Administration has traced some consignments, and laundering of drug money to a Cayman Islands bank. The whole operation would have to done in a discreet manner. The NDLF are extremely suspicious of our efforts to woo them. Saxena has closely studied their operations and also talked to some of their second line operatives."

"I strongly suggest that we use some of the corporate entities hard pressed by the NDLF activities to ferret out information from their NDLF contacts, on this reported nexus with the ISI. Sir, you are aware that the NDLF is collecting almost Rs.100 crores annually as protection money from the tea gardens and plantation owners. None of them will admit it but they are all paying. We had registered some cases against a couple of tea estates, but had to withdraw them later and look the other way. It is impossible to provide security to all the estates in that region. So we had to take a softer line. Even the CM felt it necessary to leave the estates alone and let them take care of themselves. In this process of buying protection some of their executives and managers have established good contacts with the NDLF leadership. Some payments have been arranged in foreign currency too and Bangkok and Chiang Mai have become the favourite cities for such contacts and negotiations."

Saxena paused for the PM's response, but he got a gentle nod to carry on.

"Extracting information from the NDLF cadres is a dangerous business but an intelligent and a trained agent could always get plenty out of their foot soldiers and soft contacts. There are a number of contacts of the NDLF in Bangkok and Dhaka and all negotiations for release of hostages are conducted through them. We have kept tabs on a number of tea garden and Majuli Oil executives who were making frequent trips to Bangkok and Dhaka as tourists and on business. Of late Dhaka is not easily accessible. It has tightened the visa regulations for Indian visitors, on our advice to filter out the undesirables. We could definitely use some of the corporate houses to dig out information with their contacts in Thailand. We only need your blessings for the mission, sir," added Saxena with a special emphasis on 'blessings.'

"We can put it into operation right away."

"Secondly, once contacts are developed an exercise on confidence building could help to bring them to the conference table. I don't say it can be done but I feel it is possible. At any rate the options available to us are limited. We have to somehow stall the ISI from getting a foothold in the valley."

The PM gave a wry smile. The idea of bringing the rebels into the mainstream was an old exercise. It had succeeded in the past with various warring factions and groups in the North Eastern region. These groups had also enjoyed the support of our unfriendly neighbours and had slowly but surely been won over, and joined the democratic process and formed Governments through the ballot.

The PM looked quite relieved.

"Do take all care and keep Gogoi in good humour. We want his support for the coming bye-elections to the Parliament. He should be on our side. As to his drug operations I shall have no truck. You may alert the narcotic squads and confiscate all the consignments. His network can be smashed without his name figuring in the reports. Please ensure all secrecy to this assignment. Put your best boys on it."

"We will be discreet, sir. There will be no instructions in writing and all reporting will be through briefing every Monday at your residence. No other aide will be present. Maximum security grading will be assigned and sir," Saxena turned towards Venkat, "R&AW will have the final control over the operation. We therefore will not inform the IB and the State government for the present."

The PM slipped his feet into his sandals and made a move to get up. His arthritis was again troubling him and he leaned heavily on his black ebony walking stick as Venkat extended his hand to assist him.

"Please do all that is possible, Venkat. We cannot afford to go to war at present. I am deeply worried."

It was past mid-night and a strong cold breeze was sweeping across Raisina Hill when Venkat and Saxena stepped out of South Block. The temperature was around ten degrees Celsius and that was cold for Delhi.

"Let's meet in my office at 6 pm tomorrow. This Majuli threat has to be met head on. The Rawalpindi Express will have to be derailed properly this time." Venkat winked at Saxena referring to the ISI headquarters.

"We have put our boys there on alert. They are prepared to go any length but we have limited our covert actions short of drawing blood. They had hinted that they are in position to blast the engine if we give the signal." Saxena responded by referring to the chief of the ISI.

"That project will not be approved for the present by the political set up you know. We will have to minimize its potential for mischief for the time being. Good night Saxena. We can sleep on the problem tonight and do some serious thinking tomorrow." Venkat waived him good night as he stepped into the warm interior of his car.

Ronny, his boxer welcomed him as he got out of the car. He had become a big dog at six and was unabashedly devoted to him. Chitra had no love for dogs and she just about tolerated Ronny. Ronny of course would be his frisky self with her around and insist on laying his head on her lap. She would leave it at that as any attempt to pet him and stroke him would result in Ronny jumping on her and licking her face and drooling all over, which she detested. Venkat sat down beside Ronny and played with him for while. He had returned home after two days and Ronny had missed him. Boxers like cats loved to be petted. And Ronny loved the attention he got from Venkat. He would sit with him on the sofa and get into his bed every night. Chitra would always tease him and call Ronny his mistress. Chitra was asleep when he got in. She had had a tiring day and turned in early. She stirred awake as he entered the room. It was her intuition; she always seemed to sense his presence. They chatted for long on the day's events as Venkat snuggled closer. He found her aroused with desire.

# PATTIYA

**A**nand stirred out of bed and reached for his watch. Time had lost all meaning for him. He had fallen asleep in the afternoon and didn't remember when Sreesati left him. He had met her on the golf course during his last visit to Pattiya. Alone, she had asked if she could join in; they had a good round and she played well. She was a senior executive with a travel agency in Bangkok but spent most of her time in the Pattiya office of the company. This time he informed her of his Pattiya vacation and enquired if she'd be available for a round of golf if she happened to be in town. To his surprise she had fixed up the tee time and met him punctually at three at the club. She knew the course well and they had a pleasant game. She looked happy and had enjoyed his company. Later, inviting her for a drink at the hotel, she had warmed up to his conversation. A visit to the spa led to a passionate finale as their well oiled bodies skidded on the floor in wild abandon and passion. The afternoon's lovemaking had left him wanting her more. It had been a very soothing experience.

It was almost nine when Anand stepped into the shower and scrubbed the remnants of the oil from the afternoon's massage. The smell of musk from Sreesati's body seemed to rise in the steam as the hot water flowed over his body. Anand put on his jogging suit and walking shoes and stepped out of his hotel to explore Pattiya on foot. There was a gentle breeze and the waterfront was crowded with tourists from around the world. The street vendors were busy offering their replicated souvenirs with great panache—genuine fake Rolex and Piaget watches, duplicate Chinese software and computer notebooks and what have you. The sleaze joints were busy and the girls spilt over to the foot paths, promising the exotic and the erotic. Anand walked the entire waterfront. The breeze was cool and the sky covered with a myriad of stars. It reminded him of Shillong where the clear nights made the stars so bright.

He had momentarily forgotten Sreesati and their passionate love making that afternoon. He thought of his work and made mental notes of various matters that required his immediate attention. He also decided to send a few e-mails to his deputy and review the progress of the project. He knew it was crazy to be thinking of work on vacation. But Anand could never be away from his work for long. At least he expected to be kept informed as to what was going on. Such was his nature. He had followed the straight and narrow path and rarely attempted to slip into the dark and winding corridors of the unknown world. Of late the growing aggression and militancy of the NDLF had worried him. The police had been totally ineffective. He had picked up enough gossip at the Planters Club about the protection racket being run by the local terrorists and the payoffs made by the tea companies. His company too had paid large sums to buy peace but had lately changed its policy. Majuli Oil had engaged the services of a professional security agency and had launched joint security operations with the Army and the State Police. It had worked so far but there had been threats and also a few aborted attempts at ambush. There was always tension in the air when one was traveling. He remembered the sealed confidential envelop he had been given by Brig. Sondhi with instructions to carry on all trips out of the country, especially to Bangladesh and Thailand. The seals were to be broken and the packet opened only on instructions from the head office in Mumbai. He had been trained like the others to handle weapons but had refused to carry one personally.

He came across a seafood café and decided to have his dinner there. These were real good places to eat, the food was always fresh and delicious. He had come to like Thai food and preferred it to Continental and the Chinese cuisine. The waiter came and took his order and Anand fell into a reverie staring into his glass of beer. He thoughtlessly chewed through his dinner, his mind far away from food and Pattiya. He trudged back to the hotel but could not get to sleep. He worked late into the night reading the reports on his project and redrafting some others he was writing. He wrote to his boss in Mumbai requesting for funds for the project and to his deputy for some information. His mind was still in Guwahati. Somehow getting away from the place didn't really help. He had a nagging fear of the unknown. The place did conjure up fears and paranoia.

# KANDY

Pradeep Menon drove up from Colombo into Kandy on Saturday afternoon after a hectic business trip to Johannesburg and Mauritius. He had been away from Mumbai for a whole week and now he was here to attend his company's board meeting fixed next Tuesday. His grandmother had been busy preparing for his visit. She had picked up jumbo prawns, mackerel and catfish and had wild boar meat from the Estate. There was nothing as sublime as her wild boar curry served with string hoppers. Pradeep loved to get away from Mumbai on his trips home for work and to look her up. She had refused to leave Kandy and move to Mumbai after Pradeep set up his office there. He had implored her often but she was adamant and refused to budge. At eighty five she was in the pink of health and ran the large bungalow like a sergeant major. Pradeep had always seen a bevy of servants from the gardener to the maids and the cooks since his childhood. She had retained them all and would supervise them from morning till evening.

As expected she had laid out a big lunch for him. She sat there and saw to it he had extra helpings of all she had made for him. No amount of protests from Pradeep would stop her from plying him with more. She gave him all the local news, regaled him with gossip and brought him up to date on the social events in Kandy. She also updated him about her friends and how their families were doing. The source of all the information was her Mahjong group which met every Friday and Saturday without fail. Pradeep knew she was busy but he worried about her. There had been veiled threats in the past from the Liberation Tigers of Tamil Elam (LTTE) group, but he had ignored them. The family had refused all demands for financial assistance for the cause of Tamil Elam in the past. The threats had become a little strident of late. So Pradeep got a shock when she mentioned that some persons were calling regularly on telephone and enquiring about him.

# MUMBAI

Saxena had got closely associated with Mumbai's law and order issues in the last decade or so. The events of 1992-93 that saw Mumbai plunge into a communal frenzy and shame the city for the mindless violence which killed, maimed and battered its citizens had far reaching effects. The city had in the past witnessed communal tensions in some localities over the cricket and hockey matches played between India and Pakistan. There would be lots of excitement when the rival teams met and the community would get divided on communal lines in certain vulnerable pockets of the old city. The outcome of the match would see an eruption of celebrations with fireworks and processions often leading to minor incidents of violence.

But all this was mere routine as the riot of 1992-93 were to showcase in the coming years the power of violence the mafia lords of Mumbai were capable of inflicting on this hapless city. The riots provoked a massive retaliation from the Mumbai mafia and their agent provocateurs, the ISI. Using the smuggling conduits they managed to land large consignments of deadly RDX explosives on the costal district of Alibagh and transported the same to Mumbai using their network in the city. The explosives were then packed into stolen motorcars and scooters and strategically parked in prominent locations. The resulting blasts had killed and injured hundreds of citizens. The city fortunately had held its peace after the blasts and the people refused to be traumatized or provoked to more violence as retaliation. That day the city's spirit was born; 'Salaam Mumbai' was the slogan coined for the forbearance shown by its citizens.

Saxena had been pulled out of Islamabad where he was posted as station officer and ordered to proceed to Mumbai to investigate the bomb-blasts case as it had links to external agencies. His assignment in Islamabad and information he and his boys had gathered about the involvement of the ISI had proved of immense value in the investigations. He had interrogated some of the suspects after the local police had questioned them using their usual methods. The experience of the interrogations of the suspects had only confirmed his beliefs further that intellectual approach was more productive to one that relied on physical torture alone. His methods had succeeded and he had been able to crack the case and round up the suspects available in the country. Of course the kingpins had fled on the night of the blasts and were living abroad, taking advantage of the extradition laws and the antagonistic attitude of the local governments. The Mumbai episode had left a trail of rancor and a sense of betrayal. Saxena always had a sense of unease when he thought of Mumbai. He somehow had a feeling that the city was only enjoying a temporary truce and preparations were always afoot for the next round of mayhem. The carefree and fun loving attitude of the people and their capacity to savor every moment of their lives masked the eternal fear in their hearts and the anxiety they felt every time they stepped out on the streets or took a ride on the local metro. He had always taken keen interest in the reports prepared by the IB and the Commissioner of Police on the prevailing law and order situation in the city. The reports from the CP generally highlighted the activities of the various mafia gangs or the labour unrest in city's industrial hubs. Saxena could easily identify the patterns of violence with their major objectives. While the killing of an influential and prosperous builder appeared to be a case of extortion to the local police, Saxena saw a more serious and sinister pattern emerging.

He was therefore least surprised when Venkat called and informed him about a computer diskette accidentally discovered by the Enforcement Directorate in a raid carried out in a Mumbai film producer's house. The ED, which specialised in deciphering coded data stored in computers, had some difficulty in opening the storage device. They detained Brij Kishen, the film producer for further questioning and the senior ED official in charge of the case carried the diskette home. He handed over the diskette to his son studying computer technology to see if he could open the files. The young lad took just five hours to open the folders and files in the diskette which the boys in the ED had failed to do in seven days. The officer panicked on seeing the printouts and had taken the next flight to New Delhi to hand over the papers and the diskette to his Director General. The DG too found the material too hot for comfort. He spoke to the Home Secretary and then walked over to his office in the adjoining corridor. Venkat had one look at the material and swore the DG to silence.

"You never saw this document and you never heard about the diskette. We will cover this up. A substitute will be provided to avoid any suspicion in your office at Mumbai. The young boy's computer requires to be taken care of lest some data is saved on the hard disc. You will close the case against Brij Kishen after putting him through the normal grilling. We will also send a word to the Mumbai Film Producers Guild to make some noises on the harassment by the ED staff; the newspapers will pick up the story and build up a campaign. I'll ask the Minister to make a conciliatory statement that the ED would harass no innocent person. I am calling Saxena over to do the damage control exercise and investigate the matter further."

The next day a senior official from the R&AW headquarters visited the Assistant Director's house and gained entrance carrying an identity card of a local computer-servicing agency. He removed the offending hard disc from the computer and replaced it with a new one. The Assistant Directors office had a busy day as the film producer's advocate served notice of a writ of 'habeas corpus'. The Ministers office called to say that the Chief Minister was upset and that the producer should be released after quick interrogation. Brij Kishen was the recipient of the Presidents Award for the best film three years ago and was a respectable citizen of Mumbai. The DG Enforcement Directorate also called to enquire if the damage control exercise was proceeding as discussed. Later that afternoon the office bearers of the Mumbai Film Producers Guild called on him for early release of Brij Kishen. He had a tough day answering telephones, and meeting office bearers of various associations. Two technical operatives from the R&AW with the cover ID cards of Accounts Officers from the Accountant Generals office had occupied the anteroom and had grilled Brij Kishen for almost eighteen hours. They had dug out some useful information in the last two days since their arrival.

Brij Kishen, it appeared had engaged Vijaya Choudhry a chartered accountant as a financial consultant on retainer ship basis to help him with his business accounts two years ago. She was a partner in Kabali and Talati, a firm of Chartered Accountants. Besides being a competent accountant she was young and attractive. She had over the years become a confidant of Brij and was privy to all his financial transactions. Like many other film producers in Mumbai, Brij had borrowed money in the past from some mafia overlords. The money had been plentiful and the low rates of interest had cushioned him from some initial failures. Both parties had managed to legitmise their black money and Brij had so far managed to keep his nose clean. However, after the bomb blasts incident of the mid-nineties, the Mumbai mafia was on the run and all their money laundering activities, including financing the film industry had come under the watchful eyes of the Revenue Intelligence Wing of the Enforcement Directorate. In the new environment Vijaya helped Brij Kishen to raise funds for his films by borrowing from professional money lenders in the diamond and the bullion trade. Most of these transactions were in cash and involved the collection and delivery of money by the *angadias,* traditional couriers used by diamond and other traders. The lenders were in Mumbai, Pune, Bangalore, Ahmadabad and Surat and New Delhi. However to give semblance of propriety forty percent of the borrowings was through cheques.

Vijaya kept a track of all these transactions and arranged funds for a number of projects which were concurrently in progress. She was in regular contact with the page three celebrities and had to ensure that no financial hiccups occurred in the production schedules of various films. There were *mahurat* ceremonies to be attended for launch of new film projects and promos to be organised for the release of completed ones. BK had backed some good directors and the films had been box office hits. There had been many awards and gala nights and life had been very hectic with premiers and cocktails. Vijaya had taken all this in her stride. Being the key person of B.K. Enterprise she was generally addressed as Vijayaji by the directors and the stars. With the growing success of B.K. Enterprises, Vijaya prospered with the special bonuses which Brij Kishen showered with each successful venture. He had recently gifted Vijaya a four bedroom apartment in up market Lokhandwala where she had half a dozen film stars as her neighbours.

Vijaya had long hours of work. She had to attend Brij Kishen's office as well oversee the work related to her own firm where she was a partner. The firm had a long list of corporate entities as its clients. She had a hectic schedule managing two enterprises. The work at B.K. Enterprises was, however, of a different nature. She had a small staff in Brij Kishen's office, and all cash transactions were handled by BK's trusted family retainer, Kailash Agnihotri who was addressed as munshiji. He interacted with the *angadias* and moved the money around. Every morning she would get his hand written vouchers regarding the cash received, repaid and expenses of the various projects in hand. All cheques for repayment of loans were put up for Brij's signature and Vijaya would take entries of all transactions into her laptop and give one printout to BK for his information. Thus by noon everyday BK had a picture of the borrowings, repayments and money committed to projects. All the daily reports with the statements in Excel format were maintained in small diskettes of which BK maintained one copy and a duplicate was with Vijaya. BK kept the diskettes locked up in a small safe, hidden behind the wooden paneling in his study.

The cash transactions rarely got reflected in the business accounts of B.K. Enterprises. These formed roughly thirty five percent of his overall turn over. His borrowings in cash and by cheques formed fifty percent of his investments. The rest of the money came from his company's reserve funds. Vijaya had done a wonderful job of reducing his external borrowings to half in just three years of their association. But she had to work very hard in preparing the accounts and ensuring maximum integrity of the annual financial statements. She had a knack of presenting figures and had kept the Income Tax Authorities away. Of course she had taken care of some half a dozen senior officers loading them with expensive Diwali gifts every year, as was the customary practice.

The cash transactions of B.K. Enterprises required reconciliation every three months and she conducted these personally by visiting Surat, Ahmadabad and New Delhi. The Mumbai borrowings were reconciled at meetings at Khandala. These trips were all shown as the official trips of her firm. There were corporate clients who would fix board meetings there or at the nearby Ambay Valley Resort. She would accordingly arrange meetings with her auditors from Kabali and Talati to prepare and approve their reports. The reconciliations of BK's borrowings would also be arranged during these trips. She would have lenders representatives come to her hotel and they would carry out the audit work at the business center. At times the lenders would bring the information on diskettes and the same would be exchanged by way of confirmation of the accounts. The arrangement had worked very well so far.

It was during one of her trips to Khandala that Vijaya came into contact with Pradeep Menon of Lloyds Financial Services Private Limited. B.K. Enterprises had recently borrowed a big sum from this new venture capital fund for a block buster under production. Vijaya had as usual checked in at the Hotel Hilltop when she got a message that Pradeep Menon was waiting for her in the Coffee Shop. She joined him there and was surprised by his youthful good looks. The business was over in an hour but Vijaya was so captivated by Pradeep that she could not say no to his invitation for dinner.

He came around later in the evening and picked her up. They drove down towards Pune on the old highway. The evening was beautiful and starlit and the weather, a cool balmy Sayadhari spring. They stopped at a roadside Garden Café and ordered some kebabs and biryani for dinner. The conversation soon turned from financial management and money to curious personal details as Vijaya opened up to Pradeep's gregarious personality. Pradeep it transpired had done his schooling in Kandy, Sri Lanka where the family owned tea estates and had later studied at Corpus Christi College, Oxford. He had opted for a Mathematics Tripos and after graduation joined the Barclays Bank in London where he worked as an investment banker for almost ten years. The Menon family had migrated from Kerala in the days of the erstwhile Rajas of Travancore at the beginning of the last century and had acquired and developed tea estates in the Nuwara Eliya Highlands. He had lost his father while at Oxford; his mother had passed away while he was still at school and he had been brought up by his grandmother, whom he loved dearly. He had given up his job in London and started his new venture capital fund in Mumbai after the death of his father, only to be near her.

He was a bachelor and travelled frequently to Sri Lanka to manage his tea and resort company. They drove back towards Khandala after the dinner but somewhere on the way Pradeep stopped the car. Vijaya could feel a sense of exhilaration and before she knew Pradeep had taken her in his arms and their lips met.

# PATTIYA

**A**nand was booked for his round of golf at 8.00AM. He had breakfast called to his room and logged on his computer to check out his mail. There was a long message from his assistant, Sarma. He had annexed half a dozen pie charts and other graphics with the status reports on his projects. He ran through the reports and scanned the mail. There was one from his MD, Balaraman, which informed him that there had been some delay in the renovation work to his office and the bungalow at Guwahati. He accordingly advised Anand to stay on in Pattiya for another ten days. Anand was quite confused; he had made no plans for the renovations of either his office or the bungalow. In fact there was no renovation required. He scrolled the message back and forth but found no further explanation. He had no desire to extend his vacation and was keen to get back once it was over. He typed out a message to his MD seeking further information on the renovations and expressing his surprise that the same were being carried out without his prior knowledge. He also discussed his project and requested for additional funds for some activities. He concluded by describing the beautiful golf course he had been playing in and urged Bala to take a holiday and play here sometimes. Balaraman was himself a golf addict and spent the better part of the day at the Bombay Presidency Golf Course at Chembur.

Sreesati had gone off to Bangkok to attend meetings at the head office so he was on his own today. He took the hotel limousine to the golf course around 7.45 AM. There wasn't much of a crowd and he ran into an American tourist at the pro shop and they made a twosome for the round. Bob Anderson, it turned out worked for a bank in Chicago and was holidaying with his wife and teenaged daughter. As his wife had no love for golf, she and the daughter had flown down to Phuket for some scuba diving. They teed off into the strong wind from the Gulf of Thailand and progressed through the course. In the first nine Anand led Bob by three holes but Bob slowly caught up and they ended the round, even. Later over a beer Bob expressed his surprise at the popularity golf was gaining in India. He hadn't been to India and couldn't control his excitement at the thought of playing golf in the land of elephants and snake charmers. Bob was a typical middle class American, having spent a lifetime in America's mid-west. He had worked in Milwaukee and Minnesota. Now at the senior corporate level he had moved to Chicago. He took little interest in what happened beyond his immediate surroundings and couldn't be bothered whether the elephants in India were in the zoo or they ran around loose through cities and towns. Anand felt it was futile to argue and educate such a person. He was good company for golf; and Anand decided to keep it that way.

The business of the renovation of his house and office was still niggling him. His MD's offer to stay on at Pattiya for another ten days would require more distraction than golf and Sreesati. There were four e-mails waiting for him when he got back. The first was his MD's. He was asked to standby at Pattiya for some important instructions. To start with, Gopal Reddy of Hindustan Exports would contact him. He had some proposals which had the approvals from the head office. Anand was to negotiate further details of the proposals with him. Some documents would be dispatched by courier soon and he should have them in a day or two. He had complete freedom to discuss the proposals with Gopal and he could make his travel plans as he felt necessary. Anand worked on his reports and replies through the afternoon. The round of golf with Bob had been relaxing, but the messages and reports in the emails of late had challenged his patience.

The situation was getting more confusing by the day. Bala had totally lost his sanity, Anand grumbled. He had no business and inclination to negotiate and wheel-deal for his company bosses, he argued with himself. His roles with Majuli Oil Corporation were clearly defined. But Balas recent exhortations were beyond his line of duty. He went through the other messages. These were replies on his queries from his assistant. His head was in a tizzy. His disciplined mind would not find it easy to unscramble all these unexpected developments. He was not a person who could handle emergencies. His reaction and recovery systems were very slow. Anand shut the laptop and walked out of his room. He was feeling tired, thirsty and hungry all at the same time. He walked into the bar and ordered a beer and carried it to a cozy overstuffed sofa overlooking the bay. The beer was fresh and chilled and it had a soothing effect on his troubled mind. He let his thoughts drift. There were another extra ten days gifted by Bala, at the company's expense. He might as well enjoy them. He closed his eyes and emptied out his mind of all the mundane thoughts of Guwahati and his work. By the time he ordered his second beer and some lunch he was approaching a state of ennui. He felt he was floating on the cirrus cumulus that he had sighted an hour ago over the Gulf of Thailand and he couldn't be bothered where it took him. It took him quite a while to realise that he was not alone. He could make out the hazy presence of a smart young Asian dressed in grey trousers and a Christian Dior navy blue blazer with a disarming friendly smile in the rattan chair opposite his.

"Good evening Mr. Anand. I am Gopal Reddy. I think you were expecting me. I have been trying to page you half the day. Good to see you relaxed after a round of golf. I can imagine you are enjoying your vacation."

Anand put his hand out mechanically and half raised himself to reciprocate Gopal's greetings. He was trying to focus his thoughts and remember the instructions he had received from Bala in the morning's mail. He was also trying to size up this smart fellow who had disturbed his state of peace and tranquility. The waiter came and took Gopal's order and Anand asked for another beer. They got talking about inflation and the rising price of crude oil and its impact on the developing economies. By the time their meal arrived they had established a good rapport and Anand found Gopal a likeable person. Gopal had till then studiously avoided talking business. Anand, anyhow, had no clue what it was all about. The papers promised by Bala on the proposals of Hindustan Exports had yet to arrive. The discussions drifted on to the serious law and order situation in some parts of the country and the rise in the number of terrorist outfits in the states in the eastern region. Anand was to later recall the subtlety with which Gopal had turned to this subject and the seemingly accurate detail he possessed about the terrorist organisations. They talked till late in the afternoon and decided to carry on the discussion over a round of golf the next morning.

# MUMBAI

The information deciphered by the R&AW from the diskette was placed in a file named the B.K. Dossier. R&AW found it difficult to believe initially that BK was involved with the terrorists and radical organisations across the border. There were many theories doing the rounds on the case. The Enforcement Department raids in BK's house had been the routine outcome of the normal paging of black money floating around in the film industry by the Revenue Intelligence Wing. The mystery diskette recovered in the raid in BK's office was a real bonus for the R&AW. They had had some information on the subject but nothing conclusive had been reported till now. The B.K. Dossier had changed all that. The information emerging out of the dossier was further classified with the security rating 'FOR YOUR EYES ONLY' category. This category classification was on those documents and dossiers that were made available to only seven persons in the Government. These were the PM, Cabinet Secretary, Home Secretary, the Chief of R&AW, the Director of IB, the Defense Secretary and the Chief of Staff of the Armed Forces. The document could not be read by any other person, not even the Personal Secretary to the Prime Minister, who enjoyed the same protocol as the Cabinet Secretary. With the FYEO classification on the dossier, Saxena had succeeded in isolating the Enforcement

Departments case and getting Brij Kishen off the hook. However he kept him a virtual prisoner in a safe house in Mumbai. There was real and imminent danger to him and all his office staff who were involved in the financial affairs of his company. Saxena had advised the Mumbai Police Commissioner to provide personal security cover to all senior officials of B.K.Enterprises.

Saxena was not abandoning the various theories regarding the origin of the diskette but he somehow felt that Brij Kishen was innocent. Film production had always been a risk prone activity and money was difficult to come by as banks and financial institutions were reluctant to lend to the industry. Money lenders played an important role and over the years black money had found its way into the film business. Black money had long been associated with smuggling activities of the mafia overlords and Mumbai was the epicenter of their operations in the country. The pre reform economy of import controls and exchange regulations had been the fertile ground on which the activities had prospered. Economic reforms had changed the situation dramatically and action against the mafia after the bomb blasts conspiracy had driven the criminal mafia overseas. However black money continued to grow due to weak tax administration and found illegal trade channels to be moved out to tax havens in Mauritius, the Cayman Islands and St Kitts. He had a nagging suspicion on Vijaya's role in the organization as its financial consultant. She appeared to be too smart and clever managing the crores which were funding B.K.Enterprises projects.

Vijaya had been away to Ahmadabad when the ED raid took place, but had rushed back when she got the news. She had sat for hours with the ED investigators and made available all the pen drives, files and diskettes. She had cooperated with all the officers and had impressed them with her intelligence and knowledge of the laws and regulations. However, the discovery of the B.K. Dossier diskette had totally turned the case on its head. Saxena had moved with utmost speed and diligence to cover up the raid and its aftermath and insure that all information was hushed up and nothing leaked to the media. The ED wound up their operations and withdrew their staff with utmost speed and Brij Kishen attended the gala dinner that evening for the premier of his new film 'Chandani Raat'. All rumours and stories of the ED raid were dispelled by Brij Kishen personally handling the media seniors who had come to enjoy the good booze and food. Vijaya was her charming self and deftly handled the anchors from the news channels. All rumours of house arrests were dispelled when Vijaya invited some of the media persons to Khandala the next day for an outing with the main stars of the new picture. They were visiting the Ambay Valley Resort for some promo shots of the film and would return after a days stay.

# AMBAY VALLEY

The whole complex was abuzz with activity when Vijaya arrived there early morning from Mumbai. She checked into her room and went around the complex reviewing the arrangements. She had scheduled her meetings at the resort and was also to attend a board meeting in the afternoon. She had requested Pradeep to come over and had booked a room for him too. They had not met for almost a month now after their brief holiday at the Jim Corbett National Park. Later they had driven up to Nainital. It had been an exhilarating visit away from the blistering heat in the plains. The hills were cool and lovely in May. Pradeep had been an excellent companion and she felt happy with him. She had been very lonely ever since she lost her mother to cancer three years ago. Her work had kept her too busy to develop any social relationships or seek companionship. Pradeep had arrived into her lonely world and filled the emotional void.

BK and his production team were busy organizing the promo shots with the stars for the media. Vijaya took a round of the locations and promised BK that she would meet them later over lunch. She got busy with her work and sat the whole forenoon at the business centre reconciling accounts and auditing books of the financiers. Pradeep called up to say that he'd reach at the resort by seven, and they decided to meet for dinner at the Four

Seasons bistro. She had her last visitor around noon and she was free after that to join the party. She dropped by at her cottage for a quick shower and change before joining the luncheon. The party was well attended and BK had popped enough champagne to ensure good press for his new release. Their reviews meant so much for success at the box office. Vijaya joined in the celebrations and ran straight into Sushma Reddy.

"Hi gorgeous," she charged into Vijaya, clutching her in a tight embrace and pecking flippantly on her cheeks. Vijaya managed to wriggle out of squeeze and held her by her hands.

"Sushma, unbelievable! What have you done to yourself? You are looking younger by years," she flattered Sushma to counter her. Sushma was the biggest gossip amongst the Bollywood reporters and had spread stories about her affairs with BK in the past. She had to be kept humoured but at arms length. She was good at spreading tales about the young starlets and their affairs with the stars. She had been thrashed by a stars wife for spreading wild stories about her husband's affairs. But she was incorrigible. A Botox job had done wonders to her face and she'd also lost a couple of kilos. The low cut blouse she wore displayed her ample bosom and her tightly draped sari showed off her voluptuous curves. Her kohl rimmed eyes flitted across the room, and she was soon sailing behind a screen of cigarette smoke to accost a rising star, fleetingly complimenting Vijaya for the lovely party.

Vijaya moved around meeting the guests and the media teams covering the event with BK who looked happy with the guests and regaled them with tales from Bollywood studios. She stayed on at the venue till 4.00 pm and then retired to her room after seeing off last of the invitees.

She completed her audit reports and posted all the past months transactions on the excel sheet. She felt exhausted by the time the last of the reports was saved and the laptop switched off. She fell asleep on the sofa and woke up only when Pradeep called her around 7 pm.

# NEW DELHI

Saxena had planned his strategy well to investigate the case. Like a good chess player he was covering his flanks and planning his offensive against General Ashraf Khan, the mendacious and scheming head of the ISI. After the Mumbai bombings, it had become Saxenas mission to counter Ashrafs every move and take the battle of counter terrorism to the land of the pure. He had already moved Gopal Reddy from Geneva to Bangkok to follow up on the Majuli dossier. Now he wanted more information dug out on the financial transactions revealed in the B.K. Dossier. He called up Raj Singh, station officer in Tehran and advised him to proceed to Mumbai as soon as possible. Raj was familiar with Mumbai's film industry; he had a few years ago investigated leads in the Mumbai blasts case to certain stars and starlets who were frequent visitors to the cricket championships held at Sharjha. He'd found them cozying up to mafia dons involved in anti-national activities. His investigations had also led him to couple of film financiers who brokered deals of the mafia lords holed up in the Gulf region. They had fixed up some deals for BK in the past. Brij Kishen had survived arrest and prosecution by the skin of his teeth then. It was primarily due to the secrecy and clandestine nature of the havala operations which kept no document on the transactions. The Internal Revenue Service and the

ED had, of late, found no fault with BK's accounts. These were well maintained and he had been given a clean chit. Vijaya Choudhry who looked after his financial matters was after all a competent Chartered Accountant. She was described as an independent woman and single in the case papers; nothing was known about her family background. The cyber cell in the headquarters had tried to hack her laptop to get more information and personal details but did not get beyond what was already known.

Raj spent the next five days after reaching Mumbai, studying Vijaya's official and private life. She appeared to be a fascinating personality, intelligent, smart and very suave. She had been successful in her profession and lived very well. Investigating such cases meant getting close to the suspects, their accomplices, their family members and anyone else who may be known to them, including the milkman, the news paper vendor, the housemaid and the chauffeur. In Vijaya's case, her association with Bollywood had naturally elevated her to a glamorous lifestyle and her single status, was the envy of snooping neighbours' nagging curiosity. Raj had been very discreet and careful in his investigations. At the end of the week he had little to associate her with any criminal misdemeanor. Vijaya emerged as an intelligent, practical, reticent, and a very busy person. She spent all her Sundays taking care of the household chores. She was described by casual acquaintances as charming and well groomed. There was no information available on her family background, her parents and their profession, the place she was born, the school she attended and the college she graduated from. She seemed to have no relations in the city and rarely enjoyed festival holidays. To Raj it appeared the most intriguing facet of her personality, as people usually visited their home towns and close relatives during these breaks. He also drew a blank when he checked up with the Regional Passport Offices in all the principal cities and towns. No passport had been issued in her name. Vijaya remained an enigma but Raj seemed to have developed a strange fascination for her.

Raj now planned to meet her but was equally keen to meet Saxena and get some leads on the B.K. Dossier case. He had been away to Tehran for the last two years and wanted to be briefed on the security environment. It was necessary to clear the picture and get briefed by the boss himself. Saxena was always full of ideas. He discussed and suggested lines on which investigations could proceed. He never kept anything to himself and shared his thoughts, hunches and intuitions with his officers. He never let them feel lost and would pop up every now and then like a Jack in the Box to guide them if they strayed the course in pursuing the leads. He maintained a constant presence and was involved in all the important investigations and operations. Saxena had an uncanny sixth sense always to lead you somewhere near the truth of the matter. It was as if he knew all the answers but played games with his officers and showed them only a glimpse of what the truth was. He would always appreciate it if you could fill in the blanks and complete the picture.

Raj spoke to Saxena and took an early morning flight to Delhi. There was little traffic on the road and he could reach Lodhi Road by nine. Saxena was already in his office and after a round of coffee he took Raj over the case history of the B.K. Dossier. He briefly referred to the havala transactions that were discovered during the Mumbai bomb blasts conspiracy investigations. Funds for the purchase of RDX were arranged by the Karachi based D Company. The RDX had been procured with the help of the ISI from arms dealers in Yemen and transferred by smugglers of Omani origin to an isolated coastal village in Alibagh district, which had a history of gold and silver smuggling. The local fishermen who had been the beneficiaries in the past, were duped into believing that the consignments contained cameras and watches. The presence of some conniving customs inspectors and local police from the coastal check post also assisted the transportation of the RDX to Mumbai. The same pattern appeared to be emerging in the B.K. Dossier investigations. The preliminary findings of the Enforcement Directorate revealed the elaborate care taken to camouflage the transfers of cash by superimposing on the normal borrowings by BK for his movie projects. This could only be done by an insider who was involved with the borrowing arrangements and also maintained the accounts. It was a clever act of manipulation of accounts where the receipts of these funds and their disbursements were carried out under directions of an external agent. The funds were merely parked in B.K. Enterprises to disguise their real intent. The details of these funds were, however, maintained in separate files under fictitious headings to show their utilization for funding film productions. The finger of suspicion thus was squarely on Vijaya Choudhry who was the key person handling finance and accounts matters for B.K. Enterprises.

"I have the nagging fear that the General's boys across the western borders are planning something big. We have to get to the bottom of the money trails in both directions. We have hit pay dirt as far as the disbursements are concerned-but it's only the tip of the ice-berg. We must apprehend the recipients of the fund and stop them from putting their project into operation. Gopal Reddy is already in Bangkok and he will assist Ravi Karan in Chiang Mai to neutralize the ISI plans on Majuli. We have to ensure that the NDLF does not fall for the trap laid for it by the ISI. We also plan to involve the corporate sector and build on their contacts with the NDLF to wean away a section of their cadres which are falling for the bait and are enjoying the hospitality of the ISI agents in Bangkok and Dhaka. So our task in Mumbai is going to be to unravel the B.K. Dossier further and get the Anti Terrorist Squad of the Mumbai Police to chase the local operators down and smash the cells being set up for the new terror plot. So best of luck Raj; I am sure you will crack the conundrum of the B.K. Dossier. Get Vijaya to reveal the hidden source of funds she has been manipulating since the last one year. Now with the diskettes in our possession she stands exposed. But be careful, she may not know much about the source of funds and its application. She may be just one small pawn acting out of coercion or blackmail. I am somewhat confused as I cannot see her in the role of a spy or an enemy agent. I cannot decide on her at the moment and that was just the reason I got you over from Tehran to get to the bottom of this money trail."

# MUMBAI

**R**aj took a flight back the same evening and headed home. It was well past eleven when he got back to his apartment in Bandra. He put the kettle to boil and plugged in his laptop. He opened the B.K. Dossier and scrolled down a few pages. The kettle was whistling, so he got up and poured hot water into a mug adding two bags of Lapsang Souchong. He loved the smoky flavour of the tea and had picked up some cartons at the duty free the day he took the flight out of Tehran. He sat and worked till late at night. The cryptographers at the RAW headquarters had applied various known permutations of the cipher techniques used by the ISI operatives. The one used in the B.K. Dossier appeared a unique one with its own key and perhaps a simpler mode of encryption for the benefit of the persons using the data. Raj gave up after a few attempts as fatigue overwhelmed him and he turned in.

The next day Raj was to meet with Satish Sharma, Joint Commissioner of Police, Crime Branch, Mumbai to follow up on the B.K. Dossier investigations. He got to office early as usual and put together a set of papers relevant to the B.K. Dossier case for Satish Sharma. He was about to step out of the office when Saxena called. He sounded agitated, which was rare.

"Raj have you seen the afternoon tabloids. Some Vijaya Choudhry was found brutally murdered in her room in a

Khandala Hotel this morning. I am shocked if she is the same person who was under our scanner. Can you get more details?"

Saxena was livid. He had advised the Mumbai Police Commissioner to provide security for her and the other staff. He would speak to him after he got the confirmations on the identity of the victim. Raj rushed down the six floors of the stairs without waiting for the creaky old lift to show up. The tabloid he picked up on his way to the Mumbai Police Headquarters confirmed Saxena's information on the brutality and torture. The Mid Day Mail headlines read,

## "Vijaya Choudhry of B K Films Murdered"

It appeared to be the handiwork of a mafia outfit. They must have pressed her for some information and she had paid with her life in her attempts to maintain her silence. What she had revealed, and revealed she must have, would have grave consequences on the others involved in the havala case. He was immediately concerned about Brij Kishen. If the BK dossier was the source of worry to Vijaya's killers then others faced similar threats. And Brij Kishen was certainly a marked man now. He and his family had already been moved to a safe house maintained by the R&AW on Napean Sea Road. His security would have to be upgraded now.

The office of the Joint Commissioner of Police, Mumbai located in the Police Commissioners Headquarters at the Crawford Market junction is housed in an old heritage building. Satish was waiting when Raj entered; a mug of hot coffee materialised even as he sat down. Satish had a mischievous smile on his face. They had been old buddies from the Police Academy days and had kept in touch over the last twenty years. Satish had spent most of his time in Mumbai while Raj had done his stint of district assignments in the Punjab, the Border Security Force and then moved on to the R&AW.

"So, Raj still charming girls, a dead one this time."

Satish teased him as Raj took a sip of the heavily sweetened coffee. Police canteen tea and coffee tasted the same countrywide. Raj wondered if it had something to do with the common mess all police officers shared at the police academy.

"Have you any special reason Raj to follow up on this Mata Hari. I was surprised when I learnt that R&AW had taken over the case from the ED. To me it appeared to be a case of laundering of drug money with implications of *havala* type of transactions," Satish opined.

"We have placed Bhonsle, our Senior Inspector of Crime Branch on this case. He is very experienced and is already probing various leads."

Raj pushed the folder he had prepared on the case towards Satish.

"This will give you some idea what we are probing. It's the very tip of the proverbial iceberg. Satish, this is some thing big, very big. That's why we got involved. The cover for the investigations is going to be the Enforcement Directorate's enquires into the *havala* racket. We are looking far beyond the money transfers from abroad. This is a security investigation with countrywide implications, maybe a terrorist plot. We have to proceed cautiously. We will have to show low key investigations and keep all information under wraps. There will be no press briefings without our clearance. Your local Police Station has already alerted the press. Some damage control will be required.

Make it look like a case of an estranged husband or a paramour involved in the murder. This line always goes down well with the crime reporters. Crimes of passion they call them. There is always an impotent jealous husband at the other end who can't do his home work and drives the poor wife to somebody else's arms. You tell your man to look for diaries, computer diskettes and if possible a computer notebook or a laptop."

Satish picked up the intercom and passed on some instructions to his officers. He agreed with Raj that this was a serious matter. He had been posted as Deputy Commissioner in the city when the ISI inspired blasts had rocked Mumbai and killed hundreds of innocent men and women. He himself had lost a dear friend in the blast near the Stock Exchange. Thousands others had been injured and many had lost a limb or two and had become handicapped for life. One senior Inspector in his district had gone stone deaf while patrolling on the Dalal Street. Fortunately, the impact of the blast had been absorbed by his jeep.

# PATTIYA

Anand had a pleasant round of golf with Gopal. He enjoyed the game and his company even more. Gopal had studied in Bangalore and Singapore and thereafter work had taken him to Holland, Geneva, Islamabad and Colombo. He had been a good sportsman in his student days and had played hockey and tennis. Later he had become an exercise freak and also picked up judo and was a black belt at Karate. They had lunch at the Club grill and decided to meet again the next day.

Anand was quite tired by the time he got back to his room. The afternoon sun made him drowsy. He lay back on the sofa and tried to remember all Gopal had said. He had done most of the talking and Anand had found his stories of travel quite engaging. Gopal seemed to have lived an adventurous life. Anand wondered what had brought him to Bangkok. The documents promised by Bala had still not arrived and Gopal had also not raised the matter he had wanted to discus. Anand decided to ask Gopal about the proposals he had for Majuli Oil Corporation, when they met next.

# NEW DELHI

**V**enkat had flown down to Guwahati in the R&AW Bombardier jet one Sunday morning and had a discreet meeting with the Chief Minister, Hemu Gogoi. No aides or officials were present. In fact no body in the town knew of Venkat's presence and his meeting with Gogoi. Venkat briefed Gogoi on the ISI contacts with the NDLF. He gave the names of the NDLF commanders who had made contacts with the ISI operatives in Bangkok and Dhaka. He also had voice recordings of telephonic conversations of various operatives of NDLF in contact with some ISI agents in Guwahati and Kolkata. Venkat also gave details of money transfers and drug and narcotics smuggling from Myanmar in which Gogoi's involvement figured. He then briefed the Chief Minster about the exposure of the Majuli Oil project to terrorist's threats financed and sponsored by the ISI. The NDLF's political activities he asserted were a camouflage to serious anti-national activities and it was actually guilty of treason. The NDLF was in fact planning to wage war against the State with guidance and support of the ISI. The nation could not tolerate such activities and these had to stop.

Venkat emphasized that the Prime Minister was very anguished that a political ally like Gogoi was close to the NDLF and supporting and protecting their arms and narcotics activities. He had therefore come down from

Delhi on this secret mission to convey the PM's concern. Gogoi was livid. He was in total denial mode. Using the choicest expletives against the NDLF leadership and operatives, he refused to accept any of the accusations of his involvement in drugs and arms smuggling. He however agreed to take strong measures to curb the NDLF activities.

Venkat flew back in the afternoon and met the PM in the evening. He also briefed him about the security measures taken to counter the terrorist activities in the Kashmir Valley. The army had also stepped up their vigil and deployed a Special Forces group to search and destroy the terror outfits. The Human Rights Watch was again stepping up their campaign against the police and the army operations. He had briefed his press adviser to counter all media campaigns by such groups.

The sun was setting over the Raisina Hill when Venkat drove out of the PM's villa. He realized that it was already 7.00 pm and he had promised Chitra that he would attend her Dance and Music Festival at the Siri Fort Auditorium. He gave instructions to the driver and sank deep into the plush upholstery of his Ambassador to catch some sleep. He had been up since four in the morning and was quite exhausted. He made it to Siri Fort in good time and enjoyed the concert. Chitra was most surprised to see him in the audience. She also felt sorry for him. He had hardly slept in past week and it was telling on his health now. Just the other day Dr. Bhattacharya, Venkat's physician had dropped by to chat and had warned him not to miss his medical check up. She would speak to him when they got home. He caught up with her in the lounge after the concert. Both were too exhausted by the day's events to talk and merely exchanged glances and smiles as if to say, 'Okay I know you are tired!'

There were many messages on the answering machine, but Venkat scrolled through to access the one from Suhasni. She had called from New York, where she had taken up studying Journalism at Columbia University after completing her graduation from Cambridge. Venkat looked at his watch and dialed her mobile number. She was just heading for her class when Venkat's call came through. She was her excitable self and said that she had just called to say hello and find if all was well. She hadn't called home last week and was worried. That was Suhasni. Always worried about her father and ensuring that he was well and eating on time. She had seen him come home past mid-night many a day, carrying back his lunch uneaten. This was usual when one meeting would spill over to another. Mondays were always the busiest of days when the Cabinet Secretary had his coordination and review meetings. Venkat had to take care of the subjects relating to the Intelligence Bureau, RAW and deployment of Special Forces. Security of the VVIP's was also a tricky affair with the terrorists gunning for them. The meetings would go through the forenoon into the better part of the afternoon, with endless rounds of tea, coffee and sandwiches. There was no time to eat a proper lunch and every Monday evening Suhasni would question him about what the Cabinet Secretary had served for lunch. That was the standard joke and he was at the mercy of these two women at home. She was a happy child and Venkat and Chitra had showered all their love on her. She was never lonely and the two had spent quality time with her as she grew up through school and college. Now she wanted to discuss something important, and said she would call back later in the evening after her classes. That left the two guessing as to what was so important to Suhasni that had to be discussed at leisure and not in a hurry.

# MUMBAI

Raj was heading home from the Police Commissioners office when Bunty called. They had not met for long and Bunty wanted him over at his place for dinner on Saturday evening.

'Whose birthday is it this time Bunty?' Raj enquired grinning into the mobile.

Bunty was a gay bachelor with a clutch of lady friends. He made it a point to celebrate each ones birthday when all others also got invited. They were very jealous of each other, but Bunty gave them a level playing field. He had retired some years ago after working for a Dutch multi national firm. He had gone to Cambridge to study and his folks were hopeful he would join the Indian Civil Service, but Bunty had taken a more than a friendly interest in the English girls, and spent his time pub hopping and pursuing the fair sex. He was a bright student though, and despite all his gallivanting stood first in his BSc class. These were the post war years and companies in England and Europe were recruiting talented young graduates for leveraging their businesses after the war time slump. Bunty got picked by Dutch Vulcan Tecnic which had interest in plantations and food processing. He worked from Amsterdam for almost a decade and when the company decided to set up office in Mumbai, Bunty was the natural choice to head it. On retirement Bunty received a handsome gratuity and pension and the lease of the company's flat on Malabar Hill was transferred to his name.

Raj made a mental note of Bunty's invitation and turned in early. The running around in the city and the pressure of the case had left him exhausted. The B.K. Dossier case and now the brutal murder of Vijaya Choudhry were important investigations. Saxena wanted an early closure of investigations as terrorist plots were suspected in the havala transactions revealed in the B.K. Dossier. He was a worried man and Raj knew he would have no respite till some results were achieved. Vijaya was the one person who perhaps had the most exhaustive information on the source of funds. Vijaya's brutal murder had only sharpened Saxena's suspicion of the high level of motivation and commitment on part of the conspirators. This appeared to him to be a major plot and the ISI and its proxies were busy building up their resources to strike.

# NEW DELHI

**V**enkat's mobile rang at six in the morning. It was Saxena and he had bad news, real bad news. The terrorists had struck at the Majuli Project. Peter Collins, the General Manager was missing. His Pajero was found abandoned around five thirty in the morning within the campus of Majuli Oil. His mobile and satellite phone were also missing and were not responding to calls made by the security staff. Peter Collins normally moved around Majuli with his personal security guard. The mobile security patrol which found his abandoned vehicle alerted the control room to check why it was parked on the road side. Pritam Singh his driver was located in his barrack but he had no idea how the Pajero got there. The camp hostel sentry, where Peter had his quarters, revealed that the vehicle had been driven out by Peter himself. As Peter had not entered the drilling site area any time that morning Brig Sondhi, the chief of security at Majuli Oil was alerted. An immediate search was carried out of the entire project area and also outside the perimeter fence of the Majuli Oil Camp site. There was no sign of Peter. The concertina barbed wire fence had not been breached any where. There had been no arrivals and departures at the main gate since midnight except the water tanker which supplied potable drinking water to the school outside the Majuli Campus. It had checked out of the security gate around 5.30 AM as it usually did everyday. Peter seemed to have disappeared into the thin air or he was still some where in the Camp premises. An alert was sounded and search parties fanned out in all directions. All residential premises of the staff, the labour camp, the canteens, the store rooms, warehouses, containers, and vehicles were checked. Brig. Sondhi was at his wits end. Peter could not have moved out of the camp as there was only one entry and exit gate; except the water tanker which supplied water to the school, there had been no other recorded movement there. He had interrogated the sentries on duty and a check on the CCTV records revealed no other movement since the midnight. The gate had been locked after the alert was sounded and the project area had been put under quarantine, by Brig. Sondhi. The District Police had been alerted and border check posts were monitoring all vehicular movement closely.

Venkat's enquiries with his wireless listening post at Guwahati revealed unusual activity in the early hours of the morning. The monitoring unit had also picked up signals of at least four satellite phones. The data was being deciphered with the help of service providers. It was possible that the kidnap might have some external inputs. The operatives in Bangladesh had been put on the alert by Saxena.

Venkat was shocked. Peter Collins was a leading expert on hydro-carbons and had been with Majuli Oil for the last two years. His abduction was a major set back for the Project. Venkat had a quick shower and called a car from his office. He called Saxena and requested him to come over to his office within an hour. They had to move fast and strike the enemy before he made his next move. Venkat also called the Foreign Secretary Suresh Baijal and broke the news to him. Baijal had received no information from his own sources and was happy that he had been alerted. The British Foreign Office in London it appeared was still in the dark as MI 5 had not yet got a wind of the kidnap. Baijal called Surendra Tyagi, the Indian High Commissioner in London, and informed him of Peter Collins disappearance. As nobody had claimed responsibility for the disappearance of the oil expert, it could not be classified as a kidnap, as yet. However Baijal advised Tyagi to play it low key till further information was available. He could inform the Foreign Office in Whitehall that Collins was missing and that the Government was concerned and trying to locate him.

# MAJULI

**B**rig. Sondhi had been up since he was alerted around six in the morning. He had briefed his staff and put the security drill into action; he then got to his office to consult the Majuli Security Manual to ensure that the Standard Operating Procedure was being followed. He also wanted to refresh his information about Majuli. He was sure that Peter was somewhere on the Island itself. The River Patrol Unit had been checking all boats moving in and out of the Island since the morning. The Kamlabari Ferry Point was closed down and all traffic to the mainland was shut. Sondhi switched on the digital screen in the control room and the bright green and mauve map of Majuli Island lit up the room. He had gone over the map on many occasions during briefing of his staff, the local police and the army officers of the Eastern Command headquarters who were part of the security plan drafted for safe guarding Majuli. The plan had been meticulously prepared and took care of any threats that could be faced by Majuli Oil. The armed chopper gunship and the jet speed boats had been alerted and were combing every inch of the emerald island and the river. His attention was drawn to the notes extracted from the Google site by his secretary on the geomorphology of Majuli Island and the surrounding region. He had read the notes umpteen times in the last two months. He had become very familiar with the geography of this eighty kilometer long fascinating island. He had also closely studied the ecology of the entire nine hundred square kilometers of its area.

Sondhi knew the local people well. Majuli was the home to the colourful Mishing tribe whose main occupation was agriculture. They were fun loving simple folks and there was no history of crime or militancy on the island. Majuli was also a center of Vaishnavite sect of the Hindus and had sixteen *satras* or monasteries-several of which were set up in the sixteenth century and had become the centre of Assam's music and dance. Some mischievous elements from the mainland had in the past attempted to misguide and exploit the locals but had been driven off the island. The last ten years had been peaceful and the discovery of oil had further improved the economic wellbeing of Majuli's residents. Majuli Oil had provided jobs to the youngsters, built schools and dispensaries for the islanders and contributed to substantial improvement in the quality of life of the people. Peter Collins was a popular figure on the island and was always the chief guest for various cultural functions. He had taken personal interest in making football a popular game amongst the students and now Majuli also boasted of a local soccer club, the Majuli Tigers.

Peter was very much at home in Majuli. He was born at Golaghat, the heart of the tea growing country, where his father had been a manager at a tea estate. He had been to school at Darjeeling. But then the family had moved back to London after the country became independent, when he was twelve. He had very fond memories of his childhood and readily accepted to come to Majuli when the project was started. Peter was always moving around Majuli and Sondhi was least surprised when he learnt that Peter had left his quarters at five in the morning and driven off on his own. It was nothing new for Peter to answer any call of distress or help from the project families or the islanders. It must have been something important. Captain Gogoi his Deputy was already scanning all call logs on the wireless and the Cell phone companies had been alerted. The Superintendent of Police Jorhat was also following the investigations by the state police and crime branch. The Intelligence Bureau (IB) had got the satellite phone logs and was deciphering the data. Sondhi decided to head for Kamlabari and meet the local police officers who had called the village headmen to find out if they had heard anything or seen anybody suspicious in their area the previous evening and early this morning.

# PATTIYA

The phone must have been ringing for sometime. Anand was fast asleep; the strong afternoon sun on the golf course had left him feeling groggy. By the time he stirred awake there was furtive knocking on his door. It was the front office manager with a relieved look on her face. "Sir your phone has been ringing for twenty minutes. There were urgent calls from New Delhi and Mumbai."

He picked up the phone and heard Bala's secretary at the other end.

"Sorry to disturb you sir, this is urgent. Just hold on sir."

He could hear Balaraman, speaking on the other line. He could catch words 'international incident, security considerations, yes sir, yes sir . . . sir . . . sir thank you sir'. Balaraman was talking to some senior officer in the Government. He sounded worried and at the same time excited. He came on the line and just blurted out that Peter Collins was missing since early morning. There was a major alert in the Assam Valley. Mr. Venkat Subramanian, the Home Secretary had just called and informed him that Interpol had also been alerted. Balaraman was trying to speak too fast and was sounding confused. He was trying to get lot of information off his chest.

Anand interrupted him.

"Sir, it is not wise to speak more over the phone. Phones may be tapped and we may give away information to the enemy."

He heard Bala murmur in agreement and disconnect the phone.

For the first time the word enemy sounded real. He had never used it in such a context before. He realized that he was sweating and felt a weak sensation in his knees. He reached for the bottle of whisky lying on the side board and took a swig. The warm mellow liquid left a trail of fire down his throat but he felt a little better. He took another one and then poured a large shot into a tumbler and added some ice; he enjoyed the libation better now. He peeled off his clothes, got under the shower and turned on the shower to full blast. He let the cold water flow over his body and revive him out of the stupor of sleep. He felt refreshed and his head cleared off the fog of confusion which the afternoon's siesta and Balaramans blabbering had induced. He wrapped himself in a towel and carried his drink to the terrace and slumped down on the cushioned rattan sofa.

His eyes were fixed on the horizon at the far end of the Gulf of Thailand. He started thinking of all the events that had happened since he had joined his new assignment at Guwahati, the Head Office of the Majuli Project. He especially remembered Brig. Sondhi and the security drill that had been conducted by him when he first visited Majuli. He had felt assured then that nothing could go wrong with the layers of security cordons and network of agencies involved in protecting this valuable asset of the nation. And now Peter Collins was missing. He had met Peter only a couple of times but had come to admire and respect him. Peter was a professional to the core, but unlike other professionals of the oil industry, he was soft and gentle. Anand had met many teams of professionals assigned to the various drilling sites on Majuli. Most of them were the archetypal hard drinking, foul mouthed oilmen. But Peter was a gentleman. He had last met Peter at the Golaghat Tea Estate manager's bungalow, where they were guests for lunch just a week before he took his vacation. Peter, visiting his old house where he had been born and spent his childhood, had been ecstatic then and spoke for long about his father's encounters with the wild elephants and rhinos. He remembered the servants in the house then, some of whom had taught him many secrets of the forest. He had grown up acquiring a lifelong love for the jungle and open spaces. The successive residents of the bungalow had preserved dozens of sepia prints of the Collins family. Peter's family had renovated and enlarged the old bungalow during their twenty years stay at Golaghat. They had left everything behind—the furniture, the books, the hunting trophies and the photographs when they left India in 1952 for England.

It had been a pleasant afternoon and Peter had spoken for long. The food had been excellent and there was plenty of gin and tonic to go around. Peter took his work very seriously and had worked day and night developing the oil wells of the project. He had taken just one break from his work since joining and that too was for just five days to visit his family in London. The people of Majuli owed so much to Peter and Anand hoped that he was well and still alive.

Anand almost jumped out of the chair when the phone rang again. He had become edgy and nervous after he learnt of Peters disappearance.

The front desk had called to say that Gopal was on his way up. Anand unlatched the door. They settled down on the terrace. Anand had yet to receive the documents Balaraman wanted him to discuss with Gopal. He was completely in the dark about the matter and now with Peter Collins missing he had lost interest in Gopal. He wanted to establish a safe contact with Balaraman to discuss the Collins matter further and inform him of his plans to return to Guwahati. He did not know where to begin. He was still in a state of shock and wanted to be alone. Gopal's arrival had disturbed him no end. He got up to refill his glass and go to the wash room. When he got back on the terrace, he found Gopal speaking on a satellite phone. As he stepped nearer Gopal extended the phone to Anand.

"It's Balaraman for you."

Balaraman was more composed now.

"Listen carefully; I agree we could not have spoken on the Collins matter over the normal channels. I therefore asked Gopal Reddy to meet you. We will use his satellite phone to discuss this matter and other related issues for which Gopal was advised to contact you. Gopal's business interest in Thailand is a cover for his real operations. He is a senior officer of the R&AW. He was advised to make your acquaintance as the Government wants our help to uncover the nexus between the NDLF and the ISI backed terrorists who have targeted the Majuli project. We had agreed to reveal our NDLF contacts to R&AW in order to counter the ISI agents in the Assam valley. The matter was very sensitive and required our support as in the past we had brokered peace with the NDLF to safeguard our people. We had paid protection money to their agents in Thailand and thus survived attacks. The NDLF desperately wanted money to carry on their activities and the Government also winked at and approved our actions as it gave R&AW an insight into the ISI networking in Assam. Gopal will explain everything. This operation has the approvals at the very top echelons of the Government. No funds will be spared. But be careful. Go by Gopal's advice. The operation can get messy. Even the Thai mafia has been roped in by the ISI. We will not talk more. Gopal will keep you informed about the Collins investigations. You can now open the sealed envelop given to you by Brig. Sondhi and share that information with Gopal. The envelope contains information on our NDLF contacts in Thailand. We had used these contacts to negotiate release of our executives kidnapped by them. There are some Myanmar rebels too who can be contacted in Chiang Mai. You are now part of Gopal's team. Get Collins back safe and take care."

He almost sounded like M, the legendary creation of Ian Fleming in the Bond novels

# MUMBAI

Raj reached Bunty's place on the Malabar hill around ten. Bunty's parties always went way past midnight. As usual Raj had his dinner at home before driving to Bunty's residence. He rarely ate outside his home, and was especially wary of food supplied by the caterers. The party was in full swing and as expected there were more women than men. Bunty was happy to see Raj and fixed him his drink. They chatted for a while and then Ratna came along. She was the youngest of the guests and a total stranger to Bunty's usual group. At least Raj had not met her before. She was in her mid thirties, Raj guessed. They hit it off well, and by the time dinner got served around midnight Raj had learnt that Ratna had worked for years with Gulf Air and after taking early retirement had joined a major hotel chain as their senior executive for guest relations. They left the party together and Raj offered to drop her at her Worli apartment on his way to Bandra. Ratna invited him over for a coffee. She had a small one bedroom apartment on the terrace of the building with a great view of the city. She had done a good job furnishing it. Raj was always impressed with people who kept a good house. As a bachelor he was always looking around for antique furniture to add to his collection. He was charmed by the carved antique sideboard and a matching bar in her lounge. He complimented her on the selection and suggested they should do a round of the C*hor Bazaar* together. They chatted for a while about their work and then out of the blue she asked him if he had any contacts in the police department. Raj was totally unprepared for the enquiry but asked her what the problem was. To his utter surprise Ratna wanted to have some information on the Vijaya Choudhry murder case. Why Vijaya? She turned out to be an old friend. Ratna knew more about Vijaya than what Raj had found out in the last four days of investigations. She also knew Pradeep, and had met him with Vijaya some months ago. After her murder she had called him on his mobile but got no response; a recorded message from the service provider informed that it was switched off. This was a major lead for Raj and he needled her for more information. Ratna was a little circumspect to begin with but soon got persuaded to reveal more. Pradeep it appeared was from Sri Lanka and had worked as an investment banker in London before becoming a partner with a venture capital fund in Mumbai just over a year ago.

"Pradeep is a lovely person and I was very happy when he got steady with Vijaya. I was hoping that they would settle down. Vijaya was a very lonely person with no close relatives in the city. She required a steady relationship and companionship, which only marriage could bring. Pradeep had become very attached to Vijaya. He had once told me that he was planning to inform his grandma of his intentions of marrying Vijaya. Pradeep had set up his finance company in Mumbai in partnership with Marwari investment bankers to bring in foreign funds for investment from Mauritius. He had also arranged funds for B.K. Enterprises through his company and thus got acquainted with Vijaya."

Raj took Pradeep's local address and phone numbers from Ratna before he left her place.

# PATTIYA

L ate in the evening after Gopal left, Anand received a phone and the caller identified himself as a friend of Majuli Oil. He expressed surprise at the abduction of Peter Collins and claimed that he had some information on who was behind it. He said he could help him to locate Peter and they should meet soon. He also advised him not to approach the local police or inform anybody back home about the call. He said he would contact him in a day or two and set up a meeting in Pattiya or Bangkok. Before Anand could respond, the caller had disconnected. Anand found his palms sweating. He was shaking like a leaf.

It was with some effort that Anand calmed himself. He felt trapped; his peace had been shattered. With Collins abduction and what Bala had told him, Anand saw himself being drawn into an international web of conspiracy, counter espionage and terrorism. He had never been involved in any wheeling dealing with the NDLF or its agents. In fact he knew nothing about payments made to the thugs of the NDLF by his company. Now his boss had advised him to cooperate with Gopal who appeared to be heading the operations to save Majuli and rescue Collins. The presence of R&AW agents so close at hand and his involvement in their operations was something that he had never ever imagined. He had once read about the organisation in some magazine. He had no idea what the organization did and how. He had read enough of Ian Fleming, Le'Carre and Ludlum novels in his college days. But he had never imagined himself in a situation where he would be asked to spook around in a foreign country, with people totally unfamiliar and unknown. His casual acquaintance with Gopal in the last few days had been good company for a couple of beers and a round of golf. He had found him a likable person. But beyond that he could not imagine himself involved in the cloak and dagger business that the R&AW was associated with. He was scared stiff. He had never been in any situation where he had any sort of adversarial relationship with anyone. Even in his school days there had been no scrapes with anybody and he had kept the local bullies at an arms length. Various scenarios of mortal and imminent danger were raising his anxiety and fear levels. His throat felt parched and he reached for the pitcher of water on his bedside.

Gopal had promised to join him the next morning after breakfast, but Anand wanted to speak to him right away and tell him about the call. He reached for his mobile and called his number. After a long wait a very sleepy voice responded.

"Yes Anand, any problem".

"Gopal somebody called and said he was a friend of Majuli Oil. He claimed he knows about Peter and the people who are holding him. He wants to have a meeting in a day or two."

"Anand now listen carefully. I will decide about the meeting, so do not worry for the moment. Secure your door and try and get some rest. I will meet you at nine in the morning."

Anand locked his room and fastened the security chain for added safety but he was too scared to sleep. He paced his room for long and then tried to read. He must have dozed off while reading for he woke up in the morning and found himself sprawled in the rattan chair. He had a crick in the neck and dull pain in his lower back. He got into the shower and let the hot water massage him. He felt better and went down to the coffee shop for his breakfast. It was nine by the time he finished his fried eggs and toast and was on his second cup of tea when Gopal walked in.

"Good morning Anand. Glad to see you looking fresh and cheerful. I hope the goons did not call up again."

"Morning Gopal, I was terrified yesterday. Peters kidnapping was a major shock. But I was comforted when your identity was revealed by Bala. At least I have some company now to shield me from the gangsters."

"Relax Anand. The group which picked up Peter is not interested in guys like you and me. They have very high stakes. The guy who called you was perhaps a bounty hunter. There are many small time thugs who operate in this region conning people. My hunch is that this must be one of the Indian mafia guys hiding from the police back home. We have forty known murderers, bank robbers and other absconders hiding here against whom the Interpol has issued a red corner notice on our request. They are criminals on the run and survive because they pay the local mafia. It's a dog eat dog situation. This guy who called you must have learnt of the announcement made by Majuli Oil and the Indian Police of the cash award for Peter Collins whereabouts. He is trying to get some money out of you. We will not waste our time with him; I have already spoken to the local district police chief and they are going to set up a meeting and apprehend him if he is in the Interpol list."

Anand felt relieved. He was happy to have Gopal around to explain these matters.

Gopal looked every inch a professional and Anand imagined that he probably carried a Walther PKK or a Glock automatic pistol in the waist band of his trousers. Anand was slowly getting dragged into the game. He felt confused but also appeared to be enjoying his new *avatar*. From a state of ennui just a few days ago, his being had been elevated to an arena of exciting possibilities. Stuck in Pattiya he had outlived the excitement of his vacation and had felt quarantined by Balaramans instructions to stay on. The Collins kidnapping and subsequent developments had changed his mood dramatically. He was no longer master of his destiny and in no mood to resist.

"Had a long chat with the Chief in Delhi; there is no news yet about Collins. He is sending one of our boys to Sri Lanka to follow up on one Pradeep Menon. There is a money trail that we were following in this case. There appears to be some involvement of the LTTE in the kidnapping. Saxena, our chief, wants that to be checked out. We have now to organise ourselves and move to Chiang Mai. Ravi Karan our local station officer at Chiang Mai has many irons in the fire. He is the author of the Majuli Dossier which exposed the ISI plans of sabotage using NDLF cadres. We will set base in Chiang Mai and try and get some information on Mr. Collin's whereabouts."

"Gopal tell me where do I come in all this business of hunting the abductors of Collins. I have no training in this undercover business of yours and have no skills to defend myself. I've been quite baffled since yesterday when we spoke to Balaraman and he asked me to be your understudy of sorts. Why are you exposing me to all these dangers of spying and counter espionage?"

"Relax Anand. There is no exposure to any danger here. We are not engaging in any mortal combat with terrorists. My job and the task of every R&AW officer is to gather information from various sources on strategic issues which can help us to locate and identify groups which work against our country's interest. This helps us in apprising the government of the existing and developing threat perceptions. This is the legitimate function of all our missions located abroad. Every diplomat is sensitized to pick up information and we as a specilised agency supplement their efforts."

"But Gopal, how do you explain all the accusations about the R&AW being involved in violent activities in our neighboring countries. Time and again their media names R&AW being behind car bombings, incitement of violence amongst religious minorities, rigging of the electoral process to favour particular candidates . . . ."

"Well it's just a tit for tat kind of reaction. We give them as good as we get."

"Come on now, no kidding, Gopal. Don't give me that very official line."

"Both the countries are involved in gathering intelligence and Pakistan always has some grudge or the other to keep India engaged in some aggressive posturing. They are supporting the proxy war in Kashmir so we tighten the screws on them in Balochistan and the North West Frontier Province. Anand you are right in a way, as it is said that war is an extension of diplomacy. All nations are involved in protecting their sovereign interests. The strength of a nation is not its military might alone. Its socio-political milieu, its political structures and maturity of its people and the ruling classes, its governance and ability to bring about a seamless change in its ruling formations are critical to the nation. This alone determines its economic growth by utilization of the resources of development. Economic strength and stability is, in the ultimate analysis, the real power of a nation. Intelligence gathering is the work of trained foot soldiers. In ancient India we have the shining example of Kautilya who wrote his pioneering work the *Arthashastra* a treatise in statecraft, a thousand and five hundred years ago. While he covered the entire range of subjects from administration and governance, from taxation to defense, he devoted a good portion to the designing, developing and administering the system for gathering information and networking of spies. He believed that the creation of a secret service, with spies, secret agents and specialists such as assassins, was a task of high priority for the kings. He considered the creation of entire network of secret agents was necessary for ensuring the security of the kingdom and for furthering the objective of expansion by conquest. We have a somewhat similar example in the personality of Niccolo Machiavelli in Italy who wrote extensively on the principles of statecraft and use of undercover agents to pursue political objectives."

Gopal knew a lot about espionage and he briefed Anand on the state agencies set up in the U.K., U.S.A., Russia, and Israel and of course Pakistan. He had studied the ISI very closely when he was a junior officer in the R&AW Headquarters at New Delhi. He knew the entire set up from the chief down to the caretaker of their headquarters at Rawalpindi. He knew the location of each room in the building and was a virtual walking-talking encyclopedia on ISI matters. He had been the first person in the R&AW to hack their main frame computer and the ISI were unaware of it for years till unwittingly a junior Pakistani diplomat in Washington passed on some information to a CIA mole in the Indian Mission. The information related to the presence of some Taliban sympathizers in the Pakistani Army. They talked through their lunch and Gopal gave him some information on their tradecraft. At the outset, he explained, it was very necessary in their business never to lose their cover. They had to guard their identity at any cost. Losing identity meant losing the entire plot; the operation could go of the track. It could jeopardize the entire mission and compromise the cover of the other operatives. So tradecraft was the set of practices one adopted to ensure that your cover was not lost. He gave him several examples of standing operating procedures to familiarize and to prepare him for the mission they were embarking on. Anand was fascinated by the simplicity of deception and guile that were the basic tools of the trade of espionage. The process of demystification had begun and Anand felt he had found a good teacher in Gopal to initiate him into the world of covert operations.

Anand got up from the rattan chair and bent down before Gopal in a gesture of salutation.

"I will now have to offer *gurudakshana* to you, Gopal for the first lesson on the history and art of spying."

"Yes Anand, you are welcome. I accept the offering and hereby induct and anoint you as the newest agent of the R&AW."

They both had a good laugh and ordered another round of beer to seal the contract. Anand was already feeling relieved, that there was no present and imminent danger from the drug mafia and their agents who they were to contact soon with the assistance of Ravi Karan, the Station Officer at Chiang Mai. The sun was setting over the hills and the sunbathers around the pool were slowly melting away to the refuge of their rooms. Gopal got up to leave for his hotel across the street.

"Be ready by 5.30AM. We will drive to Bangkok to catch the flight for Chiang Mai. I will get the cab and pick you up for the airport".

"Yes Guruji."

Anand smiled as he waved him good night.

# MUMBAI

**S**atish Sharma and Inspector Bhonsle from the Khandala Police Station were waiting in the lobby when Raj arrived at the Nilambari Apartments on Napean Sea Road. The chance meeting of Raj with Ratna at Bunty's party had led them to Pradeep's apartment. They took the lift to the fourteenth floor with the caretaker who let them in with the duplicate keys of the apartment. It was a spacious flat for a bachelor, but then all apartments on Malabar Hill were of similar design and dimensions.

There was nobody in and they were informed by the servants in the adjacent apartment that Pradeep's bearer cum cook, Joseph had gone off on his annual leave to Kerala, the day after Pradeep left for Sri Lanka. Pradeep's departure had been quite sudden. Normally he visited home for his annual vacation during the months of April-May, and Joseph too took his annual leave then. Pradeep had just carried a small strolley and his laptop as confirmed by his driver who had driven him to the airport. There were few documents and files in his study. Pradeep appeared to be fond of reading and had a fine collection of hard covers and paperbacks arranged in three bookshelves. He appeared to have travelled far and wide and his collection of Chinese Ming pottery and the other artifacts and paintings were indicative of his sophistication and affluence. There were a number of family portraits of his childhood with his parents and his grandmother. They could do precious little with information they gathered and thanked the caretaker and left. Satish had made some enquiries with Pradeep's assistant and the partner in his office, the Lloyds Financial Service Private Limited, but they could not confirm the date of his return. His Secretary however gave them his address and residential phone number in Kandy, Sri Lanka as well as his mobile number. There was no response from the mobile number when Satish called; it appeared to have been switched off. The mobile carried the SIM card of Vodafone and the address registered was that of Nilambari Apartments.

Raj spoke to Saxena in the afternoon and briefed him on the case.

"Raj you get ready to leave for Colombo. You already have a cover for Sri Lanka. I will get the Sri Lanka desk to update the brief for you. You should follow up this lead. I want to get to the bottom of the B.K. Dossier. There were a number of pointers to Sri Lanka in the document. I feel very uncomfortable about this. I will brief you further on Monday when we meet. I am getting your passport and other travel arrangements organised in the meanwhile."

# CHIANG MAI

There was light rain falling when they landed at Chiang Mai. The air was wonderfully fresh after the smog and vehicular pollution in Bangkok. There were verdant hills all around, and wisps of blue smoke rose from the cooking fires in the villages towards the east. The airport was teeming with tourists.

"Welcome to Chiang Mai. The rain is a good omen and your visit promises to be fruitful," Ravi greeted them in the arrival hall.

"There was a dry spell on and the local farmers were worried about their freshly transplanted paddy. But it should be fine now. We had good rain at night and the clouds were hanging low over the airport around the time your flight took off from Bangkok. I was actually expecting a delay by about half an hour."

They got into Ravi's car and drove down to the Meridian Resort at the edge of Chiang Mai city. The resort was actually a golf course with villas built around it. The main building where Ravi drove to had the resort's reception, two restaurants, coffee shop and a bar with access to the beautiful emerald green swimming pool. The guest rooms were located in the villas spread over the perimeter of the golf course and they were driven to their villa in a large golf cart. There were four suites in each villa surrounded by lawns dotted with rattan chairs and sun umbrellas. The rain had died down and a cool breeze swept across the resort; they decided to sit out in the garden and called room service for a pot of coffee and some sandwiches. Ravi had prepared a brief for them which Gopal read slowly and Ravi interrupted now and then to supplement with details and explanations for Anand's benefit. Gopal was in a pensive mood. He had closely followed the developments reported by the Chiang Mai Station chief over the last ten years. Ravi Karan's predecessor had developed the case file and had made excellent contacts amongst the local Thai Police, the village headmen in Chiang Mai as also the neighboring areas in Laos, Cambodia and Myanmar.

The original document was the generic file bearing the title, The Golden Triangle. From it had emerged a number of studies, including the Majuli Dossier outlining the threat perceptions from the ISI and NDLF nexus. These studies had networked the activities of the drug and the arms mafias operating in the triangle. The activities were known to the Interpol, the CIA and the local intelligence networks of the Thai army and police as well those of the other countries within the triangle. The biggest outfit of drug trade and armaments had been run by Kuhn Sah, who ran a parallel government, across the borders of Myanmar, Thailand and Laos. He had been apprehended by the Thai police in the past but was let off as he provided useful information on the radical groups in the region and also kept them in control. The R&AW had got wind of these activities in the mid sixties when the separatist rebels amongst the Nagas started sourcing their weapons from the region through the rebels operating in northern Myanmar. The Consulate office at Chiang Mai was set up as an outpost for the R&AW to counter the activities of the supplier groups and direct covert operations against them.

The recent developments in the Assam Valley had seen the rise of the NDLF. Its demand for statehood had seen the beginnings of a serious law and order situation in the Valley. Extortion of funds from the industry in the region had led to disruption of trade and manufacturing. The tea estates which were made the target by the NDLF protested and the state government made some noises but took no serious action. Some of the NDLF leaders were rounded up and cases filed for the threatening postures and extortion. The NDLF struck back by kidnapping some tea estate managers and released them only on receiving ransom. Such incidents multiplied and became a routine with the local police becoming the negotiators and helping in the collection of the ransom. Finally the tea estates gave up protesting as the state had failed to provide any meaningful protection and its own officials had become agents of the oppressor. Monthly sums of bribes were offered by most of the corporate establishments and the NDLF became the arbiters of peace in the state. There was of course blood shed and a very senior Assam Valley Tea Company Chief Executive was kidnapped and killed. The state and central forces were finally deployed and many extremists were killed or arrested. Some senior leaders escaped to Bangladesh and were given shelter and protection by the then unfriendly regime. They continued their campaign by smuggling weapons and explosives to their supporters back home. The bulk of the NDLF followers, however, came under the control of the moderate leadership and surrendered their weapons. They also swore to maintain peace and their leaders sought political recognition and participation, but with some degree of autonomy for their region.

The networks of the drug smugglers and gun runners in the Golden Triangle area continued to operate in small groups. They found new demands originating from the militancy of the Tamil rebels in Sri Lanka. New routes were developed through the Naga Hills, to smuggle weapons into the Chittagong hill tracts from where they were carried to the narrow coastal strip in the Bay of Bengal and then by boats to Sri Lanka. Ravi Karan had undertaken a very daring and perilous journey and trekked that entire route on foot with two carriers of the NDLF cadres whom he had managed to recruit as R&AW agents. He had disguised himself as one of the coolies and lived with them for twenty—three days, sharing their food and sleeping in the leech infested jungles. He had gone over the hills in the Chittagong Province in Bangladesh and descended on the other side to the shores of the Bay of Bengal and seen the contraband of AK-47's, Chinese Star 9 mm pistols and rocket launchers being loaded on boats bound for the Jaffna Peninsula in the Northern Sri Lanka. These routes had been surveyed by the R&AW in early 1970 and used by the Bangla rebels, the Mukti Bahini, in their struggle against the Pakistani army crackdown. The same routes were now being exploited by the ISI to aid the subversive elements in the Brahmaputra Valley. The Majuli document had highlighted the growing proximity of the NDLF leaders hiding in Bangladesh with the ISI to ferment trouble and destroy valuable economic assets in the valley.

The abduction of Peter Collins appeared to be part of the ISI master plan to forestall progress on the project. Ravi Karan had planned to use his agents in the NDLF cadres to probe the whereabouts of Collins and the group behind the whole operation. He had sent a message on the satellite phone and was hoping to catch up with his agents' codenamed Rahim and Siva soon.

# NEW DELHI

Raj was escorted to the committee room on the 8th floor after the usual formalities. Saxena's technical assistant Suresh Kumar was waiting for him with the passport and briefing documents. Raj was traveling to Sri Lanka under the cover name Vikas Shah, partner in the gems and jewelry firm, Delight Gems of Opera House, Mumbai. He had used the same cover in the past and it had worked well. Delight Gems was importing precious and semi-precious stones from Sri Lanka and Myanmar. Navnitbhai, the owner of Delight Gems had for years been a R&AW agent and had provided useful services during his business tours to Myanmar and Sri Lanka. He had developed excellent contacts with Tamil rebel sympathizers and had prevented many tragedies in the bloody conflict. His operations in Sri Lanka had successfully thwarted the efforts of the Chinese Navy getting access to the Trincomalee harbor on the east coast. He had slowed down of late due to his kidney ailments, but had continued to provide an excellent cover and network to R&AW officers visiting Myanmar and Sri Lanka.

In his new avatar as Vikas Shah, Raj had a brief from Navnitbhai to inspect some shipments of Sri Lankan emeralds, rubies and sapphires. These were required for the latest orders he had from the Tiffany's in New York. He had developed a good name in the diamond jewelry exports to the USA and was now developing a new market for the designer jewelry segment. This was a niche market, largely favored by the affluent Indian diaspora. Raj was familiar with the drill. He would be staying for a week in Colombo and make contacts with five gem exporting firms. He would then spend a week in Kandy and repeat the routine. He would have plenty of time to arrange meetings with the R&AW agents and get briefed.

Saxena joined them after Suresh Kumar completed his briefing on the logistics. This was to be a one to one meeting and after a round of coffee, Suresh took his leave.

"Raj this B.K. Dossier has opened a virtual Pandora's box. We now suspect the Tamil radicals in Sri Lanka are using the Indian havala trade channels to raise resources in Europe and the UK. Some of the money is flowing to the drug and arms mafia in the erstwhile constituent states of the Soviet Union in Central Asia. Many of these regimes have sympathies with the Jihadists and are encouraging clandestine trade and shipment of arms to Somali and other radical groups. Recently, some shipments were intercepted by the Indian Coast Guards off the coast of the Andaman' Islands. The small boats had no registration papers and are manned by crews from Bangla Desh and Myanmar. The shipments were received from a larger freighter which had sailed through the Munnar Straits after dropping anchor at Cochin, where it had picked up a general cargo of oilcakes, spices and cashew kernels. The ship was registered in Liberia and had a mixed crew of Greeks, Liberians and Chinese. The Captain was from Estonia. It was officially carrying a cargo of marine engines used by the fishing boats in the region and lubricating oil. The contraband was transshipped on to two smaller boats, south of the Andaman's under cover of darkness. A Naval

Air Surveillance aircraft had spotted some unreported sailing activity and had sent the photos taken by infra red cameras to the Naval and Coast Guard units at Port Blair and Vishakhapatnam Naval Control. The boats were given a chase and challenged. Only one could be intercepted and brought into Port Blair. A naval frigate, hundred nautical miles east of Chennai had fired warning shots to intercept the other boat, but it disappeared. The radar identified it as one of the fast vessels procured by the LTTE rebels to evade the Sri Lankan Navy Patrols. The Navy is under strict orders not to destroy and kill, but only to intercept and capture. So they could not fire the anti ship missiles. The boat intercepted by the Coast Guard and taken to Port Bair had sixty units of the Russian Stinger Missiles. This is very serious and poses a great danger to civil air transport. Our worry is that some of these lethal weapons could fall into the hands of the NDLF ultras. Secondly, this B.K. Dossier read along with the Majuli Dossier brings focus on our immediate concerns. Collins has already been abducted and we cannot afford to sit and wait for their second strike, which would undermine our intelligence and internal security. I want you to check out Pradeep Menon; he appears to be connected to this havala racket. His company's credentials are impeccable and the Securities and Exchange Board of India (SEBI) has no case against it, even of a technical infringement. His partners in the Mumbai based Lloyds Financial Services are a respectable Marwari family who also have interests in garment exports. Pradeep might be indulging in some havala business on the side to help friends back in Sri Lanka. We have already advised Thampi our station officer in Colombo to brief you on the local Intelligence inputs. He will also arrange a meeting with some moles we have amongst the LTTE rebel's. Contact me through the Indian Mission channels if you want any help or advice. Do not carry your satellite phone; but keep in touch with Navnitbhai for the gems business. He will pass on our messages and also provide you with contacts for any local assistance."

"How do I get briefed on the developments on Gopal's mission in Thailand? Could we interact and share intelligence?" Raj enquired anxiously.

"Thampi will brief you if there is any worthwhile information or enquiry from that end. Gopal's priority is locating the whereabouts of Collins and you will trace the money trail in the B.K. Dossier as well as check out whether Pradeep has any links with the LTTE."

Saxena got up to go. He had to rush to the Home Secretary's office. The secret phone had buzzed twice already, indicating the level of urgency. He half turned and raised his hand to wish Raj for his mission.

"Raj, I want this information fast, best of luck."

# KANDY

**"K**annan come, Kannan come have your tea."

Pradeep's grandmother was knocking on his door, after the maid had failed to get a response. It was the same each time; she had spoilt him and Pradeep too played along. It had been a long relationship of her playing the mother's role and their attachment had grown over the years. She had been very excited ever since he had arrived two days ago for his annual break. He usually came towards end of April and stayed on till mid May; besides his brief visits for his company's meetings. She was not prepared for this visit so his room had not been opened and aired and she had not brought his favorite fish and prawns. Pradeep too was much attached to her and always remembered the story she had told him about how his father was apprenticed into tea business.

His grandfather never believed in college education and even as Grandmother had protested Anna, his father had been sent off to the hill slopes of Nuwara Eliya to look after the new plantations as soon as he completed his school. It was a hard life those days on plantations and most of the work was done manually. The estate was growing and many hundred acres had been freshly planted and required close supervision. Anna's apprenticeship as a young planter at the age of sixteen had been tough. He had led a very hardy life but it prepared him for his life as a planter and tea producer. Grandpa had given him the new gardens for development and put Aboobaker, his trusted supervisor, to guide him and train him. Aboobaker had grown up in the estate. Abu, as Anna addressed him, was in his mid thirty those days and knew the entire estate like the back of his hand. Anna was given one of the manager's cottages on the estate and Abu helped him to settle down. There were half a dozen servants attached to the cottage, the cook, the bearer cum peon, the chamber maid, the gardner and two grooms to take care of the horses.

Anna rode out early morning everyday after a breakfast of string hoppers and spicy curry. The cook would prepare something new each day for the little master. He would make an excellent jungle fowl curry one morning and the next day surprise Anna with spicy pork curry with rice and bread. He would pack tiffin of rice, dhal and vegetables which they could have during a break from work late in the afternoon. They would ride back almost at sunset and Anna would walk into the cottage with a hot bath waiting for him. He really looked forward to soaking in the large enamel tub washing away the dirt and sweat of the day. It took him quiet a while to get used to his new life as a planter and when he did, he plunged into it with all the energy he could muster. The plantations grew and flourished under his stewardship.

In his twenty second year and just a month after his birthday Anna was engaged to Chandrika Kapuwatte a beautiful Sinhala girl from Nuwara Eliya. The families had known each other since long and Anna had met her earlier at the annual dinner which grandpa hosted every year at the estate bungalow. The Kapuwatte family was big landholders of Nuwara Eliya and they also had investments in a large tea estate and fruit orchards. The grand wedding ceremony was held in Nuwara Eliya and guests came from far and wide. The local tea community from Kandy and Nuwara Eliya was well represented and there were many ministers and parliamentarians, tea merchants and bankers from Colombo. The festivities went on for three days as per custom and tradition and there was much drinking and eating. After the nuptial ceremonies on the final day, the bride and groom were bid farewell on their way to London for their honeymoon.

Pradeep was born the same year Anna diversified his business by opening the first Plantation Resort at the estate. The opening of the resort and his arrival brought immense joy to his grandfather. He had gone into retirement after Anna expanded the tea business and stayed confined to the house in Kandy. Chandrika had moved down to Kandy from the Estate bungalow when Pradeep was three months due and she stayed on after Pradeep's birth. Now all important get togethers were held in Kandy and Anna would always drive down and stay for the weekends. With senior managers to assist him, Anna delegated lot of work to the new youngsters from Colombo. But he never stayed away from the estate for more than a day or two and would get back as early as he could.

Anna's business grew beyond tea. His resort company grew and expanded all over the country. Pradeep had just joined school then when his mother Chandrika miscarried a second time and died of complications. Anna was devastated and it was a great shock to grandmother. But seeing young Pradeep by his side she recovered soon and took over charge of the situation.

While Anna immersed himself in his work he spent most of his days in the estate cottage up in the hills and only came down to Kandy once a month. Pradeep missed him a lot but grandma did not let him feel lonely. He had missed Chandrika after she passed away, but soon got busy with his school and grandma. She was his constant companion and spent all her time planning his day for him. She never let him out of her sight after he got back from school. On weekends, if Anna was not around she would drive him to town for her weekly shopping. He learnt to buy good fish and sea food and learnt the names of all the seasonal fruits and vegetables. They would go for a walk along the lake and for a picnic to the Royal Botanical Gardens. Later when summer vacations came Anna would take Grandma and Pradeep to the estate and they would stay in the cool comfort of the Estate Bungalow for almost a month. Pradeep loved the estate and would go down to the office everyday with Anna. He would be taken on a conducted tour of the factory and was very thrilled and excited with the packaging factory.

Pradeep did well in his studies and passed his A Levels with a good percentage of marks. He got admission in Corpus Christi College Oxford University and opted for a Tripos in Mathematics. Pradeep enjoyed his stay at Oxford and travelled during vacations to Scotland and the Lake District. He visited home during the winter break and spent most of his vacations at Kandy with grandma. Anna appeared keen that Pradeep should come back home after graduating and take over the management of the estates, the tea and resort business. Pradeep had very different views on the subject and he finally shared his ideas with Anna. The year he graduated he came home to announce that he had secured a good job with the Barclays Bank in London. Pradeep had also prepared a small paper on converting the family business into a corporate entity. The business was well established and had large surpluses and reserves. It took Pradeep a while to convince Anna that it would be wise if their family owned enterprise was converted into a Public Limited company. The Blue Hill Tea and Resorts Co. Ltd. were finally incorporated in 1998 and its shares offered to the general public and corporate houses.

Pradeep expanded the operations of the company and further diversified into banking and finance. He brought ten per cent shares in The Great Mauritius Bank and invested foreign capital in various ventures in India. He had to give up his London assignment after Anna's death. He moved to Mumbai where he set up a venture capital fund and finance company. He was thus close to home and grandma and could give his undivided attention to his tea and resorts business. He took over as Chairman of the Blue Hill Tea and Resorts Company and divided his time between Mumbai and Kandy.

# COLOMBO

**R**aj was picked up at the airport by the chauffer arranged by the travel agents, who drove him to his hotel. The Grand Oriental Hotel is located at a cull de sac, where the York Street meets the walls of the Colombo Harbor. Raj marveled at the coincidence of the similar location of the Grand Hotel of Mumbai in Ballard Estate, with the wall of the Bombay Port Trust running along the road on the north-western side. He had never stayed at this hotel before. It had a grand facade and appeared very ancient. Later in the lobby he came across some sepia prints of the hotel and a marble plaque which gave a brief history of its origins. The hotel was originally built as a military barrack by the Dutch East India Company in 1837. Later the Dutch were pushed out and replaced by the British who set up their depot here to export spices. After almost a decade when the British garrison moved out, the barracks were gifted by the then Governor of Colombo to an English trader who converted it into a hotel for the visiting English traders and civilians.

Raj had just settled down when Thampi, the Station officer at Colombo called to say that he was on his way and they would meet at the Galadari Hotel for lunch. The Galadari was just a five minute walk from the Grand Oriental and Raj had noticed it while driving in from the airport. He picked up his laptop and mobile and stepped out. There was a light drizzle but it was not bothersome and Raj took long strides towards The Galadari. He walked into the lobby and with the assistance of the hostess made his way to the bar. Thampi was already there in his sartorial best. He had a fancy for Armani suits, many of which he had picked up during his stint at Dubai. Thampi had been sent there on a special mission to hunt down the Mumbai Blasts fugitives. Dubai had become a stronghold of the D company operators who provided refuge to criminals and terrorists on the run from the Indian police. Thanks to the extradition agreements between the two governments, the local police had been very cooperative and Thampi had managed to affect many arrests and had the criminals deported to Mumbai. Regrettably the main accused escaped the dragnet and had taken refuge in Karachi where they had been welcomed by the ISI and provided safe house. Thampi had won many commendations for his work in Dubai and had been assigned to Colombo to coordinate the counter espionage activities in the SAARC countries. The Chiang Mai and Colombo station officers had provide the vital intelligence inputs which had helped the state police in India to virtually wipe out the sleeper cells created by the ISI. The Majuli Dossier had however created new anxiety in the R&AW headquarters and the Home Ministry. Peter Collins's abduction had confirmed the existence of some major plot.

"Raj, hope you found the Grand Oriental comfortable. We wanted to keep your visit low key and the Grand is low profile. But the food is outstanding."

The Grand lacked the attributes which could put it into a high star category. But it was immensely popular with low budget tourists from Europe that had kept its occupancy high.

"Oh it's just fine by me. I am not here on my honeymoon . . . . ,"

"Well, when that happens we will get the best beach resort in Bentota or Beruwala lined up with a red carpet welcome for you Raj, provided you get married first."

They had a good laugh on that one. Raj had been a confirmed bachelor in the agency. He had been too much of an outdoor type to get domesticated and tied down. Since his school days in the Mussoorie Hills he had come to love the mountains. The school treks to the Bhagirathi Valley had fired a spirit of adventure in him. He had a high rank in the civil service exam and could have joined the Foreign Service, but to the surprise of all his batch mates opted for the Police Service. During his twenty years in the Police Service he had opted for deputation to the Indo-Tibetan Border Police and the Border Security Force. He had traversed the entire Himalayan Range from the Nubra Valley in Ladakh to Tawang and beyond in the Arunanchal Pradesh during his stint with these outfits. Smitten by the bug of photography, he had photographed the length and breadth of the Himalayas and the foot hills.

Raj was also perhaps the only Police Officer who had undergone the jungle warfare and commando training courses conducted by the army. He had skied on the slopes of the Siachen glacier representing the BSF against the ace skiers of the mountain warfare regiments of the Indian Army. For his skill and stamina on the icy slopes and high altitudes, he had led many teams to rescue trapped mountaineers. He had been awarded the Silver Pick Axe by the Alpine Federation in Europe and also made an honorary member of the Avalanche Rescue Group in Switzerland. Raj for all his humility and self effacing personality was very tough in determination and a resolute in character. During his four years stint in Islamabad he had managed to plant moles in the ISI headquarters and dared to install thirty five bugs in that building. The ISI could not discover the moles but five of the listening devices were compromised when the CIA 'found' that their contacts had leaked some information to the R&AW.

Raj had acquired a reputation of a spy master and was expected to rise to the top of the pyramid. It had been a career marked by competence and courage. Raj had no political mentors at New Delhi. His peers treated him with great respect and valued his advice and judgment. Thampi and Raj had been together in many missions and Saxena had considered them an effective team. Saxena understood his boys well and vice versa. Many a time they could read what was going on in his mind but rarely guess his moves. He was like those chess Grand Masters who plan five moves in advance and compel their opponent to make the wrong moves. They had closely observed him and studied his methods when he exposed the ISI backed espionage ring set up with the assistance of a Bangladesh consulate officer in Mandalay.

The young and youthful Station Officer of R&AW posted in Mandalay had fallen for the charms of a Bengali femme fatale at the Bangladesh consulate. The affair had progressed for more than six months when Headquarters smelt a rat. The intercepts on mobiles and telephones indicated some compromise of our recruits in Myanmar and the Chiang Mai region. One of our key contacts went missing and there was a major concern on the damage this could do to our counter espionage and counter terror networks. Saxena had planned the whole operation himself and no one had a clue about it. He put the listening post on high alert and flew down to Kolkata by Indian Airlines on a private visit to attend a wedding. He was to return to New Delhi the next evening, but went missing. He had actually driven to Kalaikunda Air Force Station near Kolkata after attending the wedding and camped in the mess. Early next morning the executive jet of the R&AW flew him to Yangon. The Ambassador personally received him and took him home. His visit was kept a secret even from the Indian Mission. A dummy Intel input sent by him in cipher to the Station officer at Mandalay, a day before he left New Delhi, was compromised within few hours of his arrival. The listening post picked up the entire conversation the Bangla Consulate official had with her handler in Islamabad. Saxena had also tipped off Shamim Beg, the Bangladesh Internal Security Chief, about the call and he heard it loud and clear and also recorded it. Shamim had been posted in the Bangladesh High Commission in New Delhi and had come into contact with Saxena. Saxena had cultivated him during those days and he had been helpful and cooperative since then. Saxena had a secret meeting with General Nu of the Myanmar Security service that same afternoon and exchanged valuable Intel on the anti junta rebel hideouts in the northern provinces. That same evening he flew back to New Delhi. Later our Ambassador confirmed that the Myanmar government had expelled the Bangladesh Consulate official from Myanmar, and arrested more than a dozen persons in Yangon and Mandalay. The R&AW also recalled the compromised Station Officer from Mandalay and placed him under suspension.

Thampi ordered a sumptuous Sri Lankan meal with an extra dish of fried pork curry for himself. He knew Raj did not eat pork and beef, but he never missed the opportunity of ordering it for himself. His wife was a strict vegetarian but did not object to his food habits, so long as he indulged himself away from home.

"Saxena sent a message last night. There appears to be a possibility that Collins was in Myanmar, but Ravi was waiting for a visual confirmation. There is still a mystery about the motives and the group involved. He wants Intel on the LTTE and what interest they could have with his abduction. It appears that ISI and the Tamil Tigers are both interested in this hostage situation. There appears to be an active collaboration in the situation. The ISI funded this abduction and some rogue elements of the banned outfit of NDLF infiltrated the security perimeter at Majuli Camp and snatched Collins. I have a meeting arranged with a former Tiger who has joined the moderates after leading a group of the radical forces. He fell out with LTTE Supremo on tactics employed to bomb and terrorize innocents, including the Tamils themselves. I will find out what he knows of the Collins kidnap motives. But it is equally important to trace the money trail exposed in the B.K. Dossier. This Pradeep appears to be a straight forward guy. He comes from a very respectable family of tea estate owners from the Kandy and Nuwara Eliya Hills region. His father was offered a seat in the parliament, but he had politely declined. The LTTE had also tried to arm twist him to provide funds for their activities but he kept them at a distance. Most of the tea plantation labour force you know is expatriate Tamil. The political parties in Tamil Nadu have sympathized with the LTTE and caused grief to New Delhi. The LTTE collects money from local business men here and were also trading in smuggled gems, especially rubies and emeralds from Myanmar. Navnitbhai gained favour with the last Sri Lankan President when he exposed the racket. Some rogue gem traders were arrested and prosecuted. That favour of Navnitbhai helped New Delhi persuade Colombo to keep the Chinese out of Trincomalee Harbour. Pradeep is now in Kandy and we have already alerted our Consulate there and they will take care of you. I have an assistant in the Consulate who can set up communications for us if need arises."

"I was proposing to go to Kandy on Friday afternoon after completing Navnitbhai's work here. There are already some meetings tied up with the Gem Exports Corporation and I have to inspect the consignment of emeralds for Navnitbhai. He is arranging a meeting with two of his contacts in Kandy who have information on the active LTTE agents in India. Could you arrange a one to one meeting with Pradeep?"

"I will speak to Mr. Joseph Cherian, the Deputy High Commissioner there and find out how this could be arranged. Pradeep has been taking his Indian visa from that office and surely they could always find some excuse to call him over, without causing any alarm and panic."

"Yes Thampi, it would have to be done very discreetly. Pradeep must still be under some shock of his good friend Vijaya's murder. He also left Mumbai before the police could talk to him. His sudden departure from Mumbai has raised much suspicion in the investigating officer's mind. Saxena feels his links with Vijaya could be more than a love affair. He had been lending money to B.K. Enterprises and we have found more money in the transactions than the sums borrowed from various fund managers. There is a clandestine havala operation revealed in our investigations, and outflow of funds to unknown persons. There may be sleeper cells that are being funded for some operation. The Collins abduction has also been funded by the ISI and we are not sure if there is a connection with the B.K. Dossier.

The LTTE association in that kidnap has brought the spotlight on Pradeep. Can you arrange that meeting with your LTTE contact in the afternoon tomorrow?"

"Done. I will send a word out and fix the time and venue."

The food was delicious, especially the yellow fish curry. Thankfully the cook had spared the chilies and made the fish mildly spicy. But the beads of perspiration on Thampi's pudgy face, as he gorged on the pork curry confirmed that that at least was hot and piquant! Raj too enjoyed his meal as he was famished. The morning breakfast on the flight from Mumbai had been frugal and unappetizing. He was looking forward to a good lunch and he got it at the Galadari.

The sky was clear and a gentle breeze had picked up from the Indian Ocean as he strode out of the Galadari. He decided to take a walk on the Galle Face promenade. He wanted to get some exercise and also clear his mind of the clutter of information that had accumulated since he got assigned to the B.K. Dossier investigations. Vijaya's murder had complicated matters as the key person in the havala transactions had been silenced by someone who probably was the local coordinator of the ISI plot. Vijaya's interrogation would have definitely exposed the leads to the identity of the conspirators. He was now up against a wall and did not know where to begin. Satish Sharma's efforts might locate Vijaya's killers but they would have no knowledge of the persons who were involved in the havala transfers and who actually ordered the killing. It had been his experience that all such conspiracies were generally covered by layers of plots and sub-plots which appeared to be good leads but took you nowhere. There would be many red herrings on the trails which could take one on a wild goose chase. The best bet, he felt was Pradeep as he had been closest to Vijaya. Was he involved in the money trail with her or was only a close friend? Did he have any connections with the havala transactions of the LTTE that Saxena had talked about? He had discounted Pradeep's involvement after his discussion with Thampi. Had Pradeep been involved in some clandestine money laundering operations for a terrorist outfit, he would not be taking a vacation in his home town but would have sought refuge in some hide out in London. He had a long term visa for UK and still had his work permit. Pradeep's presence in his ancestral home in Kandy did appear to clear him of any misdemeanor; but still there were some unanswered questions. Raj had a gut feeling that the plot was much more complicated than it appeared at first sight. However, Pradeep he felt could provide useful information to unravel Vijaya's personal background, her family's whereabouts, her education—in brief some clues on her contacts, her beliefs, commitments and motives. This was so important to reveal the identity and lead him closer to people behind the conspiracy to terrorize the people in the country.

His greatest regret would always be not meeting Vijaya when he could have. He had wanted to talk to her immediately he had got on to the case. Saxena had briefed him and had also arranged an invite to the mahurat party of 'Chandani Raat.' He had missed the party and was preparing to catch up with her at Khandala. But her killers had reached her before he could. There was a major void in Vijaya's dossier he was trying to construct. Ratna had provided some information. He would have to get back to Ratna for more details after he spoke to Pradeep. She could perhaps remember and corroborate what Pradeep knew about her. He had to find out more about this mysterious woman who appeared to have no relations and only a few friends. Vijaya was the critical witness and co-conspirator and perhaps had all the explanations to the coded names and flow of funds revealed in the B.K. Dossier. She was after all the designer and keeper of the accounts format developed with such cunning and guile to keep the monetary ends of the operation a secret from the regulators of the state. She may also have had some knowledge of the activities or the plot which was being funded by these transactions. The B.K. Dossier had opened a new chapter in the R&AW investigations and had alerted all station officers in Asia from Istanbul to Macau. Unfortunately she had been killed, having become inconvenient to her handlers. Her murder had flagged these investigations to the most critical category.

Raj scrolled through the mental summary of the B.K. Dossier case; he felt that there were two distinct investigations where ISI appeared to be involved. One related to the money transfers via the havala channels into a camouflaged account of the B.K. Enterprises. The second was the ISI attempts to influence the NDLF to foment trouble in the North East States and target Majuli Oil. In both these covert operations of the ISI there had been some developments. In the former, the principal associate of the conspiracy had been targeted by her controllers; and in the latter Collins had been abducted from a very secure location. Saxena was of the opinion that both the incidents were part of the same conspiracy. It was difficult to advance any reasons for this theory for the present. Did Vijaya mastermind the film financier's accounts only to fund the ISI's plan exposed by Ravi Karan in the Majuli Dossier or there was more to it than met the eye. What was the LTTE interest in these operations?

The immediate objectives of the R&AW were not only to locate Peter Collins and bring him back safe but more important, to secure the Majuli's assets. Who were the adversary, what nationality, what creed, what political entity did they represent? What objective did they work for and what master did they serve? Was it revenge for some perceived wrong, religious bigotry or blackmail for monetary gain? Maybe it was a mix of all these—a heady cocktail garnished with international intrigue, murder and mayhem.

Raj felt better after his long walk on the Galle Face sorting the clutter of information that had got stored in his memory. He could file away and store the mass of bits and bytes of the information into various files and folders of his memory and save them for future retrieval and reference. He deleted a lot of garbage and junked many theories he had fished out from the realms of his imagination. He had a good laugh as he pressed the delete button on some of them and wondered how stupid he had been to work out such scenarios. It was getting dark as dense clouds appeared over the horizon. Fearing rain Raj turned around and retraced his steps to the Grand Oriental.

# CHIANG MAI

**R**avi Karan got a message from his agents that they would be in Chiang Mai in the next two days. That gave them time to check out the contacts developed by Majuli Oil with the NDLF operatives in Thailand. Ravi read through the documents in the sealed cover with Anand but he could not make much of it. The names mentioned were perhaps assumed names and did not match the ones the R&AW had on its records. Nevertheless Ravi and Gopal picked up four at random and called on their given mobile numbers. Two appeared to be switched off and the other two numbers responded but promptly called off. Ravi decided to wait for a response—as this was the known practice amongst agents who do so to protect their cover and location. After an hour or so Ravi's mobile rang; the calling number on display was not registered on his mobile. Ravi switched the instrument on the loudspeaker mode and they could hear some heavy breathing. Then a gruff voice said, "This is Cobra calling, identify yourself."

"Cobra, this is Friend from Majuli Oil. We want to know if you have information on Peter Collins." Ravi responded.

There was a long pause but heavy breathing indicated he was still on line.

"He is not with us. But he is in Myanmar."

"Where is he at the moment, can you give us some details on his location and the people holding him?"

"We don't know his location."

"Can you find out some details on his location and identity of his captors?"

The phone was disconnected.

They again consulted the documents and picked up another four names. Ravi called the number shown against Nawab. There was no response from the other end and after a while the call was disconnected with a message "No Response." Ravi called again after ten minutes and got a response after a minute.

Short and terse the person said he would call back.

After almost an hour Ravi's mobile rang. Ravi switched it on and they could hear some people talking in the background.

"This is Friend from Majuli Oil. Can you hear me?"

"Yes, greetings Friend. What can I do for you?"

"We are trying to locate Peter Collins. Can you help us?"

"Peter Collins is in Myanmar."

"Can you tell us his exact location and details of the people who are holding him and why?"

"We are not sure about the location but one of the local Karen rebel groups is holding him captive. He was kidnapped by a NDLF faction group which is being influenced by the ISI. The Tamil Tigers are also involved and had arranged the funds for the kidnap operation."

"Can you find the location of the Karen rebel's camp where Collins is being kept? There is a good reward declared by the Company for this information."

There was a long pause and they could hear people discussing in whispers. One of the persons appeared to be angry and raised his voice. The sound got cut off suddenly as the speaker perhaps covered the mobile with his hand.

"I will call later if we have some information."

The phone was disconnected.

They made several efforts in the course of next two days to get information on Peter Collins and spoke to another three persons named in the documents prepared by Majuli Oil. All knew that he was in Myanmar but there was no information on the exact location of the Karen's rebel camp where he was kept. The whole exercise had been frustrating and exhausted them emotionally. Anand spoke to Brigadier Sondhi in Majuli to get some more details on the contacts that could help. Sondhi was helpless.

"You have already spoken to the best contacts we have in Thailand," he said. "They are from the NDLF loyalists group and they cooperate with us. They have nothing to do with the ISI agents and treat them as the country's enemies. They will definitely try and get the information on Collins and his captor's location. Just give them some time."

The meeting with Rahim and Siva was arranged in an open air restaurant located in a park adjacent to a lake. Gopal and Anand sat in the garden just outside the restaurant, while Ravi engaged the agents inside. Ravi had arranged small wireless receivers with earplugs for Gopal and Anand and they could follow all the discussions he was having with his deep cover agents. The conversation was in Hindustani, heavily accented in some Assamese dialect. The device allowed a three-way conversation and Gopal could prompt Ravi to raise some issues as the discussions progressed.

"Jai Hind, friends, how have you been?" enquired Ravi.

"Jai Hind. Jai Assom, we are well," responded the agents.

"We meet after a long time; we must have a drink, yes," suggested Ravi.

They hear Ravi call the hostess and order a bottle of whisky, one beer and some plates of chicken satay, fried pork and grilled beef.

"What is the news from the valley? Is the agreement with the Government holding? Are the rebels behaving?"

"All is well and our leaders are discussing. There is no firing or bombing. The only bad news is from Majuli Camp." said Rahim.

"The kidnapping of Mr. Collins?" remarked Ravi.

"Yes. We heard of it last week in a jungle camp in Myanmar close to the Indian border. We were in one of those 'depots' which deal with drugs and weapons. There were some boys from the KIA (Kachins Independence Army); they had come with samples of RDX to the depot. They said they had some 50 kilos, recently brought in from China. There was a lot of excitement and somebody brought out a few bottles of rum. Lot of army rum smuggled from India is available in Myanmar. The drinking went on for long. There were some drug smugglers from India, Punjabis and Nepalese. They mentioned of this British Manager from Majuli who was missing, kidnapped by the underground rebels. There was a lot of discussion and some persons appeared to know about the group involved and where Collins was being held, but they were not willing to pass on the information," reported Shiva.

"Who were these people? Myanmarees or Indians?" Ravi enquired anxiously.

"They looked like the tribal's from the Myanmar side—the Karens perhaps. They are the ones who carry the contraband across," informed Shiva.

There was a long pause. The drinks and the food had arrived and the hostess was pouring the whisky into the glasses while her assistant arranged the plates. Ravi thanked the hostess and raised his glass to cheer his agents. There was clinking of glasses and general bonhomie.

"You must get details on these Indians bringing the drugs and track the RDX. We do not want the RDX to enter into India. The ISI will like to trade it for their proxies. The NDLF rebel groups are helping the ISI, you know. You find out where it will cross the border, and we will take care of that. Send message to Post Ten. The code for the goods will be Gold."

"Yes sir. We are now going to India and will be away for six days, but we will be in contact and ask our people to keep a watch. We are tracking Collins sahib and will keep you informed. Some of our Karen friends are spreading the word amongst the local tribes. We have promised them a reward for locating Collins sahib."

"Good, we want regular alerts after you confirm he is in Myanmar. We also want information on the people who are holding him. Who they are, their nationality, motives, and their paymasters? Every bit of information you can collect. If you identify the place where Collins is being held I want you to get the co-ordinates. You already have the GPS Also let me know the existing number of NDLF loyalist cadres within Myanmar."

Gopal had followed the entire conversation. He knew what Ravi had in his mind when he asked that question. To support his idea he pressed the speak button on the wireless set and advised Ravi to check up on the weapons being carried by these men. Ravi concluded the meeting by exhorting his agents to keep up their good work. He called them patriotic soldiers of the country and thanked them for their efforts. He also handed them five lakh rupees. Indian currency was very much in demand in Myanmar.

Anand was quiet impressed with Ravi's interactions with the R&AW agents operating in Myanmar. The operation Ravi was planning was of vital interest to him and Majuli Oil. Peter Collins had to be rescued from his captivity. Anand had been very upset with Peter's captivity. He was worried ever since he got the news if Peter was well and comfortable. Were his captors treating him well? Was he getting proper food and water? He had tried putting himself in Peters place and had shuddered at the thought. He was not sure if all of this would end up satisfactorily. Gopal had made the whole business of handling terrorists and subversives too simple. Anand was not sure if they would be able to pull of the mission of rescuing Peter successfully. The Special Forces could come under heavy fire from the rebels holding Peter. They will have to fire back in self defense and there could be collateral damage. The rebels may also kill Peter if things got difficult for them. He had discussed all these doubts in his mind with Gopal and Ravi the night before. They agreed with him that there was always a chance that the mission could go horribly wrong. They were attempting to factor in all the possibilities of failure to ensure a smooth operation. In a hostage situation there is always a possibility of negotiations which is also used as a means of softening the captors. But in the present crisis there was no scope for negotiations with the captors holding Peter. They were mercenaries who were on a contract to hold Peter. They have no personal animus with him but they have an obligation to fulfill with their paymasters.

# NEW DELHI

Saxena had reviewed the brief prepared by his office on Collins abduction for the Prime Minister, and was not happy about it. The case was still in a limbo. There had been reports about Collins presence in Myanmar. He did not want to put it in the brief till he got confirmation on visual sighting from the Station Officer at Chiang Mai. This could only be done by the local agents operating in Myanmar. A group of Special Forces had already been moved to a secret airstrip in Assam with a C-130 transport aircraft standing by for the rescue mission approved by the PM. He wanted to get satellite images of the camp where Peter was being held, but the Chiang Mai source had yet to give the coordinates of the location. It could be a very difficult mission if his captors were moving Peter around to various locations to thwart attempts to rescue him. The Special Forces had to be focused on their mission. This was not a search and destroy mission for which they had been trained and equipped. They had to zero on to the spot and snatch Peter from his captors. Stealth was the strategy and they had to carry out the task without firing a shot, if possible. The idea was to minimize a showdown. Saxena had been in close contact with the Interior Minister in Yangon and had been assured full cooperation. The Myanmar Government had really no presence in the Northern provinces, where the Karens ruled and collected taxes. But under diplomatic practice and custom and of course International Law, the Sovereign Government had to be informed before entering its territory in hot pursuit of forces and rebels adverse to your interests. The NDLF cadres present in Myanmar were also being readied by Ravi Karan to provide logistic support at the ground level to the rescue mission.

Venkat had already called Saxena twice. He had included the draft brief in the PM's folder. Saxena wanted the brief to be specific to the identity of the adversary, but no agency had accepted responsibility for the abduction of Collins. It had been ten days now since Collins went missing from the Majuli Camp. The MI 5 had also drawn a blank and Scotland Yards investigators camping at Majuli had already run a complete forensic check at his camp house and his abandoned Land Rover. The abductors had left no trace of their presence which could have identified their nationality and creed. There was no hair, blood, spittle, cloth fiber from the scene of crime which could have helped the forensic experts to build up a profile of the persons involved in the criminal act. The escape route had since been identified when the tanker supplying water to the school was found abandoned at a remote site on the island, three days after Collins disappeared. That was the only vehicle that had moved from the camp that day after he disappeared. It was surmised that Peter was smuggled out of the camp, hidden in one of the empty compartments of the tanker. Similar tactics had been employed in the past by the Khalistan separatists in Punjab for transporting their hit teams around the country.

Saxena was keen to show some results, but there was nothing more to report. Venkat had during their last chat on the phone advised him to relax and not feel frustrated.

But Saxena's worry was that pained look on the PM's face when failures were reported to him. He had become very petulant with age and illness. There was a soft knock on his door and he heard the latch turn.

"May I come in Sir," that sounded like Suresh Kumar, his Technical Assistant, and Saxena looked up.

"Sir this just came in, you may like to carry it with you to the PM's security briefing." Suresh said very earnestly. Saxena opened the folder and read the brief memo from the station officer at Ulan Bator.

## TOP SECRET

To,
Secretary RAW                                    12 February 2004
New Delhi

Subject: Clandestine sale of nuclear material to suspected Qaeda/Taliban ultras.

Reports from local police and confirmed by our agents in Ulan Bator and Azerbaijan talk of sudden transfer of US Fifty Million Dollars and gold bullion to Russian mafia during the last thirty days. Suspect purchase of stolen scrap material from Soviet War Heads and Missiles dismantled under STRATEGIC ARMS LIMITATIONS TREATY (SALT). Agent in Azerbaijan confirms of major theft and disappearance of guidance systems, electronic components and miniature war heads from tactical weapons and MIRV Missiles. Russian agencies investigating and all borders alerted and sealed. Three arrests made by the Internal Security Agencies. Identities of arrested terrorists are being ascertained. Russians confirm that contraband materials still within the country with the missing terrorists.

Message No. RA/SP-XXX-2343

Sender-Ax Gangotri

TOP SECRET

This message conformed what the RAW, CIA and International Atomic Energy Agency (IAEA) Vienna had feared for sometime now. IAEA had also issued advisory on the attempts of Al Qaeda to assemble a crude nuclear device and move it into USA or some target in the UK or Europe. This message was a major alert because of the growing proximity between Qaeda and the radical groups operating within Pakistan and Afghanistan.

Saxena called Venkat and told him he had something urgent to show him and was coming over to his office.

"Yes Saxena anything new on Collins affair?" Venkat asked anxiously.

"No not Majuli or Collins. I have something more serious to show you before we go over for PM's meeting."

Venkat had one look at the message Saxena placed on his desk and whistled softly. It sounded like air escaping from a deflating balloon. He read it again and again till his peon came around with the coffee.

"This is serious, very serious indeed, Saxena. We have to take a major policy review. We cannot trust our friends across the border at all. You remember the brain storming session during the last security review when we suggested a foreign policy review and a paradigm shift for the region? We had also done a similar exercise while discussing and developing the paper on our Nuclear Doctrine. We did not get much support from the political establishment then and had to withdraw the policy paper recommending a more pro active approach. I think we will have a separate chat with the PM after our meeting and force a policy review within next ten days. I still remember that young officer you had in your policy wing. He had prepared that paper on the Durand Line and Balochistan Tribes. He was branded a hawk by the MEA boys and his suggestions ignored. Yes it was a very important policy suggestion and called for a bold approach. I am sure the Foreign Secretary would appreciate it better now."

"Yes that was Amit Sinha, a very bright officer. He is now in Washington and still recording excellent policy papers on the international terrorism. I can pull out that paper he had read at that meeting and get it updated. It was good and very well reasoned. But it did appear a very proactive policy then and put up the hackles of the MEA mandarins, schooled in the Nehru era diplomatic doctrines as they are. I think much water has flowed down the Indus and we should at least think differently in the new security environment enveloping the sub-continent and the region."

"We require a fresh look at the Nuclear Doctrine too. The Chief of Army Staff was sounding worried when we met last at that Army Day reception. He was not very happy with the missile induction programme of the Pakistan Army. Now with the non-state terrorists becoming proactive and seeking nuclear devices we better get prepared for the worst. The PM had assured us that he would have an open mind and would definitely convince the political establishment, if change was inevitable. We have to tell him that the time has come. He will have a lot of work on his plate if he agrees for a change. We will have to sound our friends overseas and garner support with the UN agencies. At the national level we will draft a major programme of educating the public, the opposition and the minority parties. Let's talk to PM first and brief him on this new development."

"Yes Venkat and no pulling off punches this time. We have had enough peace initiatives and every Prime Minister has illusions of getting the Nobel Peace Prize for bringing lasting peace and brotherhood in the sub-continent. What we have got are more war widows and disabled soldiers. Remember their Prime Minister Bhutto had threatened us with a thousand years war after their debacle in the 1971 operations. Of course he did not last long. Today our threat perceptions have mounted many times over. There is still no real civilian government across the western border. They are just puppets of the army generals who rule that country. It's so funny to see them go strutting about in their silk salwars and bending backwards to please the men in khakis.

Venkat had a big laugh.

"Saxena this is not a well kept secret of the ISI. They are shadowing the entire political class and the civil administration to blackmail them and make them toe their line."

The meeting of the Internal Security Coordination Committee at the PM's lasted about an hour. It was attended by the Ministers of Home, Tribal Affairs, Public Works and the Chairman North East Coordination Council. The Prime Minister had read all the briefs and was ready with his questions. He was very concerned with the growing violence in Andhra Pradesh by the left-wing ultras. They had again blasted the railway links in areas bordering Orissa and destroyed police stations and school buildings. A dozen policemen had lost their lives in the last two months. The Tribal Development Minister wanted more funds for development of roads in the tribal districts of Chhattisgarh and Orissa. The PM advised the Home Minister to convene a meeting of the state home ministers and their police officers to review the progress of the various schemes of training and modernisation of the police forces. A lot of money had been made available during the last five years for this purpose but the ultras were still having an upper hand.

The Majuli case was not discussed as part of the internal security meeting so Venkat and Saxena stayed back after the meeting got over. They sat in the office of Pratap Sharma, Principal Secretary to the PM waiting for the PM to call them. Pratap and Venkat had been batch mates and close friends. Pratap had spent years in the Defense Ministry and had joined the Prime Ministers Secretariat on retirement from the civil-service. He had been supportive of a more pro-active policy on the Afghanistan issue and had expressed his strong reservations on the existing Nuclear Doctrine during the last defense and foreign policy review. Venkat showed him the message Saxena had received just a couple of hours ago from Ulan Bator.

"This is precisely what you and Saxena had told the PM at the last Defense and Foreign Policy Review meeting. Our major concern was the growing menace of the ISI sponsored non-state players and it now appears they are going to raise the bar by gifting nuclear devices to them. I am sure that rogue nuclear genius Ashfaq Ahmad must be holding tutorial classes for the Taliban and the Qaeda boys. The Americans have let him off the hook so easily; I would love to see the face of the CIA chief when the Qaeda land a nuclear device in Manhattan on board a

Chinese Cargo Container. We have to convene a meeting of the Defense and Foreign Policy Review Committee immediately Venkat or we will have no answers to give to our countrymen."

"That was my reaction when Saxena dropped that message on my table. We have to give it back to these bastards. We could not do it the last time but we are a stronger economy now. We have to tell the good General next door that if he does not mend his ways we are going to make him kiss the land between the Indus and the Hindu Kush good bye. And by God we can do it now."

"Yes the Pashtun policy requires a total review. The Frontier Gandhi was let down when the British left after dividing the country. Its time we apologized and gave the Pashtuns what is theirs. You know Venkat the other day I had gone to meet Professor Prasad at the Jawaharlal Lal Nehru University. He is the Head of Department for History there and is a specialist on Pashtun affairs. He had written an article for the Harvard University Economic Review on Afghanistan's Development issues. Describing the pathetic condition of the Pashtuns on both sides of the Durand Line he has strongly advocated their unification. This indirectly implies redrawing the borders and merging parts of Balochistan along with the Pashtun dominated areas west of the Indus with Afghanistan. I feel the time has come to shake the Generals across the border."

"Pratap you have made my day for me. This is what we want to tell the PM today so we can lay down an agenda for discussion for formally declaring our intentions. Besides, before taking a decision we have to prepare the people for it. The opposition will have to be taken into confidence, the leftists have always opposed our nuclear policy but the right wing is supportive and has always criticized the

Nuclear Doctrine of no first use. We can start the campaign and up the ante by bringing up the issue in the press. There are a dozen senior defense and security analysts who keep writing on the subject. We can persuade them to turn hawkish for a change. The growing fear world wide of the terrorists groups turning nuclear would be the theme. We can also leak this message from Ulan Bator to, say, Manoj Subramanian after taking the PM's approval. We will outline a strategy to him and suggest that Subramanian kick off a press campaign to highlight the dangers faced by the nation from the growing belligerence of our neighbour and the rising influence of Al Qaeda. He could then conclude that our Nuclear Doctrine of no first use cannot defend the country from the nuclear piracy of the Qaeda. Subramanian's article will snowball the campaign and send the media into frenzy and pillory the government for answers and explanations. The right-wingers and the *Hindutava* groups will hit the streets after that and the opposition will stall proceedings in the Parliament with a demand for a White Paper on the government's response. We can then come out with a calibrated response leading to amending the nuclear doctrine and our Afghan policy."

Rajeev Pillai the PM's private secretary came in to say that the PM was ready for the Home Secretary and all three walked into the PM's private quarters.

The PM looked most relaxed; he was holding a child on his lap and was a picture of domesticity.

"Come in gentlemen; meet my great grandson Rajat, a second generation US Citizen. He may well become the President of the United States of America one day and when he visits India, the Prime Minister will have to introduce him as—'Mr. Rajat Singh the President of the United States of America, the great grand son of our former Prime Minister Late Shri Amar Singh Chauhan."

He laughed out loudly handing him over to his mother who had just walked into the room.

"Oh Dada, not again. I am sure Dada has been cracking that old joke about Rajat becoming the US President. I'll be happy even if becomes a juggler in the New York's Soho district."

"And that gentlemen, is Sujata the future Presidents mother and my loving granddaughter."

Sujata curtseyed and prepared to leave.

Venkat touched Rajat on his head and blessed him.

"God bless him and we will pray that his great grandfather's wish will come true one day."

"Venkat I am very disappointed with the states. They are doing precious little to improve the performance of their police departments even in the face of the growing menace of terror attacks. Their police departments have no special counter terrorism force. The opposition blames our intelligence agencies but the state police do not follow up on all the advisories we dispatch to them. I have advised the Home Minister to convene a meeting of the state home ministers but on second thoughts I feel I should also address them. I think in more than half the states of our Union, the Home portfolio is with the Chief Minister himself. You arrange it accordingly. Rajeev, when do we return from the US? We could arrange the meeting immediately thereafter . . . ."

"Sir we get back on the 18th March and you have no engagement till the 22nd March. We could arrange it on Monday the 20th March."

"Venkat let's keep it on the Monday 20th March. We must get tough with the state governments. We should not repeat the mistakes that were made in the North Eastern states. During my watch I want to give internal security the best resources and talent. We should learn a few lessons from the Israeli's also. The interactions with the Mossad should continue, I recall some years ago Saxena had worked on that protocol we signed with the Government of Israel, when I was Home Minister. That's working well and we have shared a lot of Intel on the Afghanistan issue."

"Sir, we have something serious to report. Saxena received this message today from our station officer in Ulan Bator."

Venkat removed the message from his folder and placed it before the PM who read through it and looked up at Saxena and exclaimed loudly.

"This has got to stop immediately. My God, are we heading for a war again. We had worked on this scenario with the Americans only last year. They had anticipated some such mischief by the Qaeda. We should alert them at once. You can call in the US Ambassador and give the details. Keep him informed of the developments. Moscow has already moved in and taken steps to prevent transfer of the material. But their border is too big and there are enough sympathizers in the Central Asian region to facilitate the concealment and movement of this dangerous cargo."

"Sir we believe it's time to enlarge this discussion and elevate it from purely an operational matter to one of policy. You recall the discussions at the last meeting of the Defense and Foreign Policy Review Committee, when the R&AW and the Army Chief of Staff had made out a strong case for a review of our declared Nuclear Doctrine of NO FIRST USE. The change was proposed on the then existing threat perceptions and the deteriorating security environment in Afghanistan and the immediate neighborhood. We had also suggested a review of our Foreign Policy vis-à-vis Balochistan and the Pashtuns on both sides of the Durand Line. We had made out a strong case in our presentation for a more proactive policy to sort out the ISI plans as well save the Balochies and the Pashtuns from the ravages of their Army pogroms'. We were branded hawks by the mandarins in the Ministry of External Affairs and the Foreign Secretary shot down both the proposals saying that such a move would jeopardize our external relations. He felt that the time was not ripe enough to get into a pro active mode. He made an excellent but a very academic presentation narrating the genesis of our foreign policy and the vision of its architect, the first Prime Minister. He went on to emphasize the importance of economic power to preamble our defense and foreign policy. He sincerely felt that India had not reached that level of economic power to bring about a paradigm shift in its defense and foreign policy."

Venkat paused to take a sip from the coffee which the bearer had placed before him.

"Sir you recall that we had discussed in a special briefing, the scenario of Qaida/LET terrorists smuggling in components of a small nuclear device and assembling it in some small town like Ranchi for example. The local police force there would have no clue about it and it could be later moved in a cargo container to New Delhi with forged documents declaring the consignment to be automobile components. They could park the container truck on Mathura Road near the Exhibition grounds and detonate it after priming it with a remote control signal. Similar was the scenario which the Homeland Security and FBI had envisioned for Manhattan, New York. There'd be very little time for our bomb disposal units and forces to react and prevent a disaster even if we are alerted about the device. The possibilities of defusing such devices by our bomb squad specialist are also remote. Similarly with our existing Nuclear Doctrine we stand no chance of preventing a disaster even if we had warning of a pre-emptive strike from across the border. The entire operation of deployment and launch, would not allow us to hit them before they strike. Today our defense forces cannot take on an airborne or a missile attack and neutralize the aggressor's first strike. The aggressor will, of course, have no advantage after his first strike as we will react fast and devastate him under our existing doctrine. Our strike force is superior and we have more powerful warheads than he has. He, however, still has the advantage of a choice of the first target."

"We have, therefore, to modify our nuclear weapons deployment and use policy and make it more proactive. We have to make it very clear that a non state combatant is a proxy of that state under our new doctrine and the state will face retaliation of an extreme measure for any acts committed by that proxy. If a non state terror outfit ever dares to deploy a device to blackmail us, we will take the battle to the enemy territory by launching our pre-emptive strike and devastate him. We have to make the game expensive for him and we should be over their crucial targets in minutes before he can launch his missile or aircraft. We have the capability and we have practiced such scenarios with dummy war heads. Secondly, we can deploy our missiles from mobile launchers and hit him hard to prevent any possibility of a retaliatory strike. We can destroy his command and control within seven minute of getting a go ahead from the PM. This would isolate his field formations from any central direction for regrouping and attack. Moreover his army would be totally overwhelmed in their eastern provinces providing relief and help to the populace who suffered our first strike. Panic in other cities and towns would have almost eighty million refugees deserting the town and cities and crowding their highways thereby reducing their ability to move their heavy assets to battle zones on their eastern borders. All this will not be possible without adopting a more pro active Nuclear Doctrine. We want to work on the amendments and we have to prepare the country for the policy measures we are going to adopt. We will have to take care of world opinion also and convince the UN and the IAEA of our threat perceptions of terror outfits being armed with nuclear devices in the neighborhood."

The PM who had patiently heard Venkat present his case, sat up and remarked, "I will speak to our party president and brief him of the new threats. I agree with you fully that the situation warrants an immediate review of our Nuclear Doctrine. We can get the policy review papers drafted urgently and we should also start a debate in the media. Let our security and defense analysts kick up a debate on the subject in the print media to start with."

"Sir, with your permission I was going to show this message to Manoj Subramanian and let him begin the process of public debate. He is one of our most prolific writers on the threats posed by Pakistani nukes and has also written a few articles in the Harvard Economic Review on the threats posed by the Qaida to the American economy. He has been dubbed a hawk by our External Affairs ministry and has not been taken seriously by us. But he deserves better appreciation. We had been hoping for a change in the political establishment of Pakistan and done so much to encourage contacts between the people. But the return of the civilian government has not brought about a paradigm shift in the government to government relations. The civilians still take their orders from the Generals. The ISI functions unhindered from the civil control and are answerable only to the army chief. They continue to train the terrorists and fund radical groups on our soil. Last year we could destroy seventy cells created to train radical students groups to make bombs and kill innocent civilians. They have continued to lure the underground movements in the northeast despite their PM's assertions in SAARC conclaves that they will destroy the terrorists groups and cooperate in their capture and prosecution. They continue to deny the presence of the absconding suspects of the Mumbai blasts case in Karachi safe houses. We have suffered them for long and have refused to interfere in their internal affairs. Our new policy should aim at raising the ghost of Khan Abdul Gaffar Khan and view sympathetically the struggles of the Pashtun and the Baluchi people against the military oppression. They have struggled bravely to get recognition and some political autonomy but they have been ill treated by the politicians and army generals who represent the Punjabi landlords. We have to set the cat amongst the pigeons to show them that we too can play the game like they do in Kashmir. If you gave a free hand to Saxenas boys, they can set fire to the region between the Indus and the Hindu Kush in no time. Let's see how the Generals save the region from breaking away in a year.

We want your permission to take this issue also to the press. Professor Prasad of the JNU has recently published an article describing the sorry plight of the Pashtuns on both sides of the Durand line recommending the reunification of Pashtunistan. Similar studies have been conducted by Professor Alka Gadgil, Head of the Department of Asian Historical Studies at the JNU. She has written an excellent treatise on the tribal's of Pakistan and has made out a case for the redrawing the Durand Line which was a British conspiracy to divide and weaken the invincible Pashtuns. She has made out a strong case for the independence of the Balochistan and merging of erstwhile North West Frontier Provinces with Afghanistan. We could ask her to write her story in some prominent newspaper and this could be followed up with a major debate on the TV news channels. All this ought to send a strong message across the border and shake them up a bit. We must call off their bluff once for all."

"Venkat I agree with you. Try and get the press campaign going before I reach New York. Let us take the message to the UN that we are changing. A strong economy gives us the opportunity to flex our muscles. India has to project herself as an emerging power. We cannot be tied down by a bunch of armed thugs from across the border. Please go ahead and keep the Foreign Secretary informed of these discussions. Let him come and meet me also when he gets back from Moscow."

# COLOMBO

**R**aj completed his appointments with the gem and jewel traders in the forenoon and headed for his meeting with a former LTTE commander. Thampi had asked him to come to the office of Spice Trading Corporation located behind the Noritake showroom on the Galle Face Road. Raj took some time to locate the Corporation's office. The passage behind the Noritake shop was a parking lot. Some twenty meters into the passage he found the narrow corridor leading to a flight of stairs with the wall on one side covered with signboards of perhaps a dozen offices. Most of the signboards were in Sinhala, but he could find one with the Spice Corporations office address in Sinhala and English. He climbed the poorly lit staircase to the third floor. An elderly person with a stoop answered the call bell and beckoned him inside. Raj followed him and was led through the premises which appeared as a storehouse of spices with a strong aroma of cloves and cardamoms. Raj saw two women staff working on ledgers and registers in very dingy surroundings. He was led to a room with a balcony overlooking the road. He surmised they were in a room right above the Noritake showroom.

Thampi was there with a very athletic looking man in his mid fifties attired in a shirt and a white *dhoti* tied like a sarong.

"Raj this is Comrade Balu, a good friend and former Member of Parliament. He has worked very hard to secure peace in the country. I was telling him about your mission and the threat of growing terrorism in the sub continent. I have also briefed him about the kidnapping of Peter Collins and the suspected LTTE involvement. You must listen to the information he has."

"Mr. Raj there is a major involvement of the ISI in arms procurement by the LTTE. They have arranged supplies of 500 AK 47 rifles from the Taliban sources in Pakistan and Afghanistan. Some wireless communication sets of Chinese origin have also come through that source. The trading in weapons is tied up with the drugs trade, especially heroin, from Afghanistan. The LTTE has a good network of contacts in France, Germany, Switzerland and some Scandinavian countries where Tamils from Sri Lanka have acquired refugee status. They have become a natural conduit for smuggling the heroin through the gulf ports and Yemen into Europe. The drug money is used for purchase of weapons. The banking arrangements are done by LTTE front companies in Mauritius. The Mauritius route is also used to legitimize the illegal funds into clean currency and has been invested in various businesses in India, especially in Tamil Nadu and Kerala; in Mumbai and Bangalore most of the funds have been invested in real estate. Some funds have also made their way into the film industry in Chennai and Mumbai. Pradeep's family has never come near any business which is illegal. Pradeep has funds in various companies in Mauritius and is a partner in a major banking corporation which has invested in his company in India. They are a very respectable family and they have done good work in employing and educating the ethnic Tamil labour in the Kandy and the Nuwara Eliya

Hills tea estates. But yes LTTE'S funds have been invested in the Mumbai film industry."

"Comrade, what would be the LTTE'S interest in Myanmar and why are they interested in Peter Collins?" Thampi asked after a long pause.

"Peter is a British national. The British are not very sympathetic to the LTTE cause. Moreover a large number of Sri Lankan Tamils are in jail in the UK and possibly the hostage situation is created for demanding a release of one of them. However, I cannot personally recall any body important enough to warrant such a daring and dastardly act on part of the LTTE. Maybe the ISI is interested in somebody's release and the Tigers are helping with their contacts in Myanmar and Bangla Desh."

# KANDY

Thampi had booked a room for Raj in the Amaya Hills Hotel in Kandy. This was a pleasant hotel overlooking the town of Kandy and at a distance of little over three kilometers from the city center. Raj called Mr. Tilakaratne of the Kandy Jewels Corporation and fixed up his meetings. They had got Navnitbhai's message and had most of the articles ready for inspection. They decided to meet at four in the afternoon. Raj next called the office of the Deputy High Commissioner of India in Kandy and was immediately connected to Joseph Cherian.

"Raj, what are you doing in the evening. I have a small party at my place and I have also invited Pradeep, so please do join us for dinner."

Raj was pleasantly surprised by the patronizing air of Cherian, but was pleased at the arrangement of meeting his key 'witness' in such an informal manner. He thanked Joseph and noted his address.

Raj went down to the dining hall and ordered fish koftas with rice for lunch. His mind was on the information he wanted out of Pradeep on Vijaya and his financial transactions with B.K.Enterprises. The fish koftas served with rice were crispy and delicately flavored; the flavors of mint and black pepper came through well. Raj washed down the meal with a glass of chilled beer and felt satiated. Having a sumptuous meal on overseas assignments was one way of keeping anxiety at bay. The long drive from Colombo and the spicy curry and rice made Raj drowsy and he couldn't keep his eyes open for a minute. He dropped on his bed and dozed off. He got up with a start around three thirty and splashed some cold water on his face to freshen up. He would have loved a cup of tea but there was no time. He called for his car and drove into town.

The meeting with the gem traders was pleasant and he got his cup of steaming Dilmah Earl Gray Tea as soon as he arrived. Mr. Tilakaratne was waiting for him. Navnitbhai had been a valued client for over a decade and their annual sales to his Company were presently valued at over twenty million Sri Lanka rupees. The business discussions were a mere formality. Tilakaratne's assistants brought in the samples of the gems ordered by Navnitbhai for Raj's approval. The trust and business ethics amongst the diamond and gems traders was of a high order and most of the time purchase orders were made by word of mouth. You placed the order and the consignment would be delivered. There was no scope for cheating and fraud and when it happened, which was rarely, it would mean end of dealings for the trader who indulged is such practice as he would lose face in the gem trading fraternity. Business concluded they signed off the documents required for custom clearances, freight and insurance and Tilakaratne ordered another round of tea.

Tilakaratne reminded Raj of the Dickensian character, Micawber in David Copperfield, constantly washing his hands in the air, bowing and genuflecting, overeager to please. Raj felt a little embarrassed by the attention he was getting and he made all efforts to put Tilakaratne at ease. They talked about the weather and then the current visit of the Sri Lankan cricket team to India. He seemed to be a great admirer of Sachin Tendulkar, the great Indian batsman and told Raj that he was a hero to the younger generation in Sri Lanka. Raj added that he too was a keen cricketer and had played for his college but now his passion was limited to following the game on the TV.

They chatted long about cricket, Tamil insurgency and the political scenario. Then Raj casually asked him about the tea industry and exports. The discussion progressed into the conditions of plantation labour and then to the families who owned the plantations. Pradeep Menon's company it appeared had the biggest plantations. They were developed largely by Pradeep's grandfather who was one of the pioneers of the modern tea industry in Sri Lanka. Pradeep's father had carried on the tradition. The present Chairman Pradeep was the face of growing globalisation of the Sri Lankan trade and industry. He led the expansion of his group into banking and finance.

Raj took leave of Tilakaratne and drove back to the hotel. He picked up his swimming drawers and took the lift to the pool. The water was crystal clear and he could see the patterns on the tiles at the bottom. He changed and dived in. There were only three young girls in the water and the rest, mostly foreign guests were all sitting around or reclining on beach chairs in various stages of acquiring a tan. Their glistening bodies filmed with tan lotions and sun blocs, indicated that most were past their prime. Raj did half a dozen lengths to get some exercise and then stopped to catch his breath. The water was cool and pleasant and he continued his exercise by doing another half a dozen lengths of breast stroke. He felt good and relaxed and hung around at the shallow end admiring the girls frolicking in the water. They must be in their early teens and were chattering away in German. He remembered his visits to Munich a few years ago to attend a seminar on drug trafficking organised by the Interpol. He had managed to get enough time on the weekend for some sightseeing in the old city area and visit the English Gardens. He also managed a visit to the Holfbrauhaus, the famous historical watering hole of Munich where beer was served in the one liter steins, by buxom Bavarian waitresses dressed in their traditional dresses.

Raj got back to his room showered and changed into a fresh shirt. Dinner at the house of the Deputy High Commissioners he thought, ought to be a formal affair, so he put on a tie and carried his blazer to the car. The residence of Joseph Cherian was a large villa on the hill above the lake. There was armed security at the gate, a reminder of the troubled times the country was passing through. He was ushered in by Cherian's bearer to a large hall at the rear end of the villa. There were a dozen guests present. Cherian broke from the group and came up to greet Raj.

"Good evening Raj and welcome. I hope you had a pleasant day and all your meetings went off well."

He introduced him to his wife Tara and others present. The guests were a sprinkling of city's business community and local district officials. The ladies were all dressed in saris in the Sri Lankan fashion. The Principal of the local college was also present and his wife was the sole exception who wore a skirt and blouse. She was a charming lady and Raj got talking to her. Sheetal was from Mauritius and was a practicing gynecologist. She had graduated in medicine from Grant Medical College in Mumbai and chatted endlessly of her student days. Her family belonged to migrants who had gone to Mauritius from Kolhapur district in Maharashtra a hundred years ago. Raj helped himself to a scotch and soda when Cherian came along and told him that Pradeep had called and informed that he would be here within half an hour. He had gone away to his tea estate to attend an urgent meeting and got held up on the way back in a traffic jam on the highway.

Raj caught up with Tara Cherian who had been busy playing the hostess. She was from Chennai and had been a national level hockey player. She had represented India and had accompanied the national team to Malaysia and Canada but had to give up playing after she got married to Joseph when he was posted in Spain. Sri Lanka was the second foreign station for her and she liked the place. She was very proud of the villa which had been the official residence of the prime minister of the erstwhile State of Kandy and had been designed by a Dutch Architect in 1891. She promised to take him around on a conducted tour of the house if he came around the next day.

"Here is the most eligible bachelor of Kandy," she said and moved over to welcome a handsome young man as he was ushered into the hall by the bearer.

Pradeep needed no introduction to most of the guests present so Joseph brought him over to Raj.

"Pradeep this is Vikas Shah from Mumbai, representing Navnitbhai, jewelers from Mumbai. He is visiting us for a few days to buy the beautiful gems of Sri Lanka. You must persuade him to buy some tea from your estate too."

"Welcome to Kandy, Vikas. How long are you planning to stay? We must take you around and show you the beautiful hills of Nuwara Eliya."

Pradeep helped himself to a glass of beer and raised it to Raj.

"For a pleasant trip. And now tell me besides gems and jewels, what attracts you to Sri Lanka."

"Well that's a long story and will require telling beyond this pleasant evening. So I will tell you the short one while we enjoy Cherian's hospitality."

"You appear to be a very interesting man I must say, Vikas."

"I have the immediate task of buying gems for our company. We are the largest importers of gems and semi-precious stones from Sri Lanka and have been so for the last twenty years. Navnitbhai does not travel much these days so he asked me to check out some consignments of rubies and emeralds which he had ordered. I finished the task in the afternoon and now I am looking forward to some tourism here and in Nuwara Eliya. Then depending on how fast I tell you the other part of the story, will move on to Bentota for a day or two to check out the beautiful beach resorts there."

"This suspense is too much and now you have made me more curious. Tell me your plans and we can decide to meet accordingly. Where are you staying in Nuwara Eliya? The Grand Hotel is it?"

"No I have not yet tied up my plans beyond today. I thought I'd consult Joseph Cherian for Nuwara Eliya. He has been helping me with my travel plans."

"Listen I am going back to my tea estate tomorrow morning and I intend to stay there for next three days. This place is fifteen kilometers short of Nuwara Eliya. We have our family cottage there and it's more comfortable and scenic than any hotel in Nuwara. Why not stay there and be my guest and look around and see what we do to make some of the finest teas in the world. We will have plenty of time to relax and admire those beautiful hills, and in the bargain you can tell me your long story."

Raj couldn't believe his luck and accepted Pradeep's offer promptly.

"Thank you, that's very gracious of you."

Dinner was announced and Cherian caught up with them wondering what the two bachelor boys were up to. He was happy that Raj could meet Pradeep and hoped all was well. He had known Pradeep for just a year but he was sure he could give him a clean chit. He was certain that he was not involved in any matter which could bring trouble to his door step. Thampi had just mentioned that the RA&W was on some serious investigation involving national security issues and Raj was to check out on information Pradeep may have been privy to.

The meal was a combined fare of Sinhala and Indian preparations but it was so difficult to differentiate. The names of the preparations were the same and most of the spices similar. But all the dishes were spicy and hot enough to make you perspire under the collar even in the cool, salubrious weather of Kandy. Raj had taken a liking to the pork preparations, as these were seldom served in restaurants in India. The sambar was spicy and went well with the string hoppers and the chicken curry. Pradeep joined him after helping himself from the buffet. They found a table in the far corner of the dining hall still unoccupied and they moved over to enjoy the wonderful meal in peace. They talked about food and Pradeep remarked that he had been just a week out of Mumbai and was missing the samosas, dhokla and vada pau already. He was just waiting to get back to those tasty snacks again. They lingered over their dessert and the coffee and talked about Mumbai.

Raj was up early next morning and walked over to the
dining hall for some breakfast. Last evening's dinner party
had been good and he had indulged and enjoyed himself
thoroughly. The food and company had both been excellent
and he had met some interesting people. He felt a little
sluggish and decided to have something different. He had
been enjoying the string hoppers and curry for breakfast
ever since he landed in Colombo and ordered some toast
and poached eggs for a change. He helped himself to some
fruit from the buffet and had some light tea to wash it all
down. He got back to his room and finished his packing.
Waiting for Pradeep to arrive he switched on the cable
TV and paged the BBC news. The headlines were about
the Russian Secret Service, the FSB busting a mafia
group trying to sell nuclear material to an Islamic terrorist
group. Some of the terrorist killed and arrested were from
Afghanistan working for Al Qaeda. The material offered
on sale had been salvaged from the dismantled missiles and
nuclear warheads under the SALT agreement. It was still
not clear from reports released by the Russian Government
if any material had crossed their borders. The news was
followed by a round table discussion on terrorism with a
Russian nuclear scientist, the Director of the IAEA, and a
Major General of the NATO forces posted in Afghanistan.
Fears were expressed by the participants that this material
would find its way into the hands of the rogue scientists
who had helped Dr. Ashfaq Ahmad proliferate nuclear
technology to Iran, Iraq and North Korea. After the
arrest of Dr. Ahmad, some of these scientists had taken
political asylum in North Korea, Libya and Myanmar.
Their present whereabouts were not known to the IAEA
but they still posed a potential threat to world peace.
There had been unconfirmed reports that some were still

working on clandestine projects to develop nuclear devices for weapons of mass destruction. Material smuggled from dismantled warheads could help them achieve their objective. Raj switched off the TV and went down to the lobby and cleared his bills. The receptionist handed him a sealed envelop which had been delivered in the morning by courier. Raj saw it was from Delight Gems and opened the packet. There was a brief message from Navnitbhai.

"Rupees fifty million transferred from a Mauritius Bank to the party you are meeting today for the gems that went missing. Confirm the transaction made and on what account."

That was the first clue Saxena was giving him about a transaction traced from the B.K. Dossier to Pradeep. The funds were given to Vijaya. Saxena was keen to trace the LTTE hand in this transaction. Comrade Balu had also hinted that LTTE was parking its funds in construction business and the film industry and then through their channels via the havala route to the arms smugglers in middle east and eastern Europe.

He wheeled his bag out of the lobby just as Pradeep drove his Land Rover on to the porch.

"Good morning Pradeep, looks as if we are going to have some rain today."

"Good morning Vikas, yes we are expecting rain and we need it desperately. We have had scanty rainfall so far which is affecting our new plantations." responded Pradeep as he drove out of the hotel and headed for the road to Nuwara Eliya.

"We are replacing some of the bushes which are almost a hundred years old. My grandfather had purchased that part of the estate from a Scotsman in 1945 when he decided to quit and go back; twenty acres of that plantation has now been replanted. We need rains desperately for the plants to survive."

They drove through the outskirts of Kandy and passed a number of large villages with roadside shops and motor repair garages. They were soon driving through hilly terrain full of thick vegetative cover. The road went past a few plantations of rubber and spices and jungles of tropical forests. The tea plantations came to view as they reached the higher altitude. The valley view was breath taking as they neared Nuwara Eliya. There were waterfalls and mountain streams and far off in the distance they could see a river debouch into the plains.

"The Kandy and Nuwara Hills are the catchment area of the two major rivers of Sri Lanka, the Kelan and the Mahaveli and are the source of hydro electric power and irrigation systems," informed Pradeep, as they entered the Estates of the Blue Hills Tea and Resorts Co. Ltd. There were tea plantations covering the entire hillsides as far as the eye could see. They drove another kilometer or so through the plantations and estate offices till they came to an open area with factory buildings and parking lot for trucks and various types of tractors and other farm equipment. Pradeep waved out to some officials in the courtyard and slowed down to say that he would see them later in the afternoon. He drove on through the lush green rows of tea bushes beautifully trimmed and manicured by women labour which was working between the bushes, expertly plucking the two leaves and a bud which constituted the essence of the tea industry.

Almost at the top of the ridge on the road beyond Raj could now see at the very crest, a beautiful bungalow surrounded by trees.

"There it is, the Estate Bungalow our home built by my grandfather who spent most of his working life here. My father, Anna of course renovated it extensively and made it what it is today. He added three more bedrooms to the existing four, and enlarged the living room to accommodate more guests for his famous dinner parties. He also added a library which is my favorite haunt today."

They were welcomed at the porch by the caretaker, the gardner and two other servants who took care of their bags and disappeared into the house. Pradeep showed Raj to his room and they decided to meet in the library after a wash.

# CHIANG MAI

The meeting with the deep cover agents had provided valuable information but visual confirmations and coordinates of the rebel's camp were needed before sending in the Special Forces to rescue Collins. The mission was somewhat complicated as the operations would be carried out in a sovereign independent country ruled by a military junta. The country was also in a state of civil war. There were many regional nationalities and their militias involved in the conflict. The Kachins Independence Army (KIA) was the largest outfit fighting the Myanmar government for independence. The other ethnic groups involved in the civil war were the Karen National Union (KNU) and the National Union party of Arakan (NUPA) both fighting for a homeland for their people. Some of these movements dated back to the days when Burma was still a colony of Britain, like India.

The insurgents held sway over the country north of Mandalay. Even before the Junta took over from the civil government, the insurgents ruled the area, collected taxes and traded weapons. They had also provided shelter and help to the rebel Naga and Mizo insurgents in the past. Now that the Nagas and Mizos had found political recognition in India, the Karens and the Arakanese insurgents looked up to India to broker peace for them with the Generals in Yangon. They could be relied upon to turn Peter Collins over if he was being held by some of their factions. But it was a difficult situation as there was no unified command amongst the insurgents and there was some amount of competition when it came to drugs and the arms business. The Junta Government was in no position to take on these rebels as they had no support of the people. The Myanmar army was mortally afraid to go on patrols in the territory held by the Kachins, Karens and Arakanese rebels and the entire country was in a state of economic and political stalemate. Ravi had worked in this beautiful country of gentle and peaceful people and felt sad to see the unyielding generals holding on to power and keeping all important leaders of the National League for Democracy (NLD) under house arrest.

Ravi had a number of messages awaiting him when he got back to his office. One was a summary of the story emerging from the Russian media, the Interpol and IAEA regarding the clandestine trade in nuclear scrap, including the fissile material from the former Soviet Republics territories. IAEA and Interpol had issued a fresh look out notice in respect of missing nuclear scientists associated with the rogue Pakistani nuclear scientist and bomb maker, Dr. Ashfaq Ahmad. There were five Pakistani, three North Koreans, two Sri Lankans, two Egyptians, three Iranians and one South African named in the notice. Of these one Korean, two Pakistanis, one Iranian and the South African were specialists in designing the nuclear core material and one Sri Lankan and two North Koreans were experts in developing the trigger mechanisms for nuclear devices. The rest were metallurgical engineers. It was also Interpol's information that one Pakistani, one Iranian and two North Koreans were probably working secretly in their country's nuclear weapons programme. All were fugitives from law and wanted in half a dozen countries for smuggling contraband goods. They were also suspected to be involved in clandestine nuclear proliferation and transfer of technology and equipment. They had now been declared as nuclear terrorists by the IAEA.

Ravi had during his posting in Yangon discovered that one of the Sri Lankan scientists was living in Myanmar. He had been given political asylum and was understood to be part of a secret project of Myanmar's junta. His whereabouts were not known and it rumored that he had married a local girl and was in contact with some nuclear scientists in North Korea. Ravi decided to activate his local informants amongst the Karen rebels. He left messages on the rebel's wireless network to contact some of his agents in Imphal, Manipur. Imphal, the capital of the eastern most state of Manipur with a preponderance of Hindu population, was a relatively peaceful area in the troubled eastern region. There were some issues with a splinter group of Nagas but the land was free of insurgencies. The R&AW had a number of safe houses in Imphal which had become a meeting point for the Karen and the Arakanese factions fighting for their homeland in Myanmar. Some of the rebel factions had been providing the R&AW with useful information on developments in Myanmar. They could be quite useful in providing logistics support to the Special Forces in the operation planned to rescue Peter Collins.

# NEW DELHI

Venkat managed to organise a meeting with Manoj Subramanian over cocktails and dinner at his college buddy Rakesh Puri's farm house in Qutab Enclave. Rakesh was resident editor of The Asia Journal published from Singapore. The journal primarily focused on financial and economic matters in the region and regularly carried articles on strategic studies with special emphasis on the growing belligerence of China and its mentoring role in North Korea and Pakistan. Manoj was a regular contributor to the journal. They discussed the recent terror attacks carried out by the LET proxies in Jaipur and New Delhi. Manoj wanted the Border Security Force to conduct hot pursuit of the LET terrorists across the LOC and destroy their terror camps in Pakistan Occupied Kashmir. The Indian army could provide cover and firepower by the low flying MI-17 Helicopter Gunships which could interdict the camps with rockets. One swift attack would not start a war but would also put Pakistanis on notice that we were prepared to take risks to put end to the cross border terror attacks. The international law recognized the rights of the littoral states to hot pursuit if attacked but India had unfortunately not utilized this soft option available to it.

Venkat reminded Manoj about the paper he had presented some years ago on the subject—'Support to the Pashtun movement and the Baloch rebels as an option available to India, besides a war, to counter Pakistan on the Kashmir', at a seminar organised in the National Defense College.

"Manoj what is your advice today on the policy options available to India to pursue an aggressive policy on the Pashtun and the Baloch issue?"

"I stand by what I said that day that India can only have peace on its western borders if there is fire within Pakistan. I would add that we can follow a policy to rewrite Pakistan's western borders between the Indus and the Hindu Kush mountains by creating a greater Pashtunistan and Balochistan, to include the Pashtuns homeland on both sides of the Durand Line. Such a border will bring peace to Afghanistan and strengthen the hands of the Sind politicians by cutting the aggressive Punjabis to size. We can then take over the Kashmir areas lost in 1949 and reintegrate the entire state with a promise of more political autonomy to permanently silence the separatists and their cause," exhorted Manoj.

"Why don't you write and publish your treatise on the subject in the prominent dailies, as the present situation on the ground warrants reorganizations of some borders in the sub-continent?" asked Venkat anxiously.

"And be branded a hawk again by the mandarins in the South Block who have grown up on Panditji's policies and the doctrine of Panchsheela?"

"Manoj, listen I am serious. We have to make a paradigm shift in our foreign policy and project ourselves as a super power in the region. We could not do so in the past decade as our economy was weak and we had still to acquire the status of a developed country. Today the world recognizes us as an economic power house with a robust financial and industrial system. We are pioneering development in so many areas that the US, France, Israel and UK want us to collaborate with their strategic industry and save their corporate worlds from disaster. The growing terrorism in the Islamic heartland has shaken them up. We cannot sit on the fence eternally while the ISI and its foot soldiers attack us at will and kill our innocent citizens. Pakistan is a nuclear powered nation and a failed state to boot. The world is not sure of its ability and its capacity to safeguard the nuclear arsenal from the terror outfits."

He reached into the inner pocket of his jacket and pulled out a copy of the message they had received from Ulan Bator a week back and handed it over to Manoj.

"I brought this along to show you how close we are to nuclear terrorism and blackmail. You must have followed the news on the BBC and our news channels too. We have been anticipating this since long and had got the story even before the Russians did. I have had no sleep since we got that message. We are not sure how far the Russians have succeeded in preventing the material from moving out of their borders. They are only concerned about the material falling into the hands of the Chechen rebels. So they have secured their borders with Chechnya. Tomorrow it may surface in Peshawar and Dr. Ashfaq Ahmad or his boys will get busy in making devices for the terror outfits to blackmail us and the world. Our nuclear doctrine in its present form is incapable of dealing with the non-state nuclear terrorists. We have to review our foreign policy as well as our nuclear policy doctrine in this post 9/11 scenario as we have become vulnerable to bigger threats that do not lend themselves to conventional solutions. We have to anticipate nuclear threats and blackmail from non-state combatants. The time has now come to tell the Pakistani Generals that it takes two to play this game.

We should create sleepless nights for them by declaring total support for the Pashtuns and the Baloch cause. Simultaneously we have to develop a proactive nuclear doctrine to counter acts of threat and black-mail from the non-state agents."

"Come Venkat let me get you a refill."

Rakesh took Venkat's glass and poured a large shot of Glenlivet and topped it with ice; that was Venkat's favorite single malt and he liked it on the rocks.

"Yes Manoj let's all recharge our glasses before we hear your side of the Islamabad story."

The story Rakesh referred to was the attempt by the ISI to blackmail him by the honey trap route. Manoj had been with a delegation of Indian journalists to Pakistan a few years ago as part of the confidence building measures. They were dined and wined all the way from Lahore to Islamabad. And then after one late evening when Manoj returned to his hotel, he got a call from the front desk that the local correspondent from the Daily Jung wanted to interview him on the delegation's tour of Pakistan. Manoj was surprised that someone would approach him at such a late hour but decided to go as refusing would have amounted to insulting the local hosts. At the lobby he was directed to the bar, which at this late hour had just a couple of American Air Force personnel having a night cap before turning in. As he entered the bar the steward showed him to a corner table occupied by a stunning beauty.

"Thank you for coming Mr. Subramanian. I am Shehnaz from the Jung. So sorry for disturbing you at this late hour; I've been trying to get through to you all day but our press guild kept you so busy that I could catch up with you only at this late hour."

She gushed in impeccable convent school accent. Manoj guessed that she was in her mid thirties. The salwar suit she wore was very smart with a low neckline, low enough to reveal her ample bosom. Manoj had had a fair amount of scotch at the party earlier in the evening but felt that he urgently required another to face this new challenge. He ordered a double scotch. They talked for long on the delegation's visit and she told him that she would be visiting India to cover the special session of SAARC convention on trade and commerce in Mumbai, coming December. By the time Manoj order his second drink she had slipped across the table to Manoj's side. Manoj could smell the expensive perfume she wore and was quite excited by the thought that Shehnaz was probably playing the role of Mata Hari for her ISI masters. He decided to take on the challenge and play along to see how far his guess was correct. He put his arm behind her head and let it slide slowly till it came into contact with her bare back. Her leg had moved and now rested along his and when he put his hand on hers she giggled and remarked that he was quite naughty. When he suggested that they go up to his room to record their interview on the delegations visits on his lap top, she readily agreed.

Shehnaz was a real professional and slipped into the bathroom when they reached his room. Manoj pulled out his lap top and a small hand held device he always carried which could locate listening devices and hidden cameras. By the time Shehnaz emerged from the bathroom with just a towel wrapped around, Manoj had exposed the ISI plot and located two closed circuit cameras targeted on the bed. One was hidden in the flower pot on the writing desk and the other was on the overhead air-conditioning duct. Manoj reached out for the spare toothpaste tube he carried in his suitcase and smeared the paste liberally on the camera lenses totally blinding them. There was only one listening bug placed under the side of the bed. Manoj shouted some half a dozen Punjabi obscenities into the bug for the benefit of the ISI Chief, before crushing the device under the heel of his boot.

Manoj narrated the tale to his delegation next day on the flight back to New Delhi but cut out the details on Shehnaz. He would laugh it off and say that there was no video or audio of the event; but he could not disappoint his hosts by refusing the exclusive gift they offered him. And so the story remained with a few red faces in the snoops and dirty tricks department of the ISI. The Chief wanted to see and hear what happened and against all advice, heard the brief and curt message of Manoj before the recording was interrupted and killed by Manoj's size nine boots stomping the bug out of life.

Venkat had a good laugh as he had not heard the story before. He raised a toast and complimented him on getting one up on the ISI.

"Manoj we want you to do the lead story on the need for a change in the nuclear doctrine and I am requesting Dr. Alka Gadgil of the School of Asian Historical Studies JNU, to do a comprehensive policy document on foreign policy review and new policy initiatives on Pashtun and Balochistan homeland demands. We want the matter in the national press and the international media for a month at least before our scheduled meeting of the foreign policy review committee. Yours and Alka's story has to hit the media the day the Prime Minister arrives in New York to address the UN General Assembly. He will not discuss the proposals in his address but the international press will raise the matter definitely at his press conference. We want to get maximum coverage on the expected paradigm shift in our foreign policy at this conference. He will not skirt the issue this time but refer to the charged environment and the threats from Qaeda to the world at large. He will speak of the activities of the terror groups in Kashmir and of the proxy war unleashed on India by the ISI. He will bring out the country's concerns on nuclear proliferation and the nuclear arsenal build up in Pakistan He will also highlight the terrorist group's threats and the weak civilian control in that country and question the safety of their nukes. The real dangers posed by the trade in nuclear scrap, will be addressed by him to emphasize the need for a change in our nuclear doctrine. After Alka's and your article appear in print there would be considerable discussions in various forums. The TV News and Current Affairs Channels would be a good forum to carry the discussions forward. We are updating the list of defense experts, former diplomats, security experts, foreign policy commentators for being invited to these debates. We must bring out the message loud and clear that we are moving into zero tolerance mode as far as threats to our security are concerned. Our nuclear doctrine will factor in the threats from the non state agencies. We want to leave the Pakistan Civilian government and their power center, the Army and the ISI with no doubts in their mind that we will hit them before they or their proxies strike us. There will be no hiding behind the excuse of non state agents in future."

# KANDY

Raj was impressed by the beautiful location of the Estate Bungalow. It was on the crest of the ridge above the tea gardens which stretched for miles around. The air was fresh, tinged with the smell of wood smoke rising from the cooking fires of the outhouses and tenements of the tea workers, located in the valley behind the bungalow and the ridge. One had to walk to the very edge of the ridge behind the bungalow to see the roof tops of these habitats. In the bungalow it was the library that was most impressive. Like the rooms it was paneled with oak wood and had solid Burma teak wood pillars and rafters. The pillars had been finished smooth and beautifully varnished. The capital of the pillars was carved lotus shape and supported the frame on which the rafters had been laid out. The library had book shelves covering the wall on one side. There must have been over three thousand books of all sizes. The old ones were leather bound, some gazetteers of Kandy district, many volumes on pest control, flora and fauna of Ceylon and a couple of old shipping and Lloyds Insurance Manuals. Behind the solid teak desk with a green beige cover was a glass paneled gun display containing a dozen weapons. The oldest were two muzzle loaders and the finest appeared to be the two James Purdey guns. These were beautiful weapons. Raj had only read about them but never seen them.

"Sorry Vikas I got a little held up. There were a few calls from Colombo and one from our office in Mumbai. I was told by my secretary that the Mumbai Police are making enquiries about my return and my flat has also been kept under watch and a police patrol car parked outside the gate. Oh yes I must show you those guns. My Grandpa and my father were both good hunters. They grew up in this wilderness. The plantations abounded with sambar, leopards, wild boar, deer and host of wild cats and foxes. Game meat was a regular feature on our table. While in school I went on a few hunting trips and night drives and loved the excitement, but never got to shoot much. We will open the gun cabinet in the evening after we get back from a round of the plantation. I will call Aboobaker who was the plantations' supervisor and my father's gun man; he always accompanied him on shikar. He was the last senior supervisor from my grandfather's days and retired well over twenty years ago. My father would not let him go back to his village and gave him a place to stay in the plantation. He has always been a member of the family and gets all his meals from the bungalow kitchen."

One of the bearers walked in and Pradeep asked him to get two beers. They moved over and settled down on the leather stuffed sofas facing the wide glass windows overlooking the rolling green hills of the tea plantation. The beer was chilled and fresh and Pradeep gulped a mouthful and asked Raj to tell him his long story that brought him to Kandy.

"Last month I met Ratna at a party and we got into a friendly conversation, the usual party chatter and gossip. She asked me if I had friends in the police. When I asked her why she wanted police help, she told me about her friend Vijaya Choudhry, who was found dead in a hotel

155

at Khandala. The papers had speculated a love triangle but then the police appeared tight lipped and volunteered no information at the Police Commissioner's weekly briefing. Ratna also mentioned you and said that you were a very good friend of Vijaya's and that you were proposing to marry her. She appeared worried that she could not reach you on the phone when she learnt about Vijaya's tragic murder. I spoke to my friend Satish Sharma, the Joint Commissioner of Police, Mumbai and he could only confirm that Vijaya had indeed been murdered, rather brutally and it appeared to be a professional job. The culprits had tortured her possibly to extract some information. The poor girl had suffered a lot and her body lay in the police mortuary as no one had come forward to claim it. The police could get no information about her family from her office. Ratna appeared very upset and was very keen to know why her good friend, Vijaya was killed. Satish also mentioned that you were required for investigation in the case as you appeared to know her and you two had been meeting frequently in Khandala. There were a few financial transactions between your company and Vijaya's firm which were cause of some concern to the police authorities. They wanted you to reveal the source of those funds. When this business trip got organised I called Ratna to find out if she had your address in Kandy. She said it would not be difficult to locate you as you were a prominent person in the city. And then we met at Cherian's dinner party."

"Yes Vijaya was an enigma. Although we came close and I had proposed marriage, Vijaya was non-committal. She would always avoid the question and wanted to continue with the existing arrangements. She never spoke of her childhood or her school and college days. She was a loner with very few friends, except Ratna. I think Ratna was very close and she may have confided in her."

"She said that you were going to announce your marriage plans after you told your grandmother about Vijaya."

"Oh yes that's what I had told Vijaya when we discussed marriage. My grandma had brought me up and she is almost ninety years old now. She is the nearest surviving relation of mine besides my maternal grand parents who live in Nuwara Eliya. I had told Vijaya that grandma had been persuading me to get married for years now and had a list of eligible girls lined up. She had known most of the families and some were close relations of my mother. I therefore could not marry her without her knowledge; she would have been very happy to meet her."

Pradeep paused as memories of Vijaya overtook him.

"I was serious about Vijaya. She had a tragic loneliness about her which I admired. She was a very fine person but never gave any hint of fear or panic or of something amiss or gone wrong so seriously that she would lose her life in this manner. I was very shocked and upset and could not bear to go back to Khandala after I saw the reports of her death in the papers. I thought of getting away from Mumbai by taking an early vacation. It's been very difficult for me to put this episode behind me. That's why I am spending more time at work here than in Kandy. Grandma must be wondering what's come over me. She is still full of energy but she refuses to leave Kandy. I had got her passport to take her for a holiday to India but she refuses to budge from Kandy. I gave up my job in London and moved to Mumbai to be close to her. We had diversified into banking and finance and I found investments in India were promising good returns. My company has this joint venture, Lloyds Financial Services and we have clients in industry trade and commerce."

"I am sorry about Vijaya, Pradeep. When you get back to Mumbai I will take you personally to Satish. They feel you could provide them some information on her personal background and family, her business rivals or enemies. Besides there is the matter of the funds you loaned to her firm. You could prepare yourself for some serious questioning. There was record of financial transactions found with her boss that has become a matter of serious enquiry with the Revenue and Police Departments. Anyway Satish will brief you when you get to Mumbai. They have nothing against you but Vijaya's name is linked with some irregular monetary transactions. They want to know if you have any information."

The bearer came in to announce that lunch was ready and they walked into the dining hall.

The meal was an elaborate affair and Raj could see fish and prawns fried in rich reddish brown spice paste placed in small shallow bowls next to his plate. Then there were two curries; one yellow and the other fiery red topped with chopped coriander. There was a tureen of dhal, lentils cooked with green chilies and ginger, platters of rice, string hoppers and dosas.

"Vikas don't be surprised by the number of dishes on the table. This has been the Estate Bungalow tradition since my grandfather's days. He always invited guests over, often without notice. He was a great host. That tradition has endured. My father Anna was also like that too. He could never have a meal without being surrounded by people. As our family was small, there were friends dropping by to enjoy a good meal and my fathers company. He just loved good food. In his early days he would survive with just rice and dhal for days while working on the plantations, but once he got back home the meals had to be sumptuous."

The food was outstanding though a trifle hot for Raj but he enjoyed it. He had eaten a lot in Sri Lanka but the flavor of this cooking was very different. The very distinct flavors of spices and herbs overrode the sharpness of the chilies. The pork curry had a very strong aftertaste of coriander and turmeric and the fried chicken was loaded with ginger and cardamom. The prawns had diced garlic, ginger and loads of fresh green pepper. The meal was finished with an excellent baked Custard pudding, a remnant of the colonial era. After lunch it was siesta time and Raj decided to take a nap, while Pradeep said that he would go down to his office and have a chat with his management team to finalize the agenda for the next board meeting of his company he was proposing to hold before returning to Mumbai.

"I will get back by five so if you like we will take a walk in the hills."

"I would love that."

"Good, the bearer will get you tea around four thirty. I will meet you in the garden."

# PONDA

**D**r. Alka Gadgil, Venkat found was on a year's deputation to the University of Panaji, Goa for setting up their new Department of Historical Studies. Venkat called Pundit Vishnu Bandotkar in Ponda, Goa to have the meeting arranged with Alka. Vishnu had studied with Venkat at Cambridge and they had become good friends. He had done exceedingly well and was offered an academic position after his PhD, but he was keen to get back. So he returned and went straight to Pune where he applied and accepted an assignment in the Department of Mathematics at the University. Vishnu's father had been a Vedic scholar and a renowned physician in Belgaum. He had also been an old member of the Rastriya Swayamsevak Sangh (RSS) and headed the erstwhile South Bombay State Chapter which included the districts of Belgaum, Satara, Kolhapur, Sangli and Pune. Vishnu too was drawn into politics and was advised by his father to lead the movement for the liberation of Goa which was a colony of Portugal in 1961. He exploited the angst amongst the Marathi and Konkani speaking students in the districts of Ratnagiri and Belgaum and raised the standard of revolt against the Portuguese rule. The local authorities were determined to break the movement and brutally assaulted the agitators who tried to enter Goa from the Vengurla border of the erstwhile state of Bombay. Many were jailed and tortured. Vishnu carried on the movement regardless and started a newspaper 'Swaraj Gomantak' from Ponda till he was arrested and jailed in 1961, months before the Indian Armed forces liberated Goa in a swift action from Portuguese occupation.

He moved to Ponda after his retirement from the Pune University and was promptly appointed the Chairman of the Academic Council of the newly constituted Goa University at Panaji. He continued to guide PhD scholars and one of his brightest and successful students had been Dr. Alka Gadgil of the Jawaharlal Nehru University at New Delhi. Alka's family came from Dharwar in Karnataka and was distantly related to his wife. He was therefore quite excited when his good friend Venkat suggested that he organise a meeting with Alka at his house in Ponda, on a matter of urgent national interest.

"Vishnu we are coming for lunch and the meeting is incidental. We have not even informed the Government of Goa. We are travelling under assumed names and would be staying at Dabolim. So do ensure that you give us some good Saraswat food."

Vishnu and Saxena travelled to Dabolim airport in the Bombardier Challenger 850 jet of the R&AW. It was a two hours fifteen minutes flight from New Delhi's Palam Airport. For the last half hour of the flight the pilot flew low over the Western Maharashtra coast as instructed by Venkat, who wanted to have an aerial view of the new mega atomic power plant coming up in Sindhudurg district. This was the second major atomic power project under the Indo-US agreement-Atoms for Peace. The first mega project of 2500 megawatt capacity had already been commissioned in the state of Uttar Pradesh. The Bombardier flew at an altitude of eight thousand feet and gave a bird's eye view of the project sight which was bustling with activity. The power station was nearing completion and the atomic core was to go critical in six months time. The picturesque coastline was doted with spas and resorts connected to the coastal highway that ran almost parallel along the beach from Ganpatiphule in Ratnagiri to Vengurla on the Goa border.

After landing at the Dabolim, the pilot taxied the aircraft to the Indian Navy's Technical Area. They were received by a Naval Police Officer and driven in a staff car to the Naval Mess where the rooms had been reserved for them as visiting Defense Auditors. They left for Ponda soon after for their lunch appointment with Vishnu Bandotkar.

# KANDY

Raj was strolling in the garden when Pradeep drove up to the bungalow to pick him up for their evening walk.

"We will drive for five kilometers on the highway and then take the trail along the stream. The path is mostly uphill—a short hike through the woods till we get to a ridge. We then traverse the ridge to the Planters Bungalow on the other side. We have a very large plantation there and the bungalow is located almost over the waterfall. I am sure you will enjoy this walk."

"I love the hills, Pradeep. I am an avid trekker and return to the Himalayas each year, to its many unknown trails. I was looking forward to walking on these hills when I planned my visit to Colombo. I am lucky that I found you as my local guide."

"Oh that's great. I would say I am lucky that you came by. I want to do some serious trekking myself in the Garhwal hills. Two years ago I had gone to Rishikesh and Uttarkashi. I managed to get a guide who took me to Gangotri. It was a beautiful drive with the River Bhagirathi flowing on one side of the road all along the route. I was not prepared for the trek to Gaumukh and postponed it for a later day. Now that I have met you I would love to join your next outing in the Himalayas."

163

The trail was getting steeper and they had to walk single file as the bushes and small trees closed in on the narrow bridle path. It was very pleasant, and a gentle breeze had picked up. The wood cock was calling and there were a host of other game birds in the undergrowth. As they negotiated a clump of stunted oak trees they came to small stream and surprised a pair of sambar drinking water. Pradeep who was walking ahead stopped suddenly and crouched down. He signaled Raj to do the same. He then beckoned him to walk up slowly to the spot where he stood behind an oak. The deer had got alerted and were restless, but had not moved from the stream. It was a beautiful sight and the rays from the setting sun reflected on the animal's shiny brown coat. They dipped their heads once more into the water and the next moment they bounded off into the thicket of trees on the far side.

"Grandpa used to carry his twelve gauge gun on these walks and never missed an opportunity of a good hunt. But he was a conservator too and did not allow indiscriminate poaching by the local villagers. He used to regularly organise meetings of the village headmen and the forest rangers to ensure that the animals did not damage the plantations and the crops in the village. If the deer population went up they would inform the rangers who allowed periodic culling."

They had reached the top of the ridge and westward the sky was turning orange in hue with the setting sun. They could also hear now the crashing sounds of the waterfall which was still some distance away. They took the downhill trail. Jungle fowl rose from the bushes disturbed by their sudden appearance as they walked briskly through the path. It was getting dark but Pradeep knew the track well and they soon reached the spot from where the bungalow was visible.

Kumar Rajapaksa, the Plantation Manager was waiting to welcome them. They walked around the bungalow to the rear side from where they got a panoramic view of the waterfall. In the failing light of the evening the water appeared like milk flowing over. It was a wonderful sight. The whole countryside was so beautiful and serene. Kumar had arranged tea in the garden facing the bungalow and they enjoyed the fragrant brew with some freshly baked cake.

"Broken Orange Pekoe from our very own estate Vikas; I have asked my secretary to keep a few packets of tea for you to carry back to Mumbai. You will remember this walk when you have that tea every morning."

On return the conversation turned to tea brewing and Pradeep recalled the tea he once had at a roadside shop on his way to Shimla. The concoction was heavily laced with ginger, which had perhaps been crushed and boiled with the tea and good full cream milk added with couple of teaspoons of sugar. It was wonderfully refreshing in the crisp cold October morning and Vijaya who was with him had three cups of that brew.

"She said that as a Bengali she loved tea but this one totally surprised her. In Shimla she insisted on having the adrak chai, as they called it, every morning and afternoon. My Malyali cook in Mumbai has also picked up the recipe and serves me the same every morning."

Vijaya Choudhry a Bengali! That one surprised Raj. The available information on her had identified her as a local Maharashtrian from Jalgaon district, born and brought up in Mumbai. It appeared that Satish Sharma's boys had slipped up again in their investigation. Pradeep had revealed an important facet of her personality and this could lead them closer in deciphering the B.K. Dossier. Vijaya's true identity could lead them closer to the money trail and the terror nexus. Her murder and the manner in which it had been carried out revealed the panic and fear of discovery by the perpetrators. They had discovered that the diskette which contained the vital information of the financial transactions of their nefarious activities had been compromised and they had got into a damage control mode. Vijaya was perhaps the key operator in the money transfers and the laundering racket, who received the funds from overseas and deployed them in various investments till these were required for funding the illegal activities of her handlers. She was a plant, deep under cover enemy agent who had managed to embed herself in the civil society of Mumbai. Her charming personality, her demure and petit looks, and her professional competence had carved for her respect and acceptability in Mumbai's upper crust circles. Her handlers had some diabolical plans up their sleeves and it was very essential to unmask her background to get close to them. For Raj, Vijaya dead or alive was the principal prosecution witness in the present case. He had to get to Saxena also and pass on the leads on Vijaya. He felt that Pradeep would know more, but he would have to proceed very cautiously. Ratna might also remember more after all they were good friends and lots of personal information does get exchanged amongst close acquaintances. He decided he must take her out for dinner to tell her about his visit to Kandy and Pradeep's tea estates. She might recall something about Vijaya that could be valuable for his investigations.

They had reached the Estate Bungalow and Raj found the ridge was abuzz with the shrill chattering of cicadas and the glitter of hundreds of fireflies that flitted about like falling stars against the dark sky.

"Let's meet in the library say in half an hour's time, Vikas. I am sure you will enjoy a hot shower after that brisk exercise."

Raj went up to his room and stripped down to his skin. There was a little chill in the air but the walk had perked up his system. He stepped into the shower and soaked himself. His mind was racing ahead and he tried to recall a dossier he had read some years ago, on the deep undercover KGB agents which the Soviets had planted in the US. One of these agents had lived in Manhattan New York for thirty long years and carried on his activities undetected. He had made friends in various US government organisations and collected valuable information on defense and science projects. He spent his afternoons walking and exercising at Central Park and would be seen feeding the pigeons and mixing with the regulars. The FBI later discovered that he had developed five designated drops in the park where his informants regularly placed nuggets of information on weapons systems, electronic devices, industrial equipment and double agents behind the Iron Curtain.

Raj dressed for dinner and put on a light pullover he had carried for the stay in Kandy and Nuwara Eliya. Pradeep was already in the library and the embers of a dying fire glowed in the grate making the room warm and smug.

"Some Glenfiddich, Vikas? I picked up this bottle from the duty free at Mumbai airport and was waiting for an occasion to open it. I think you deserve this after that great workout. I too had not exercised since I came to Kandy and it has been one big eating orgy since then. My grandma insists on making four course meals like she used to for grandpa and my father and stuffs me with food whenever I am here. She is always complaining that I do not eat enough in Mumbai and that I should marry a good Kandian girl who will make spicy pork curry as she does."

He handed Raj his glass of whisky and they retired to the cozy sofas by the fireside.

"It's appropriate that we are having Glenfiddich after sighting the deer in my valley. You know Vikas, Glenfiddich is the name borrowed from the Glen of Fiddich which in the ancient Gaelic language stands for the Valley of the Deer. I learnt this when I visited their distillery in Scotland during my stay at Oxford. Cheers".

"Cheers and thanks Pradeep. It's been a wonderful day and its turning out to be a memorable holiday too. I had been looking forward to a break and this has been very exciting."

"I am glad we met. With your experience and expertise on trekking, I am sure I will get a chance to see the beautiful mountains in the Himalayan Ranges and the flora and fauna in the valleys. I have seen a bit of the Jim Corbett National Park and heard amazing stories of the Englishman's adventures in the jungles and foot hills of the Terai region. I had spent a few days with Vijaya at the National Park and then driven up to the famed hill stations of Nainital and Ranikhet. Vijaya was so impressed that she compared the hills to the ones in Vermont she had visited with her mom years ago after she finished school. You know she was a US citizen by birth and was brought to Kolkata by her mom when she was seven months old. Her first visit after that was to Vermont for a short holiday and New York where her mother was invited to a workshop and a lecture tour by Columbia University. Later she worked as a consultant in Chicago before opening her partnership firm in Mumbai"

Raj was excited as these gems of information got revealed by Pradeep unsolicited. He was glad that he got invited by him to visit the tea estate.

"Vijaya was such a level headed and successful person but she too suffered from lot of stress. She never spoke about her personal problems and her family; but in the year or so I had known her, I found her on many occasions lost in her thoughts, silent and moody for days. It was as if something was gnawing her soul. I am sure there was something seriously amiss in her personal life which led her to her cruel end. I am as interested in finding out the causes of her tragic death myself as perhaps your friend Satish Sharma is."

There was a knock on the door and the flow of information on Vijaya was interrupted as a tall dark man, with weathered features topped with a jungle floppy hat, entered the library.

"Come in Abu," Pradeep got up from his seat and warmly embraced the old family retainer. He enquired about his health and wellbeing and Abu responded with a grateful smile and moist eyes.

"Vikas this is Aboobaker, my Abu who was a constant companion to my father Anna right from the day he was inducted to work on the plantation. Anna was sent to work on the new plantation and lived all alone at the Planters Bungalow we visited today. Abu showed him the ropes and looked after him day and night. He taught him all that a planter needed to know to become a successful tea producer. Anna learnt a lot from Abu's apprenticeship; Abu also taught him about the jungle and its inhabitants. The whole plantation area was full of wild life those days, leopards, deer, sambhars, wild boars, foxes and a variety of game birds. The wild boars were destructive animals and created lot of havoc with the new plantations. They would dig up the saplings and destroy the young bushes. Anna learnt to hunt the wild boar and its meat became his favourite food. I called Abu to show us the guns and tell us some stories of the jungle."

Raj shook Abu's hand which had become lined with age and coarse with the hard work at the plantation. Abu opened the gun display cupboard and took out the weapons one by one. The James Purdey guns, the 300 Express and the twelve gauge double barreled were real beauties of remarkable workmanship. Abu was as enthusiastic as a sixteen year old and narrated the stories of shikar with Anna with great aplomb. Pradeep had to request him to slow down as he had to translate his narration into English for the benefit of his guest. Raj had a thrilling exposition of the hunting exploits of Grandpa and Anna in the wild hills of Nuwara Eliya. Most of the hunting those days was done on foot as there were no roads and horses could not traverse the steep slopes of these mountains. The story telling session ended with dinner being announced; they thanked Abu and proceeded to the dining hall.

Pradeep was unusually quiet during the meal. The good whisky had mellowed him somewhat and Abu's jungle stories had put him in a nostalgic mood. Abu's tales had revived memories of his childhood, his grandfather and his parents. He suddenly felt very lonely and remembered his grandmother living all by herself in Kandy. He had felt very happy with Vijaya but she was taken away from him in such a tragic manner. He remembered each day he spent with her and felt a pain deep in his heart. Was he somehow responsible for what happened to her? There was that fear gnawing at his heart. He had tried to put away the thoughts but memories were revived since the arrival of Raj. He wanted a broad shoulder to unburden himself but he could not use grandma for what he wanted to say now.

They finished the meal in thoughtful silence with Raj wondering if he should raise the matter of the funds with Pradeep and Pradeep in turn wondering if he could trust a stranger with information which could put him into difficulties later. Pradeep asked his bearer to bring the coffee to the library.

It had been a good day for Raj but he was totally unprepared for what was to come. Pradeep who had been in a pensive mood throughout the meal, only replying to Raj in monosyllables suddenly opened up.

"Vikas I was wondering if you could help me out with Satish. There has been a lapse on my part but I was under tremendous pressure. You talked about the police wanting details of some financial transactions I had done with Vijaya's firm. There was one which I had carried out very reluctantly. I was not involved with the fund transfer, but allowed this party to use my company's account to pass over funds to B.K. Enterprises. I never realised that there was some irregularity in the matter then. Lots of money comes into Mumbai for films and realty investments. The channel is of course what you call 'havala' in India. After Vijaya was murdered I was worried that we had got involved inadvertently in some serious criminal transaction. I am sure Vijaya herself knew nothing about it. I feel very guilty because Vijaya lost her life and I cannot fathom what went wrong."

Pradeep paused and sipped his coffee. He appeared very tense and Raj could see beads of perspiration on his forehead.

"Vikas you must advice me on what I should do now. As a family we have had a long history and tradition of being good citizens and honest businessmen. We have never sought any favours from the government of the day and grandfather developed our tea estates with sheer hard work and the sweat of his brow. My father expanded the business and diversified into hotels and resorts and I have added banking and finance. Kandy has a very large population of Tamil expatriates who were brought in by the British to work in the tea gardens. Over the years some have done well, got educated and opened their own business in transport and retail. This country has seen a growing conflict between the ethnic Sinhala and the expat Tamils which has reached tragic proportions in the last two decades. The homeland or the Eelam demand by the Liberation Tigers movement has led to clashes and blood shed. We were approached by the Tamil leaders to support their movement, but we kept them at an arms distance. My family had a name and reputation and we were offered positions in the Government. But we declined politely and continued to expand business and maintain good relations with all."

Pradeep paused again and poured himself another cup of coffee.

"After I expanded our company's holdings into banking and purchased a majority holding in a Mauritius bank I was approached by a few LTTE financiers to invest some of their money in India. I refused. Last December I was again approached by a LTTE politician who wanted my help to place some funds in the Mumbai film industry. When I refused I was told that my denial to help may jeopardize the safety of my family. That was shocking, as it was a direct threat to my grandmother. I was under tremendous pressure. I thought of taking her to Mumbai and got her a passport and a visa for India. She however did not wish to move out of Kandy and I could not tell her the reason for my insistence. I had to make extra security arrangements to protect her from the LTTE thugs but she would not follow the advice of the security guarding her. She would not allow anybody to travel with her in the car and she would go around in the market as she had always done for nearly seventy years of her adult life. She would always complain when I called from Mumbai and insisted that I get rid of these security guards. I was at my wits end and under such coercion and blackmail I agreed to make a one time transfer of their funds from Mauritius to India. They insisted that the transfer be made in cash to B.K.Enterprises who had already been borrowing from our finance company in Mumbai. Their other condition was that we should make no entry of the said amount in our records and that B.K Enterprise would also not arrange any repayment of the sums through our company. I had no choice in the matter and felt that it was a transaction with no record and would be safe. We had given many loans to the B.K.Enterprises and their repayments were prompt. Their account with us was very good and they were our valued clients. Due to our business with B.K. Enterprises I came into contact with Vijaya. She handled all the finances of BK's firm and we soon became friends. That friendship soon blossomed into intimacy. Now I am worried that this one lone transfer of funds for the LTTE may have figured in the books of B.K.Enterprises which has put the spotlight of the Mumbai police on me. I am innocent Vikas, and I am sure Vijaya was not involved in any criminal activity. Her murder has left me shattered and now this police enquiry has got me worried. What I did for the LTTE was under coercion. I felt the transaction was for a commercial purpose. I am not aware if that money was utilized for any other purpose against the laws of your country. I am willing to confess this before your police."

"Pradeep I am not aware of this case at all. Satish Sharma is a fine officer. He will give you full opportunity to explain yourself. I am sure he will understand the compulsions which made you commit the transaction. You come down to Mumbai and I will take you to him."

# PONDA

**V**enkat and Saxena ran into a host of exotic aromas when they reached Vishnu's house. He clasped Venkat to his bosom and held him there for a few minutes. The last meeting had been a decade ago in Pune where Venkat had gone to preside over a National Seminar on Narcotics.

"Welcome Venkat I was so pleased when you told me to arrange this meeting with Alka. She is like my daughter and had not been home for so long. When I called her she readily agreed. But I am sad that you are rushing back to Delhi. I wish you could have stayed for a day or two. There is so much to talk about."

Saxena was introduced to Vishnu and Alka as Dilip Sehgal from the Information Ministry. The lunch was delicious and Venkat spoke freely like a Hindu zealot briefing Alka on what was expected of her. Saxena and Vishnu were surprised by what he said, but it was true. He spoke about the spirit of tolerance of the Hindu society over the centuries and its ability to accept other faiths. He spoke about the Mughal Empire which was built on secular tradition that accepted and tolerated all religious beliefs and practices by most of its rulers. It survived till the British arrived because the Mughal rulers accepted the Hindus as their subjects and not enemies. The Mughals did not come as conquerors but sought refuge from their fratricidal disputes at home in Fergana. They were different to the raiders from Iran and Afghanistan who made periodic raids only to take the riches and women away. The Mughals were not an army in occupation. They appointed the Rajput princes as Governors of provinces and their armies were commanded by Rajput royalty. The civil administrators were from all faiths and there was no persecution on basis of race and caste or community. He went on to add that the Pakistani rulers considered themselves the successors of Mughal royalty and claim the Red Fort and the Taj Mahal but they have not maintained even a modicum of the secular traditions and polity promised by their founder and first President. The Sunnis treat the Shias and other Muslim denominations as non believers, who are periodically attacked and their places of worship desecrated. The surviving Hindus had no place in their society and live as second class citizens. They had carried on the anti Hindu and anti India propaganda since partition and raised the Taliban militia and various terrorist organisations to wage war against India. We had been subjected to brutal attacks by these brainwashed zombies let loose on our cities and they have even tried to subvert the Indian Muslims to turn against their country. Despite all efforts on our part to normalize relations as good neighbours, they had kept alive the propaganda of hate and misinformation. He concluded by expressing the fear that they may pass on the nukes to the terrorists for use against India.

"Alka you must bring out these latent fears of the Nation and propose a proactive policy of quid pro quo. We must do to them what they have been doing to us for last sixty years. We must sow the seeds of dissension and treason and seek further balkanization of that state by supporting the cause of the Pashtuns and the Baloch people. The hate levels should go up to provoke the Pashtuns to attack the cities of Karachi, Islamabad and Rawalpindi till they bring the Generals on their knees. The Punjabi oligarchy that rules the country must be destroyed. We will have peace only when the home land for the Pashtuns and Baloch are created. The Durand Line needs to be redrawn to unite the Pashtuns on both sides. Durand Line was another creation of the British to divide the Pashtuns and weaken them. We must make amends to the Frontier Gandhi who stood by us during our freedom struggle. Unfortunately the partition threw the Pashtuns and Baloch to the wolves of Punjab."

Saxena who was enjoying his fish curry in coconut milk with rice, added that Pakistan as a failed state has become a danger to the entire world. Its people have failed to create robust institutions to protect democracy and the Generals have ruled the country for most of its history. They have usurped all state functions gradually and today pose a mortal threat to our country through its sponsored non state agents.

Alka who had patiently heard Venkat and Saxena was curious to know as to which news paper group would publish her articles.

"Alka you leave that to us. This will be the beginning of a major debate which will engage the entire country. We have many pacifists who will attack you in letters to the editor or bring out their own views on the subject. All will be encouraged in the best traditions of our policy of freedom of speech, discussion and publication. There will be external pressures and comments. The British Foreign Secretary would make a flying visit to New Delhi to consult his counter part and convey his governments concern at these new developments. Similarly the Secretary of State in Washington would request meeting with our Ambassador in Washington and convey the Presidents concern at the growing belligerence of Hindu Fundamentalist groups and intellectuals. We will handle all the issues as and when they arise."

# NEW DELHI

**R**aj's report to Saxena sent via Joseph Cherian was received with some amount of alacrity at the R&AW Headquarters. The R&AW had a special division dealing with nuclear piracy and terrorism and Saxena put the division head to check out the Atomic Energy Commission of Pakistan, (AECP) staffers list for possible presence of Bangladeshi scientists. The R&AW had built up this file in close coordination with the Atomic Energy Commission of India and the International Atomic Energy Agency, (IAEA). It contained complete details of all scientists working with the Commission in Pakistan, with their specializations and deployments. The current staffers list did not show any Bangladeshi scientist and it was presumed that after 1971, all Bengali personnel were deported or left on their own. A check was therefore run on the information available on pre 1971 staffers. The list contained names of three scientists belonging to the erstwhile East Pakistan province. These were Prof. Mizanur Rehman, Dr. Rashid Jallaludin and Dr. M.Humayun Kabir. A cross check with latest IAEA data bank revealed that Dr. Rashid Jallaludin had recently retired as the Deputy Chairman of the Bangladesh Nuclear Research Centre, Dacca and was residing in his ancestral home in Chittagong. Prof. Mizanur Rehman had returned to USA and was Assistant Dean at the College of Medicine in the University of Illinois, Chicago.

There was no information on the current whereabouts of Dr. M.Humayun Kabir who had held senior position in the Atomic Energy Commission of Pakistan (AECP). His last position was that of Specialist Fuel Cell Division at the Nuclear Research Center, Kahuta. The IAEA had made efforts to locate him in Pakistan after 1971 without success. He seemed to have disappeared into thin air. The IAEA had information on all the personnel secretly deployed on nuclear weapon development program, but Dr. Kabir did not figure in that list either. He was last seen at the regional seminar held at University of Dhaka in early 1971 on fabrication of nuclear fuels for power plants. The seminar had been attended by delegates from India, Australia, Pakistan, China and the Philippines. Dr. Kabir had presented a paper on safe handling procedures of nuclear materials. He was not seen after that date. Those were the days when East Pakistan was witnessing a political upheaval. This ethnically divided province of Pakistan was going through serious political turmoil and soon came under military administration after the provincial government had been dismissed and leaders arrested on charges of treason and conspiracy. The repression had led to a civilian uprising which was crushed brutally and all notable among intelligentsia either killed or thrown into prison. There was a major exodus of population and millions fled the province and took shelter in the neighboring states of West Bengal and Tripura in India. The Pakistani officials at the AECP had informed the IAEA that Dr. Kabir was absconding and had not reported for duty at the Kahuta facility after attending the Dhaka Seminar. It had been alleged by the Pakistani Government that Dr. Kabir was a traitor and had joined the rebels who were agitating for a separate Bangla homeland.

The RAW dossier on Dr. Kabir updated till around his disappearance revealed that he had graduated in Mathematics and Physics from the University of Dacca. He was appointed a lecturer in the Physics Department and also pursued his higher studies, collecting an MSc and an M.Phil. Later that year, he was awarded a Government scholarship to study at the Columbia University, New York. Dr. Kabir was a scholar at Columbia University for five years and was awarded a PhD. in Nuclear Physics on his dissertation on fabrication of fuels for nuclear reactors. He continued to do post doctoral research in Columbia and later moved to the University of Illinois, Chicago and joined the physics department as research fellow. He later applied for the post of scientific officer in the Atomic Energy Commission of Pakistan and was selected, joining his assignment in early 1970 at the Kahuta research facility.

What the dossier did not contain were the personal details of Dr. Kabir's life. During his stay in New York he had met Payal Choudhry, a journalist from The Statesman Newspaper in Kolkata, who was studying at the Graduate School of Journalism. They became good friends and soon that friendship blossomed into love. They got married at a temple in New Jersey months before Dr. Kabir got an appointment at the Atomic Energy Commission of Pakistan (AECP) as a junior scientist and left for Islamabad. Payal stayed back in New York to complete her programme at Columbia. About six months after Kabir left for Islamabad, Payal gave birth to a baby girl and she named her Vijaya. Payal finished her course and decided on Dr. Kabir's advice to return to Kolkata and not join him at Islamabad. Payal had written to her parents and informed them of her marriage with Dr. Kabir. There were some angry exchanges but soon the family objections to the marriage died down and there appeared some reconciliation when Payal announced her intention to return to Kolkata and not go to Islamabad to join her husband. The family rallied around and welcomed her home. Payal soon rejoined the Statesman as an assistant editor.

Dr. M.Humayun Kabir was promoted as Specialist, Fuel Cell Division at the Nuclear Research Center, Kahuta but he was not a happy man. He felt lonely and homesick. He had not met Payal for over two years and had yet to set his eyes on his young child Vijaya. He decided to set up home and applied for a visa for Payal. After some enquiries his case was recommended to the Home Department by the AECP and Payal was granted a limited visa for six months. The Statesman reassigned her in Islamabad as a special correspondent and the Kabir family settled down to quiet domesticity.

However, politically Pakistan was in turmoil. The eastern province was getting vocal and matters came to a head during the 1970-71 elections to the National Assembly when the Awami League won all the East Pakistan seats and gained a majority in the house to form a government. The prospect of a National Government headed by Awami League, a party of ethnic Bengalis was unthinkable to the Punjabi political elite and the President, a former Pakistani General. Dr. Kabir realized, like other East Pakistani civil and military officials that situation may turn difficult and ugly as the Punjabi politicians and army generals were not well disposed towards their Bengali brethren. He felt a Bengali had no future in Pakistan if East Pakistan was to break away and secede. In February 1971 came the opportunity he was looking for. He was invited to present a paper at a seminar organised at Dhaka by the University and the IAEA. He made up his mind to go back to the USA if things got ugly, and in the meanwhile decided to send Payal and Vijaya to Kolkata. He put them on a flight to New Delhi and headed for Dhaka.

# DHAKA

The Seminar at Dhaka was a great success with some good discussion and exchange of valuable information. The city of Dhaka was by now on the boil with political rallies and street corner gatherings of people of various political factions. The mood was belligerent and defiant of the authorities as the Awami League chief and popular political leader of the province was not invited to form the government after the results of the National Assembly were declared. The Bengali pride was hurt and everybody felt cheated by the attitude of the Punjabi and the Sindhi political leaders. Dr. Kabir, who had taken a few days leave at the end of the seminar to visit his folks, realized it would be suicidal to go back. While he was still enjoying his leave, the army cracked down on the agitators and arrested the Awami League leaders all over the province. Curfew was imposed in Dhaka and all major towns and cities. The radio station was shut down and censorship imposed on the press. Almost all newspapers ceased publication by way of protest. Telephone services were cut with the outside world and there was practically no communication within the province. Humayun Kabir had been in daily touch with Payal at Kolkata till the telephone exchanges were taken over by the army. She had been worried and had beseeched him to come over. Refugees were crossing the borders in hundreds and there were harrowing stories of rape, murder and torture in all the Indian newspapers and broadcasts of the All India Radio. But for Dr. Kabir there was no question of walking out of the house. All Bengali officers of the national and provincial governments were suspect and were to be arrested and jailed as traitors. The senior most had special warrants of arrest issued in their name. Many had been shot along with their families. On the tenth day after the crackdown an official vehicle drove over to Dr. Kabir's parental home and took him away to a detention center. He was identified by an officer of the AECP posted in Dhaka and put on a military plane the next day and transported to Islamabad where he was held in detention. For the world at large Dr. M. Humayun Kabir, a nuclear scientist at the AECP facility at Kahuta, had disappeared from the face of the earth.

# KOLKATA

The shocking army crackdown in East Pakistan traumatized the people of West Bengal who shared language and cultural affinity with their eastern neighbours. The refugees pouring in were a pathetic sight and sapped all the resources of the local administration. In Kolkata Payal continued her efforts with the visiting foreign correspondents to get some news of Humayun. He was after all a senior scientist and a member of the intellectual elite of the country; and Payal believed he could not be harmed. There was no information on the detainees and the list of people who died in the disturbances was not made available by the army. Payal waited patiently for the situation to normalize but there was no phone call from Dhaka even after the Pakistani army surrendered. The Statesman deputed her to Dhaka to cover the aftermath of the struggle and the birth of the new nation. She was in Dhaka for more than three weeks and her International Press card gave her unlimited access. She got to meet Dr. Kabir's aging parents but they had no news of him after he was taken away by the military police. The Pakistani army had burned all the office files and records before the surrender. There were no records of Dr. Kabir's arrest and detention. She wrote to the Ministry of External Affair, New Delhi to request the Indian High Commissioner in Islamabad to locate her husband with the help of the

AECP. The AECP said they had no information on Dr. Kabir who had gone missing after attending the seminar in Dhaka. They had declared him as absent from duty. Payal tried to get information from the US Embassy on behalf of Vijaya who was after all a US citizen. She got the same response as from The Indian High Commission in Islamabad. Payal could not bring herself to believe that her husband Humayun had died during the Pakistani Army operations in Dhaka. She kept hope alive in her heart and looked after young Vijaya's upbringing as a single parent. She put her into a convent school just off Park Street and continued her work with the Statesman. She read all the reports of the commissions which enquired into the Dhaka killings and followed up the investigations of the World Human Rights Groups. But she got no news about her husband.

# NEW DELHI

Saxena was in Venkat's office for vetting the brief on the Collins investigations for the PM's meeting. Saxena had got a positive report on the location of Collins captivity in Myanmar and the group which was holding him. There were indications that the ISI had planned and bankrolled the entire operation and that the kidnapping had been carried out by the NDLF rogues. The LTTE appeared to be interested in the hostage crisis but its motives were not clear for the present. By a process of elimination Saxena had put forth his theory that the LTTE wanted the British Government to act in some way for obtaining release of Collins. It had been a very dangerous and audacious kidnapping. Meticulous planning had gone into the abduction and transporting him across the border into Myanmar. Once the border was crossed there was no big deal. The Karen rebels were gun running for the LTTE for a decade and the links were well established. The Karen group that was holding Collins had been identified but they were not willing to talk business with Saxena's agents in Myanmar. They would hold Collins and await LTTE's instructions. Saxena was holding back on giving the go ahead to the Special Forces group till he got the nod from the British Foreign Office and some clue on the LTTE motives.

Venkat's secret phone rang and as he reached for it he made a sign pointing his index finger to the ceiling to say that it was the PM.

"Yes Sir we were waiting for instructions. Yes Saxena is with me. No sir the Special Forces are still on standby. Yes sir we understand. We will set up a hot line within an hour with the British High Commissioner. We will not act till we hear from the British Government. Yes sir we have to be very careful. We have already issued an advisory to all State Governments after we got the alert from Ulan Bator. Sir all our Atomic Energy Commission establishments are on alert and have put the Emergency Plan A into action. Their mobile units are scanning suspected locations for radiation footprints. The remote sensing authority has also undertaken aerial surveys but there is no indication of any unauthorized nuclear material in the likely urban and rural locations. We are maintaining the vigil Sir, and we will keep you informed on all developments."

"That was the PM. He had a call from the British PM that the Commissioner of Police in London received a mail by local post demanding the release of a Sri Lankan Tamil engineer, Kripanidhi, who is in jail in London. He is one of the specialists who worked in Ashfaq Ahmad's team and was arrested in London trying to smuggle sensitive electronic components which could find their way to nuclear labs for fabricating trigger switches for devices. The communication has demanded his release for Collins freedom. The British Government is reviewing the demand and has requested us to put on hold the Special Forces mission."

"This is serious, Venkat; we must put the Sri Lanka Government also on the alert. The LTTE is attempting to raise the ante in its civil war for Eelam. We have to guard our own interests first. I am not very happy with the developments we have witnessed in the past two weeks. The Russians have still not given any report on the extent and quantity of nuclear materials smuggled out in the recent transactions by the Russian and Kazak mafia. You must request the Foreign Secretary to put some pressure on the Russian Ambassador to confide on their findings. This is a very serious situation. It now appears that the LTTE has also joined in the clandestine operations to fabricate small nuclear devices to further their political objectives. The ISI has been collaborating with the LTTE since long. They have fabricated the suicide bombers jackets using the LTTE technology. The LTTE has used these jackets very successfully for carrying out their assassination missions and killed over a dozen political leaders and senior Sri Lankan defense personnel. Our own Prime Minister was a victim of such a suicide mission. Now it is payback time for the ISI. They appear to be behind all these furtive efforts of the ultras to acquire the materials and get Ashfaq Ahmad's team to fabricate a few devices to blackmail us, the Sri Lankans and perhaps the US."

"The MI 5 must be aware of all these developments and should factor this into account when they decide on Collins case. I am not surprised at the Americans silence. They must have assessed the situation by now. They were keeping a very close tab on the SALT agreement follow up and have two dedicated military satellites watching all the operations day and night. In fact it was they who had warned the Russians six months ago of suspicious non operational activities in the vicinity of one of the dismantling sites. Their night vision and the very high resolution satellite cameras had picked up images of some civilian vehicles carrying unauthorized personnel.

An instant alert sent by the US SALT monitors led the Russian security chasing and apprehending Chechen rebels and one junior technician from the facility. The Russians had thereafter tightened the security around the dismantling sites. However, the situation was very difficult in locations outside the Russian State where the weapons had been deployed during the cold war era. The dismantling process was in progress under the SALT treaty, when Gorbachev implemented his Glasnost and started the demolition of the Soviet Union. The breakaway states in the Central Asian region had Muslim majority and though they had no cause to support Jihadist fundamentalist and their radical supporters, they were under some pressure. The developments in breakaway Chechnya and the uprising of the Uyghur's in China's Sinkiang province had found some supporters amongst the Jihadists. Moreover the White Russians had always been viewed as imperialists in these regions. All these factors had created a situation which did not encourage complete integrity of operations in the Russian led SALT treaty compliance procedures."

"I think the Americans will not issue an advisory unless they have specific inputs on India. The CIA and the FBI and now the Department of Homeland Security are focused on threats to the US. We may get some advisory only if they have a specific input. Saxena, we can counter threats of nuclear blackmail only if we can show that we have a proactive nuclear doctrine. The Americans had their B-52 bombers on nuclear patrol over the Arctic Circle twenty four hours of the day and their ICBMs were kept ready for firing in silos located across the US. Their nuclear submarines were deployed across the globe to launch the nuclear minuteman missiles without surfacing. Their nuclear triad insured that the Soviets leaders could never surprise the Americans by launching a pre-emptive strike. The present scenario is worse than what the Americans or the Soviets faced during the cold war days. We have a faceless enemy who is stateless by choice; he owes no moral responsibility to any people or society. He is a pariah to his people and a menace to the whole world. He is brutal in behavior and totally mindless of the consequences of his acts and behavior. We have to have the capacity to bring unimaginable calamity on the country and people who shelter him and provide a platform to attack us. They should not hide behind the excuse that the act of terrorism was carried out by a non-state agency over which it had no control. It was understandable till such acts were limited to conventional weapons. With nuclear devices coming into operation—they better watch out. We may attack on reasonable apprehensions of impending attacks and destroy them. It should be in their own interest to control the Jihadis and eliminate them to ensure their own safety and survival."

"Venkat, I better get going and speak to Special Forces Team to stand down till we hear from London again. You let me know when you want me back to brief PM further."

Saxena walked across the forecourt of the North Block and strode across Rajpath to his office in the Cabinet Secretariat, as was his habit. He spent most of his working hours in his office and visited his R&AW headquarters for staff meetings and administrative work. Winter was practically over and Delhi was enjoying the wonderful short spring. The flower beds were blooming with sweet smelling flox, snap dragons, colorful dahlias and calendula. There were sweet peas on trellises and chrysanthemums in pots and bushes of marigolds in all shades of yellow. He felt relaxed when he took this walk from his office to Venkat's in the North Block or the PM's in the South Block. He was in a relaxed mood today though he felt very worried about Jihadist militants and their dangerous plans. He decided to send Raj across to Dhaka to check out on Dr. Kabir and his family's whereabouts. He had married this Bengali girl from Kolkata. What happened to her?

# MUMBAI

Raj found almost a dozen mails in his inbox, as the cab drove him out of the airport. He scanned through them and pointed the cursor to the one with the user ID Kailash. That was from Saxena himself and indicated the urgency of the instructions from the chief. Generally he got all the official messages from Saxenas staff officer but the rare ones from the chief meant 'drop everything on hand and move'. This one wanted him to report to the station officer at Dhaka. Raj knew that he had to move immediately. He called Saxenas office to find out the arrangements for his Dhaka visit.

"Sir you can get to Delhi by 6 pm. The Dhaka flight via Kolkata departs at 8.00pm. I will meet you at the airport with your passport and documents. The boss has already approved the briefs and has a special message in a sealed folder."

Raj had sufficient time to shower, change and pack his bag. Bahadur, his bearer-cum-cook was happy to see him home after a week and got busy preparing his lunch. He had been with Raj for over ten years now and had travelled with him all over including the overseas postings. Like Raj he was still single and totally devoted to him. He had enjoyed his stay in Tehran and learnt to cook a few local dishes. He was disappointed when Raj had to move suddenly to Mumbai to take up his new assignment. Ever since they moved to Mumbai life had become too hectic for Raj and he was never home for lunch. He was happy that today Raj would leave home only after eating his lunch. He knew he would be away for a few days, so he had prepared his favourite vegetarian dishes. He laid out the table just as Raj finished dressing and called him to fetch his shoes. Raj enjoyed his meal and reminded Bahadur to get his clothes laundered. He signed some cheques and asked Bahadur to collect the cash and pay off the bills.

Raj boarded the Jet Airways flight for Delhi at 4 pm. Suresh Kumar received him and they moved into the reserved lounge. Suresh handed him his air ticket by a Biman flight leaving at eight for Dhaka via Kolkata and a fresh passport with a business visa. Raj was visiting Dhaka as a representative of a large retail store specializing in labeled garments. His visits to two garment factories were arranged. The rest of his stay was to be coordinated by the Commercial attaché in the Indian High Commission. There were still two hours for the flight but Suresh decided to drop him at the International terminal. At the Departure gate he handed Raj the sealed envelope containing Saxena's special message.

"Sir read it and destroy it."

Raj walked into the terminal and checked himself in. He completed the other formalities, went through immigration and settled down in the departure hall. He took out the envelope and removed Saxena's note. There were just a few words typed on an A6 size sheet.

"Dr. M.Humayun Kabir married Payal from Kolkata while they were studying at Columbia University, New York. She returned to Kolkata after completing her programme at Columbia. She joined the Statesman and worked as Assistant Editor for around a year. She was deputed to Islamabad in late 1970 as a Special correspondent as Dr. Kabir managed to secure a short term visa for her to join him in Islamabad. She returned from Islamabad in February 1971 shortly before Dr. Kabir's disappearance and rejoined The Statesman. She worked for the paper till mid 1994 when she resigned due to terminal illness. She expired in June 2001. Find out more about her and if she had any children-perhaps, a daughter?"

The flight from Kolkata reached Dhaka just past midnight. Raj checked into the Radisson Hotel and hit the bed. He had been travelling for over eighteen hours now, starting from Colombo with brief stopovers at Mumbai, Delhi and Kolkata. He just wanted to sleep for the next ten hours if possible. He had a long days work ahead and he would have to start early. He was however clueless about his plans; numb with fatigue he just drifted into unconsciousness.

# NEW DELHI

Dr. Alka Gadgil's article entitled 'Homeland for the Baloch and Pashtun tribal's in Pakistan and Afghanistan' first appeared in the Economic and Foreign Policy Weekly published by the Lokshakti group of newspapers and journals. The group had long been identified with right of center political thinkers and had a sizable patronage amongst academicians, industrial and commercial houses. In the weeks that followed there were severe editorial comments in the more conservative of newspapers that still believed in the Nehruvian dialectics of the cold war era of non alignment and non—interference. They criticized Gadgil's article as a grave provocation challenging the historical settlements, one even propounding that a proactive foreign policy was totally against Gandhian philosophy. Some others described her as a RSS hawk in a secular polity. Many foreign commentators commended her approach as original and recommended that her suggestion of redrawing the Durand Line be taken seriously as this would have a moderating impact on the situation in Afghanistan. An internal paper prepared by the Ministry of External Affairs, South Asia Desk took her to task for attempting to disturb the efforts to normalize relations between the two countries and described her suggestion of policy change as chauvinistic.

The debate carried on further in the TV news channels and picked up some momentum and heat as the days went by. The guest editors from Pakistan were confused whether to condemn the idea totally as being anti national or praise it as having some merit for consideration. A major support though guarded came, from the Pashtun intellectuals who appreciated the concern expressed by a Hindu right wing thinker for their harassed and oppressed brethren, but felt that this may be a new Hindu scheme to destroy Pakistan. The Government spokesman maintained that India respected the freedom of speech and expression and found nothing outrageous with what was written. Dr. Alka Gadgil was an academic and a researcher and what she had said was a historical fact. The Pashtun people had indeed been divided by the Durand Line in 1894 and it had then been the trump card of Colonial British India's policy to establish the "Great Game" buffer zone between the British and Russian interests in the region. With growing nationalism and integration of ethnic groups in various regions of the world, including in Europe, it was but natural for the Pashtuns and the Baloch tribal's to aspire for a homeland of their own. Had not Pakistan been raising the standard of revolt in Kashmir for the last sixty years by calls of independence for the oppressed, and fighting a proxy war?

The reaction in the media across the borders was on expected lines. The hawks went ballistic calling for a jihad to destroy the Hindus. The intelligentsia was divided in its condemnation. The general approach seemed to be that the tribal areas required more development and Government should commit money for education and infrastructure. More representation in the government bodies would also involve their leaders in the governance of their own people.

This was especially true of the Pashtuns who had suffered during the Soviet intervention in Afghanistan and later at the hands of the Taliban groups. The official line was that the matter was being taken up with the Government of India, but the country was prepared to face any challenge. The US Ambassador called on the Foreign Secretary and was assured that there was no move to change the existing policy and that our academics enjoyed freedom of speech in the best democratic traditions enshrined in the constitution. The government had no policy of press censorship and the media was free to air their views on any subject affecting the country's integrity and peaceful development. Dr. Gadgil had written with great moderation and she had not distorted or misrepresented facts. In fact she had been critical of the leadership of the ruling party leaders who were at the helm of affairs when the British were pushing the partition idea. That the Baloch and Pashtuns got a raw deal in the Partition was a fact which evens the British historians had conceded.

The British High Commissioner also called on the Foreign Secretary and expressed his concern at media reactions on both sides of the border. He said the British Government was concerned that heightening of tensions may disturb the peace in the region. He was offered the usual courtesies and informed that the government had no proposal to gag the press or curtail academic freedom. There was nothing provocative or unwarranted in what the article had contained. The facts were well known to the British Government as it had officially endorsed the agreement signed in 1893 between Amir Abdur Rehman Khan of Afghanistan and Henry Mortimer Durand, the then Foreign Secretary of British India, which laid the Durand Line boundary in 1894. Similar was the status of the McMahon Line, India's' boundary with Tibet which had already been challenged by the Chinese Government. The High Commissioner was also reminded that successive authorities and governments in Afghanistan, including the present one have condemned the Agreement of 1893 and refused to accept the Durand Line as their country's eastern border. Dr. Alka Gadgil had not erred in the presentation of the facts.

The Pakistan Foreign Secretary lodged a protest on behalf of his government. He was politely informed that if he referred to Dr. Alka Gadgil's article and the subsequent debate generated in the media, he was only protesting against the exercise of fundamental rights insured by the country's Constitution. Nothing had been said which was not a historical fact. The government had made no announcement so far that it supported the cause of the Baloch and Pashtuns to have a homeland of their own.

The debate in the press and the electronic media gave Venkat immense satisfaction. He was sure that the subject would be debated in the next session of the Parliament. The approach might appear reactionary to the left of center parties but would find support amongst the more vocal right wingers.

# DHAKA

Raj was up early and ready by 9.00. He walked down to the coffee shop helped himself to fruit and a croissant at the buffet breakfast, and was through his second cup of tea when the restaurant hostess paged him with a message from the front desk that his taxi had reported. Raj finished his tea, picked up the local newspapers and walked to the exit. His taxi driver Debu appeared cheerful and fresh and gave him a military salute as he stepped into the vehicle. Raj gave him the address and relaxed back scanning the headlines in the English dailies, The Daily Star and the New Age. There was news on debates in the Bangla Parliament on education reforms, pension for school teachers and construction of new school buildings in district places. The garment workers were demanding better wages and working conditions and there was an editorial on the rising import bill and the balance of payment crisis. Sonar Bangla International, the first garment export house he was visiting, was located in the Narayanganj area. It took almost an hour to get there through the slow moving traffic. The business office of the company was located within the factory compound itself. He was stopped at the gate by the security but once he gave his name and visiting card, he was allowed to proceed to a small double storied building of recent origin. The receptionist, a young lady in pants and a printed flowery top escorted Raj to the Chief Executives office. Sabina Ahmad turned out to be a charming lady. She was happy to see Raj and thanked him for the business they had received from his company. She spoke with a marked American accent and appeared to have spent some years in the US. A sorority emblem on her table indicated she had been to Wharton Business School. She showed him some new samples of ladies garments. Raj handed her letters from his head office, some placing fresh orders and others regarding bank transactions. The meeting over Raj thanked Sabina and invited her to visit Delhi. He had an appointment with the station officer R&AW at 3 p.m. and asked the driver to take him back to the hotel.

Shubir Dutta the station officer in Dhaka was an old R&AW hand in Bangladesh and had been posted with Raj in Copenhagen in 1992. He had located Dr. Kabir's ancestral home but learnt that both his parents were no more. The house was presently occupied by a maternal aunt of Dr. Kabir. Shubir had made efforts with the local authorities to get some information on Dr. Kabir but had drawn a blank. They decided to take a chance and visit the lady. Shubir dismissed Raj's taxi and asked Debu to come to the hotel the next morning.

The house was in the Hazaribagh area. They had some difficulty in finding it though Shubir had got the details of its location from a local agent. The lady who answered the door turned out to be Samina Begum, the spinster aunt of Dr. Kabir. She seemed to be in her mid-fifties and appeared well educated as she replied in English when Shubir enquired in Bengali. Introductions done she invited them to the living room which was modestly furnished. There were many framed photographs of family members and Samina Begum introduced the photographs by touching them reverently. There were photos of Dr. Kabir's father who had been district judge of the Provincial Services of Pakistan, a group photograph of the family taken before Dr. Kabir's departure for the US, of Dr. Kabir in the convocation gown after he received his PhD and there was one of Dr. Kabir and his wife Payal after they got married in New York. Samina Begum said she had some more photographs of Payal and her daughter and she rummaged in the drawers till she found an old yellow manila envelop. There were perhaps a dozen photos and she handed them one by one to Shubir explaining that these were the surviving snaps of Dr. Kabir's family. They showed Dr. Kabir, his wife Payal holding a small child, another with Payal playing with their baby daughter and one with Dr. Kabir holding the child.

"These are very old pictures; don't you have any later ones?" enquired Shubir.

Samina Begum was close to tears. In a voice choked with emotion she said that they had lost contact with Dr. Kabir in April 1971 when the Pakistani army arrested him. All efforts to locate him failed and the Pakistani Government declared him a rebel and a traitor. After Bangladesh became independent, the family made many efforts to get some news of Dr. Kabir. Payal who was in Kolkata came to Dhaka after the surrender of the Pakistani army and made every effort but got no news about Dr. Kabir. After 1971 Payal wrote regularly to Baba, Dr. Kabir's father. She came over when Baba died in 1980 but after that we lost contact with her. Baba kept all her correspondence in this desk and read the letters over and over again. He was very fond of his grandchild although he met her only once when she was two and half years old in December 1971, when Payal came to locate her husband.

"Could we see those letters please as we are trying to locate Payal's family?" Raj asked anxiously.

"Yes, I will just find them while you have some tea."

Samina Begum got busy sifting through the papers in the desk drawers while Shubir and Raj helped themselves to the tea brought in by her maid. Samina thumbed through a number of envelopes of various shapes and sizes in the drawer and finally pulled out a large one which had a number of smaller envelopes bearing Indian postage stamps. She handed them over to Shubir and Raj. The letters were all in English and addressed to Dr. Kabir's father as 'Dear Respected Baba.' Raj suddenly felt weak and nervous. There in the very first letter he felt he was closer to solving the mystery of Vijaya Choudhry. Payal had written about the progress of her child in school and addressed her as Vijaya. The name appeared in every letter she wrote to Baba. One envelope contained a short letter written on school note book paper by Vijaya to her Dadu. There was also a group photograph of schoolgirls in their pinafores and Payal had identified young Vijaya by a small ball pen dot for Dadu's benefit. Samina Begum was most surprised as she had never opened that packet and seen Vijaya's photo. Vijaya must have been around eleven years old then. Behind the photo Payal had written—'Vijaya with her friends at St Mary's School, Park Street, Kolkata'.

"Samina Begum, we are very concerned about Dr. Kabir's whereabouts. We do not hold out any hope for now, but we feel he might be alive. We have to find out more about Payal Kabir and Vijaya before we can proceed further. We would like to have copies of all these letters and this photo to further investigate his disappearance. As you said Payal had settled down in Kolkata and these letters also bear the postage cancellation at the Kolkata

GPO. We want to visit Payal's home and find out about her and Vijaya."

"Sir, you can have them. I beg you with folded hands to get some news about Humayun Dada."

Samina Begum was overwhelmed remembering the fateful days of 1971. She could not contain herself and broke down.

"I am sorry Didi. I reopened the wounds of those fateful days. I know the burden of the tragedy all of you carry."

"You did not remind me of the tragedy; we have refused to forget those difficult days. I was a young student in 1971 and we were all at the forefront of the Sonar Bangla movement. When the army cracked down in our town of Sylhet they took away all the girls and locked them up in the local barrack. Most of the boys were shot. I lost my brother who was a student leader. They tortured him for three days and left his body hanging in our college compound. The fate of us girls was even worse. We were left mentally and physically broken."

# NEW DELHI

Saxena had been following up the B.K. Dossier investigations and the Vijaya Choudhry murder case with the Mumbai Police Commissioner. He got a call from him the day Raj met Samina Begum in Dhaka, and was informed that Satish Sharma had been able to recover some pen drives and a personal diary from Vijaya's apartment in the Lokhandwala. Satish would discuss the case with Raj after he returned to Mumbai. Venkat called next to inform that Manoj Subramanian was with him with the draft of the article on the Nuclear doctrine and wanted advice and approval. They agreed to meet at 7.00 pm in Venkat's office and Saxena got busy with his staff officer discussing the proposals for fresh deployments and postings.

Later in the afternoon he got a message from Shubir Dutta in Dhaka that Raj had taken a flight for Kolkata. His message folder had routine reports from Copenhagen on the LTTE and Sri Lanka peace talks, from Myanmar on the growing disenchantment amongst the young students on the Army Junta's attempts to introduce their brand of democracy in the country. There was one from Kathmandu regarding arrest of some traders dealing in counterfeit Indian currency. Thirty lakhs worth Rupee Five hundred currency notes had been seized by the Narcotics Bureau of Nepal and three Nepalese and two Indians had been arrested. He marked a copy to Economic offence Division for follow up. At five thirty he had his Divisional officers briefing which generally lasted till past six thirty. Just as he was leaving his office he saw a message marked "URGENT" in his courier folder. He cut open the sealed packet and pulled out a priority message from the R&AW Station Officer in Kathmandu.

## TOP SECRET

To,
The Secretary R&AW                                    16th March 2004
NEW DELHI

Agent from Pokhra reported an unusual gathering of Hindu activists from various organisations, political and social. The Group leader is one Raghunath Bhide of Indore. He noticed arrival of this group which drove up in a mini-bus all the way from Indore to the Vishnu Temple on the outskirts of Pokhra Town. They camped out in tents and were met by the local right wing activists of the Gurkha Union Party. On Tuesday the 5th May they were met by Colonel Adhikari and Major Virender Singh, both serving officers of the Dogra regiment. They are travelling under assumed names Raj Tilak and Gurbachan Singh to Pokhra. Both stayed at Hotel Shangri-La in Kathmandu and Hotel Lake View at Pokhra. Identities confirmed from Indian Airlines arrival desk Kathmandu Airport.

The group held a meeting late night at the camp site when Col Adhikari briefed them on ISI's plans to attack Hindu pilgrimage centers during yatras and festivals. Plans to kill Hindus by remote controlled IED's explained. Col Adhikari emphasised that the Government is in appeasement mode and will not go to war on ISI terror strikes. It was therefore necessary that Hindus organise to save their Dharma. As attack was the better form of defense their trained force should destroy mosques and Madarssa's as acts of revenge for Hindu blood spilt by ISI terror groups. There was unanimous support in the gathering. Col Adhikari assured training and supply of all materials for manufacturing explosive devices. He said that the Hindu activists should motivate committed young men and women to be ready for sacrifices. He was assured all support by Raghunath Bhide. They decided to draw up detailed plans for their strikes in their next meeting in the Balak Baba Akhada in Indore in August.

Raf/35/# 67/Range

Everest

Top Secret

Saxena pocketed the message and walked out of his office around ten minutes to seven and strode across to Venkat's office.

There was no news from London as yet. Venkat asked his staff to send Manoj in and serve the tea and snacks. This was the usual drill in Venkat's office. All meetings starting after six thirty had a high tea arranged and his staff would ensure that they got the best snacks in town. There were samosas, medu wadas, cheese sandwiches and delicious Bengali sweets. Manoj regaled them with Taliban jokes he had heard recently in Washington where he had gone to attend a meeting with the Rand Foundation on the source of funds of Al Qaida. Manoj then made a presentation of his article wherein he argued that the Draft Nuclear

Doctrine under consideration of the National Security Council stipulates that you deploy the nuclear triad—the land, sea and air based nuclear delivery system as a secured second strike capability. He reminded that though the drafting committee had considered the role of the non-state combatants, it had not taken their interventions as a serious threat. Now in the background of the recent incidents and growing concerns of threats of nuclear terrorism posed by the Lashkar-e-Taiba, Al-Qaeda and Jaish-e-Mohammed terror groups, it had become necessary to factor in their existence. The need to review the 'no first use clause' in the doctrine aught to be considered seriously as coercion and blackmail could be used by these groups by smuggling a nuclear device into the country. He was of the considered opinion that only a threat of preemptive strike by the nuclear triad could neutralize such threats. The existing doctrine gave the impression that the country was willing to suffer an initial nuclear strike, however crippling it might be before striking back in retaliation. Such a situation was unacceptable as the reaction time after an attack was launched by the enemy would be just seven to eight minutes which could leave the command centers paralyzed and incapable of reacting effectively. The retaliatory strike might not be as effective as envisaged and leave our security compromised and the conventional forces demoralized. The scenario had become even more daunting now with the possibility of the non state players acquiring nuclear devices.

"Let's consider a scenario where the ISI succeeds in putting a group together who smuggle in a small device as big as a portable generator, in a dissembled state, say to a suburb of Delhi like Faridabad and re-assemble it in an abandoned factory shed. While this group awaits the arrival of the fissile core and trigger, a threat is conveyed from one of the identified terror groups with past record of involvement in India, that all armed forces and Para military forces be withdrawn from the Kashmir valley and the region of Ladakh within fifteen days failing which a nuclear device would be set off in New Delhi. How will you tackle the threat?

A) Protest to Pakistan? They will raise their hands and say sorry these are non-state players and not their citizens.

B) Threaten to bomb them in retaliation? They will raise cries of nuclear threat and blackmail, declare Jihad and operationally prepare their own weapons for a strike.

The terrorists will anyway set off the device in the capital and cause enough casualties to set off panic in the other Metros. So what are the options available to you?"

Manoj paused to nibble a cheese sandwich and sip his tea.

"Emphasize in the preamble of the Doctrine Document that the distinction between State and non-State combatants does not exist. Therefore any hostile act by a non-State player invites retaliation as an act of hostility by the enemy State. Revise your Doctrine and use of the Nuclear Triad and give a go ahead to the Nuclear Command Administration (NCA) to deploy on threat or a perceived threat. The NCA will place the AGNI V nuclear missiles on the mobile launchers in attack mode and scramble the BRAHMOS cruise missile platform of the Sukhoi 30 jets. Two nuclear submarines capable of launching twenty nuclear missiles within a space of thirty minutes will be at their launch stations in the Arabian

Sea. Simultaneously our Military Satellites Rakshak I & II will monitor their air bases, nuclear facilities and missile batteries. Any attempts by their forces to move their missile launchers, or put their bombers in air should invite immediate attack by the Triad."

Manoj paused, got up from the sofa, helped himself to another cheese sandwich and poured himself a fresh cup of tea from the sideboard. He took a satisfying sip of the excellent tea; Venkat always offered the best.

"Broken orange pekoe from the Nuwara Eliya Hills in Sri Lanka, isn't it Venkat?"

"You are a real connoisseur of good tea, Manoj; that's what Chitra got for me from her visit to Colombo last week."

"Manoj your hypothesis is faultless. According to it we have to become pro active and totally unpredictable in the use of our nuclear capability. We arm ourselves to our teeth and become belligerent. Yes, it does pay to overawe the bully. Your hypothesis is also based on the premise that we can never expect to have normal relations with that country and therefore we indulge in this brinkmanship. Will our people ever accept this? One would live in constant fear of being nuked. We may also fry them in the process but where does that get us?"

"The situation is not of our own making, Venkat. We are being subjected to the bullying tactics by that State and its proxies. So long it is conventional weapons it's manageable. They bomb us and kill the innocent in cities; we chase them and kill their Jihadis. But the emergence of nuclear capable terrorist outfits is a different ball game altogether. They are raising the ante in the expectation that we will leave the matter at the protest level. No sir, they should know that the non-state nuclear capable combatant will be treated on par with their regular forces in future. If you threaten us by that route you risk getting nuked. They should know that our nuclear doctrine has been revised and also been ratified by the parliament. The state will protect its citizen from any mischief by the enemy. We should be prepared to live in nuclear bunkers like the Americans and the Europeans did at the height of the cold war. Each house in Geneva, where I stayed for three years, had a nuclear capable bunker in the basement, kept provisioned with food, water and essential medicine supplies all round the year. It was mandatory and every resident had to comply. Now it's all over as both the Americans and the Russians realized it was futile to out bomb each other. They signed a peace treaty and decided to dismantle their weapons. We will have to reach that stage one day when the worthy Generals on the other side of the border realize that they would like their children and grandchildren to live in peace with their neighbours."

Saxena got up and gave a standing ovation when Manoj concluded his presentation.

"Bravo Manoj that was well said."

Saxena showed the message from his Station Officer in Kathmandu to Venkat after the meeting was over and others had left.

"This was what we have anticipated all the while. You remember when last year the Muslim Majlis Party in Hyderabad blamed the Hindu Jagran Party for the blasts in the Mecca Masjid. Politically the ruling party is not willing to accept any blame on the Hindus. That, you mark my words Saxena will be the beginning of fresh round of bloodletting between the two communities unless we take strong measures now. I will put our IB man at Indore after Raghunath Bhide and also advise Army Chief to put his two Dogra regiment boys on a watch list of the MI.

# KOLKATA

**R**aj flew into Kolkata on a late afternoon Biman flight and checked into the Park Hotel. He opened the blue plastic file Shubir had compiled for him containing copies of the letters they had retrieved from Dr. Kabir's home in Dhaka. Raj read through the letters written by Payal Kabir to her father-in-law as a dutiful son would have written himself to his aging father. She spoke about Dr. Kabir's work in Columbia and the Chicago Universities and how he had missed his home especially during Eid and Durga Puja. She spoke about their marriage and birth of Vijaya while she was still in New York and Dr. Kabir had taken up the assignment with the AECP in Islamabad. She was a doting mother and in every letter she gave news about Vijaya's progress as she grew up and learnt to walk. Her letter to Baba describing Vijaya's first steps as she learnt to stand and walk was an emotion filled moment of joy of a single parent as well as of anguish that her father was not around to share these moments.

Raj read through the file till past mid-night. He could not sleep for hours thereafter as he felt disturbed. He could not bring himself to imagine that she might be the same person. Through the letters he could virtually see little Vijaya emerge before him. But the picture was incomplete as the correspondence stopped after Dec1980. The last letter from Payal remained unread. She had learnt about his illness and had wished for his speedy recovery, but the letter reached Dhaka a day after he passed away. Now he had to find out about Payal and her daughter from 1980 till the present day. He knew from Saxena's note that Payal had possibly passed away sometimes in 2001; so he guessed that Vijaya must have graduated by then and working in the US and would have been around thirty one years old. The gaps in the jig saw were slowly closing and all the patchworks merging. He had the latter part of the picture pretty clear. The interactions with Pradeep during the brief visit to his tea estate had fleshed in the personality to a great extent. Vijaya had emerged as a young professional with a disturbed childhood living with a mother who was emotionally lost in the search of her missing husband. She had a vague idea about her father and had been close to her mother. There was a gap of twenty years in that picture which required to be explained. These years had been crucial. Something or some events had intervened and touched her life and disturbed her. Pradeep talked about days when she was deeply disturbed but would not discuss her problems. Why was she in Mumbai? What made her stay back in the country or come back from Chicago where she had taken up a good job? What were the compulsions to get involved in questionable transactions involving tainted money? And what was the need for secrecy and subterfuge in clothing the transactions in the manner she had done. The B.K. Dossier was turning out to be the proverbial Pandora's Box. Was she innocent or was she involved with the terror outfits who had meticulously planned this havala network to bring in money for funding terror strikes? Raj could not believe it was true. He was not ready to condemn Vijaya yet. From all accounts he had gathered so far from her friends and her Dhaka kin, he could not imagine her capable of intrigue and falsehood. He had a nagging feeling that Dr. Kabir her father might perhaps be the cause of her travails and her sad death. Raj was getting a headache now. His mind was in a conflict. He decided to shower and get some sleep. He stood under the cold shower for a few minutes and then turned on the hot water till steam filled the shower cabinet. He felt refreshed and somewhat relaxed as he emerged from the bath.

Raj had obtained Payal's address in Kolkata from the letters she wrote to Baba. Payal had in fact written her address on all the letters she sent to Baba. So Raj gave the same address to the taxi driver who picked him up at the hotel. The locality on Rafi Ahmad Kidwai Road was just half an hour's drive through the chaotic Kolkata traffic, but Raj had some trouble locating Ruby Mansion where Payal had stayed with her parents on returning from New York. He got out of the taxi and walked around asking for directions from the shopkeepers and the cycle rickshaw drivers who were crowding the narrow lanes around Ruby Mansion. Ruby Mansion was a large apartment house constructed sometimes in the mid fifties. It had seen better days and appeared desperately in need of a coat of paint. In fact its condition was not dissimilar to most of the structures in the area. Raj enquired about Payal Kabir's flat from the watchman in the compound. He seemed to be lost and said that no person of that name lived in the flat Raj had mentioned. Raj explained that he was aware that the lady in question had expired some years ago; he wanted to meet her relatives who lived in the flat now. The watchman appeared to be new so he decided to accompany Raj to the fourth floor where the flat was located. They took the elevator and knocked on the door. After a while the door was opened by an elderly gentleman who appeared to have been disturbed from his siesta. The watchman spoke to him in Bengali, but the gentleman did not follow him. The watchman now raised his voice and said that the visitor wanted to meet him. He followed it this time and looked at Raj enquiringly and spoke in English.

"Yes, what do you want?"

Raj said he was tracing Dr. Humayun Kabir's family and had some enquiries to make about Payal Kabir and her daughter Vijaya. The gentleman gestured him to come inside and Raj followed him to a spacious living room filled with stuffed sofas and gleaming period furniture made of teak wood. A large glass enclosed book case covered practically one wall of the room which was filled with hard covers and some leather bound volumes. This was the home of an affluent and well read middle class family, Raj surmised. The old man gestured Raj to sit on the sofa and seated himself close to him.

"You must have noticed by now that I am some what hard of hearing," he said and laughed amusingly at himself.

"You wanted to know about Payal. Well she passed away six years ago. She suffered from cancer. She endured a lot and I had to give her pain killing injections. I am a doctor, but I don't practice now. She was my niece, her father Dr. Arun Kumar Choudhry was my elder brother. I was a bachelor, so when I retired from the Army Medical Corps, Arun dada asked me to come and stay here. I had the company of Payal and her charming daughter Vijaya for years. Then Payal passed away. Vijaya kept visiting me every now and then but I have had no news of her for almost two months now. She always wrote to me during Puja festival and came over sometimes—not every year though. Last year she called and said that she could not get leave due to pressure of work but promised she would come during Holi."

"Sir, I am from the Human Rights Watch organisation and we are still trying to trace some people who were reported missing during 1971 disturbances in Bangladesh. We have received a request from our Pakistan Chapter to get some information on Dr. M.Humayun Kabir's family. He is still reported missing by their government agencies."

"He was killed by the Pakistan army during those disturbances; their army destroyed all the intelligentsia in that country. Payal made so much effort to locate him but without any result. You know Vijaya was born in New York and is an American citizen by birth. Her US passport has her name as Vijaya Humayun Choudhry-Kabir. However when Payal admitted her in school here she registered her name as Vijaya Choudhry and that name remained in her school leaving certificate as also her B.Com degree and her Chartered Accountants Certificates. She is still an American Citizen; her passport was renewed by Payal when she took her to the USA for a seminar she was invited to attend at Columbia University. Later Vijaya took up a brief assignment with a Chartered Accountants firm in Chicago but came back after three years due to Payal's illness and set up her own firm in Mumbai. I advised her to go back and work in the US after Payal passed away; she was very lonely and depressed at times but she stayed on."

"No Dada", she would say, "I have work to do. Baba may come back some day . . . ."

"Payal never lost hope on Humayun. She always said that he will return one day. During the later years of her illness she would talk about him all the time. She convinced Vijaya that her Baba was alive and that he would come home one day. I always cheered her and never questioned her why she felt so. It was good to see her happy and cheerful in her condition as it was good therapy for one terminally ill with cancer; but I knew there was little hope. She was sinking all the while"

Debi Kumar Choudhry, Vijayas closest surviving relative got up and returned with a packet of family photographs and letters. He showed them one by one to Raj. There were photos of Payal and Vijaya with Payal's father as Dr. Debi Kumar explained. There were some of Vijaya with Payal and also of Payal alone. Vijaya looked a charming and as vivacious a person as Pradeep had described her. Raj selected five recent photographs which could provide a good sample for the forensics to match with the ones taken after she was murdered. He requested Dr. Debi Kumar to lend the same to him for a day to make copies.

# MUMBAI

**R**aj headed for his office after his flight landed in Mumbai. He had lot of paper work to complete before his meeting with Satish Sharma at 4 p.m. Sandra Lobo, his secretary, handed him a folder of correspondence from the head office. She had already replied to the routine correspondence and only the top secret classified mail in sealed covers awaited Raj's attention. Raj slit open the packets one by one and read through the correspondence. He made notes in his personal diary and kept some of the letters in one pile. The rest he got Sandra to put in the shredder. That was the routine procedure in his office; no files were made of important cases. After a report was sent all papers were shredded and burnt to ashes in a furnace and flushed into the municipal sewers.

There were some routine letters to be written to the Commissioner of Police and the Coast Guard Commandant which he dictated to Sandra, and while she typed them he pulled out his laptop and started completing his notes on the information he had collected in Colombo, Kandy and Pradeep's guest house in the Nuwara Eliya Hills. He made his assessments on the intelligence inputs. He did a similar exercise on the information gathered in Dhaka and Kolkata. He felt quite satisfied with the progress made so far in tracing the family background of Vijaya Choudhry. He had still to get the confirmation from Satish Sharma about the identity of the corpse in the police mortuary. He had asked Satish for a DNA report to be prepared for final confirmation. He signed off the letters Sandra had typed and drove down to the Police Headquarters.

Satish had called the investigating officer Inspector Bhonsle with the related papers and they got down to examining them. The forensic report on the identification was still awaited but was expected soon. The coroner's office had put their best boys on the job and they would call Satish as soon as they had a confirmation or otherwise. The most crucial piece of evidence found by Inspector Bhonsle was a personal diary maintained by Vijaya. She wrote about the pressures she was working under and prayed for strength for Baba's sake. There were many references to her father in the diary and it appeared that she was being subjected to blackmail and coercion to do things beyond her will. At one place she had written that her tormentors had harassed her ailing mother too. Raj read through the diary at random but he required more time to analyse this conundrum. He requested Satish to lend him the diary for a few days. They then proceeded to open the pen drives which were also found along with the diary. Satish loaded one on to his lap top and opened the first file. There were some names which appeared to be in code. Others were names of popular stars in the film industry. Each name had some amount mentioned against it. The amounts ranged between five to ten lakh rupees. These went upwards of fifty five lakhs in each cycle of payment. The payments were made once every week. There was repetition of some names in all the files in that pen drive. Inspector Bhonsle handed over another pen drive saying that it contained data of a different kind that he had not been able to figure out. Raj opened the drive and found five entries in the first file. Each entry had a date and the time in the twenty four hour format. The next file too had similar information; each month of the year had two dates selected at random. Then there was a third drive with dates along with the name of a city. There were three entries for Khandala, two for of Ahmadabad and Bangalore and one each of Ranchi and Lucknow. Inspector Bhonsle had not figured out this piece of information, except perhaps that they could be the meeting venues on the dates indicated. The fact that Khandala figured in the pen drive indicated a pattern for Bhonsle. He however had no explanation for the fact that the pen drive did not mention the day on which Vijaya was murdered in Khandala. Vijaya and Pradeep had been meeting regularly in Khandala, but the day before she was killed they had stayed at the Ambay Valley Resort. According to the resort reception they had checked out the next day after breakfast and Pradeep left for Mumbai in his car. Vijaya had stayed back for a meeting with the press correspondents and the media crew who had attended the promo the evening before. The Resort Travel Desk had confirmed that later in the afternoon, Vijaya took their cab for a drop at the Hotel Hilltop, Khandala. The Hotel had also confirmed that Vijaya had checked in around 3.00 pm and that she had visitors around five in the afternoon. Her body was found the next day by the housekeeping attendant who went to clean and make her room.

Raj requested Satish for copies of all the pen drives and promptly loaded them on to his laptop. After Bhonsle left Raj told Satish of his meeting with Pradeep in Sri Lanka. He said he would bring him around next week when he returned and requested that Pradeep should not be called for questioning by Inspector Bhonsle. Raj assured him that Pradeep was clean as far as Vijaya's case was concerned. He informed Satish that the Vijaya Choudhry murder mystery was a small piece in the larger puzzle which his organisation was trying to solve. It had international security dimensions and his best guess was that it could finally be laid on the table of the ISI. Satish let off a soft whistle and assured Raj that the entire police force was at his disposal.

Raj spent the next two days reading Vijaya Choudhry's diary. He was reminded of what Pradeep told him during his stay at his tea estate. Vijaya had appeared being under pressure but never talked about it to him and when he pressed her she would just say it was nothing, but she appeared worried. The many references she made to Baba in her diary reinforced Raj's conjecture that Dr. Kabir might be alive and the reason, ironically for Vijaya's travails. Where could he be, what were the compulsions on Vijaya to suffer the way she had? Then what were the explanations for all the data stored in the pen drives; these definitely had some linkage to the diskette discovered with Brij Kishen. He ran the pen drive which had a list of dates and time indicated against each. Could this be a timetable for calling somebody or for receiving calls? He made a note in his diary to get more information about Vijaya's mobile from Satish. The mobile was reported missing from the room after her body was discovered.

Raj was beginning to believe that Dr. Kabir was alive and perhaps a hostage of the ISI. He was visiting Dhaka to participate in the Regional Seminar hosted by the IAEA and Dhaka University when he had been picked up from his ancestral home by the Military Police. He was not heard of after that. The AECP maintained that he was absconding while the Pakistan government had taken a stand that he had joined the Bangladesh rebel leaders and their freedom movement. His body was never found and the Human Rights Watch still had his name in the list of intellectuals missing after the Dhaka disturbances of March 1971. Raj felt that the ISI might be using Dr. Kabir to work on some secret armaments project of the AECP on threat of eliminating his wife and daughter in India if he failed to cooperate. They must have secretly taken photographs of his family and coerced him to work for them. Dr. Kabir had been one of the few renowned scientists who had specialised in processing and fabricating fuel for nuclear reactors and had worked for over two years in the nuclear plant at Kahuta. He had been the blue eyed boy of Dr. Ashfaq Ahmad and had probably been abducted from Dhaka at Dr. Ahmad's behest. It now appeared to Raj that Dr. Kabir's wife and daughter had perhaps been coerced to work for the ISI to keep Dr. Kabir alive. As Vijaya was a child and would not have remembered her father after he disappeared, she must have learnt about his captivity from Payal before she died. It was Vijaya who became the real victim of this tragedy. Perhaps Vijaya had been used as a safe conduit to funnel money to the sleeper cells of the ISI. The financial deals of B.K.Enterprises were used as a cover to bring in the havala money to fund their agents. Vijaya had been compelled into doing what she did to protect her father from harm. The investigations into the Vijaya murder case and the B.K. Dossier were interlinked. The B.K. Dossier, Raj feared was like the Rosetta stone containing the key to decipher the data in the pen drives. He had to meet Satish urgently to fill the missing gaps in Inspector Bhonsle's investigations and also felt the need to consult Saxena and apprise him of his conclusions.

# MUMBAI

Satish had most of the information ready by the time Raj reached his office. Inspector Bhonsle had some results to show after Satish threatened to have him transferred to a remote district in the state if he failed to produce results in his investigations. Bhonsle managed to trace two mobile numbers and also produced the bills recovered from Vijaya's flat. One of the two numbers was the same Raj had retrieved from Pradeep and Ratna. This was the one she normally used in her official and private communication. The other was the one which Satish and Raj felt worth following up. Very few calls had been made from this number. Most calls received on this number were from Dubai and Karachi. Both the phones had disappeared after Vijaya's murder but surprisingly her personal phone continued to function for another week or so. The calls made were to local numbers in Khandala but a few were to Mumbai. There were a few return calls from the numbers called in Khandala and Mumbai. Satish asked Bhonsle to rush to Khandala and pick up the room boy who had discovered Vijaya's body. His hunch was that he had picked up her mobile phone the day he found her body and kept it for himself.

Raj passed on the other mobile number and the details of calls received on it to the special cell in his office in Delhi to trace the users in Dubai and Karachi. He had already passed on the B.K. Dossier documents to Satish and a task force had been constituted by the Mumbai Commissioner to decipher the documents and the pen drives. Satish had also received the coroner's report but it did not confirm the identity. The photographs obtained by Satish from Kolkata could not be matched as the face of the victim had been badly disfigured. Satish however kept the report confidential and asked Bhonsle to get the DNA tests expedited.

The investigations had so far proceeded in the right directions and they had more or less come to a conclusion that Vijaya's murder was planned as her handlers feared that their plot had been exposed and their network of sleeper cells compromised. They also did not want her to reveal the secret of Dr. Kabir to the world at large. She of course would never have jeopardized the safety of her father, but it appeared to Raj that the ISI operatives had perhaps panicked and ordered her elimination.

The discovery of the net working, money trail and havala transactions uncovered was indicative of some long term project and team building activity. The clever and ingenious efforts made to conceal the funds and engage an innocent person by threat of blackmail and coercion was indicative of the dimensions of planning and management. Satish proposed to rename the case file as-'The Cuckoo's nest'. The lazy cuckoo never builds its own nest, but lays its eggs in other birds nest, preferably the crows. The female crow sits on the eggs till they hatch and nurses the chicks along with her own without knowing the difference as they all look alike. The ISI had used Brij Kishen's film financing model to superimpose their own network of payments to their cells without attracting any attention till the raid carried out by the Enforcement Directorate exposed it.

They had a willing partner in Vijaya Choudhry who had been coerced and blackmailed by threats to her hostage father's wellbeing. Had the diskette not been discovered by the ED, the plot would never have been exposed.

Raj finalized the draft summary of his investigations and flew down to Delhi the next day. He wanted a brain storming session with Saxena and others involved in the case to get guidance and plan the follow up action. The Commissioner of Police and his sleuths were working to trace and arrest the people who had received money through Vijaya. Raj also learnt from Satish that the room boy of the hotel in Khandala had confessed to stealing Vijaya's mobile from her room after discovering her body. He was looking for her purse to steal some money and found the mobile on a bed side drawer. After some steady interrogation he also revealed that he had seen two strangers outside her room earlier in the evening, but before he could alert the hotel security he saw them moving out of the premises. He thought they were some contractor's men who were carrying out repairs to the air conditioning system. They carried bags usually seen with electricians. The hotel security revealed that the work on the air conditioner had been completed two days back and no contractor's men were supposed to be on the premises on that evening. Fortunately the room boy who had had a good look at the two men cooperated with the Crime Branch artist to help develop the sketches of the two men.

# MUMBAI

The identity kit sketches of the two suspects of the Khandala murder led to a man hunt which yielded good results for the crime branch. The two suspects, known criminals, were arrested near Sawantwadi while trying to flee to Goa. They confessed to the murder but denied that they came to kill Vijaya; they wanted information but she was very stubborn and would not talk. They had been promised fifteen lakhs rupees to extract some information from her and had been paid five lakhs as advance. They said they could identify the persons who gave them the contract as they had been approached through some associate of theirs. Detailed interrogation had led to the arrest of a number of suspects from Mumbai, Jaipur, Ranchi, Hyderabad and Coimbatore. The special team set up by the Mumbai Police Commissioner to decipher the names in the B.K. Dossier and the pen drives, questioned the arrested suspects for one whole week. This was the toughest case Mumbai Police had handled for sometime now. The names in the B.K. Dossier were cleverly concealed in characters of various heroes of films produced by Brij Kishen. Some of the B grade films had heroes who had adopted new names for their film career. They however still maintained their original names for signing of contracts and receiving payments. In Brij Kishen's account books the payments were shown to the stars in their assumed names which appeared in film titles and publicity material, while account payee cheques had actually been issued, partly in the original names and partly in the assumed names to give scope for tax avoidance. This had become possible as the Income Tax Department had issued more than one Permanent Account Number (PAN) to the same person. The error had been discovered later and the entire programme had been recast to prevent such a fraud being repeated. However, the earlier error had not been fully rectified and some people continued to use duplicate PAN accounts to take advantage of the system. The documentation was very complicated and parallel accounts maintained to avoid payment of Income and Service Taxes. To this system of accounting, Vijaya had been coerced to add another layer cleverly designed by the ISI with the active help of the Mumbai mafia holed up in Karachi. The investigations came up with five names to start with but they were not sure whether these were the actual names or the assumed ones. A check on the data in the police computers did not match up on the name or aliases. These names were also shown to the arrested suspects but they had no clue. Their interrogation gave no information to the crime branch and they appeared to be just the foot soldiers on the fringes of the cells created for the project. They were held over as suspects and sent to jail for protective custody. The investigators were in a blind alley and no idea how to proceed further.

# KHANDALA

The following Monday Satish decided to drive down to the Hilltop Hotel in Khandala which Vijaya had used during her visits and where her body was found. He checked into the hotel as a guest. Satish called the resident manager and with his assistance went over the records of the hotel especially the ones which had details of Vijaya's stay. There was information relating to check ins and check outs, bills paid by her credit cards, information of messages forwarded to her by the telephone operators and a complete log of incoming and out going calls. Bhonsle had already verified most of this data and the calls had generally related to her office work in Mumbai, and some personal calls to her friends and associates including Pradeep. Actually most of her business calls had been made from her mobile phone which had also been separately verified and checked. It was late in the afternoon when Satish, tired of sitting in his room decided to take a walk. He put on his jogging shoes and took the garden exit behind the swimming pool to get to the hillside. The weather was getting warm now and the gulmohor trees were starting to flower. Satish jogged to the bottom of the shallow valley which brought him to a stream of crystal clear water. He had taken almost forty minutes coming down the hill and the uphill climb back would take him more. He climbed at a steady pace and made it back to the hotel entrance and front desk in an hour. The lobby was under maintenance he had noticed last evening when he had checked in and some portions of the false ceiling had been removed exposing the wiring, AC ducts and fire control pipes. He started wondering why the hotel was tearing down their front lobby for renovation, when it appeared to be in a good condition. It was such a waste of money he felt. Satish had come to the hotel maybe a dozen times in the course of last three years with his family. It was a good hotel and their rates were very reasonable. They had a decent restaurant and the children enjoyed the swimming pool and the indoor activities provided at the games centre.

He picked up a bottle of water at the bar and on his way to his room he stopped at the reception desk and asked the manager why they were ripping up the wood work in the lobby area.

"Sir, we had some problem with the security CCTV cameras and the maintenance people found that termites had damaged some panels on which the wiring had been carried out. We just finished a pest control operations and replaced the wood work in some sections of the lobby."

"How many cameras do you have in the hotel," enquired Satish curiously.

"Sir we have forty-five cameras in various locations as advised by our security consultants."

"What about the recordings, do you maintain them and for how long?"

"Sir as advised we keep these for a year to start with, for audit purposes."

"Bingo! We may be some luck at last," murmured Satish, as he rushed back to his room for a shower. He later called Bhonsle and informed him of the security cameras and advised him to pick all the recordings they had during the days when Vijaya stayed at the hotel. These could be scanned to identify the people Vijaya met in the business center or the coffee shop. The selected discs could be copied for further investigation by the forensics cell in Mumbai. While Bhonsle got busy identifying the recordings, Satish returned to Mumbai the next morning.

# NEW DELHI

Saxena had two messages from Vikram Singh, his station officer at Kabul. One was extremely encouraging as it reported the reactions of various Pashtun group to Alka Gadgil's articles. It appeared that one of the Pashtun leaders from Kabul had a son studying at the Symbiosis College in Pune on a government fellowship. He had meticulously collected cuttings of various reports which appeared after Alka published her article and carried these to Kabul when he visited home for his vacation. He translated these for the benefit of his father and his friends. Soon word had spread that India was giving recognition to the Pashtun demand for reunification and supported the redrawing of the Durand Line. *Jirga* meetings were held to discuss this development. The information had been picked by the Pakistan military intelligence officers and created a panic in the Director General of Military Operations (DGMO) headquarters in Rawalpindi. The government had been informed that discontent was brewing and there might be an uprising amongst the tribes. He passed on the message to Venkat for his information.

The second message was somewhat disturbing. One of the deep penetration counter insurgency agents keeping tabs on the Lashkar-e-Taiba and other India centric terrorist organisation had reported unusual activity in the town of Dadyal bordering Pakistan in occupied Kashmir

(POK). This town was just about two hours drive from the AECP facility at Kahuta, and had seen regular traffic of official vehicles driving senior officials in and out of town since a month. The center of activity was located in an old mansion which belonged to an erstwhile Aga, a prominent business family with large holdings of agricultural land and orchards, which had migrated to Srinagar in 1948 after the frontier tribesmen invaded this area. The vehicles were escorted by armed police guards and would stay at the facility till the convoy returned back to Kahuta in the evening. Invariably there were two staff vehicles and one police escort. Saxena asked his staff officer to check out the coordinates of Dadyal with the ones given by the agent from his GPS readings. The information confirmed, Saxena spoke to Venkat and sounded him on the aerial survey he was organizing of Dadyal town in POK and its surroundings. He also passed on the coordinates of the Aga's house in Dadyal to the Military Intelligence (MI) requesting for high resolution images from their satellite Rakshak II, positioned over the Western border.

The Bombardier surveillance jet of the RAW made a dozen sorties on a flight course parallel to the LOC the next day and took a number of photographs of the target area. The sorties were mounted from seven in the morning till 10 pm using infra red cameras for the night runs. In all some four hundred images were developed from the very high resolution surveillance cameras used in the Bombardiers photo suites. The photos showed the arrival of the three vehicles around 8.30 am. Two of the vehicles were Toyota Lexus SUV's, the types used by the Military Intelligence and the ISI. The escort jeep was a Land Rover of the Police department. In the first vehicle there were three officials; in the second there were two police officials in uniforms escorting the third who wore a light suit. The person appeared to be around five feet six inches tall and wore dark horn rimmed spectacles. He also appeared to be somewhat darker in complexion to the rest fair skinned Punjabi civilians and police officers. The satellite images received from the MI further confirmed this information with more graphic details.

Photographs of all the civilian and police officers were sent to the photo archives branch. A diplomatic courier bag with copies of selected photos taken by the Bombardier was sent to the Islamabad station officer in the Indian Embassy to verify the identity of the officials. The photos taken by the Bombardier had also shown some local civilians being escorted to the mansion and leaving the place just before the team returned to Islamabad. Copies of these photos were sent to Vikram Singh in Kabul for being passed on to the agent in POK with instructions to identify these civilians and extract some information out of them. Saxena also sent word to the Air Surveillance team to keep the flights going for another five days to observe the pattern of activities at the Dadyal premises.

Saxena had kept the entire afternoon free for Raj. He had seen his draft report on the Vijaya murder case and the money trail investigations. He was more than satisfied with what Raj had achieved so far. Now a lot depended on the work being done by Satish Sharma and his team of officers. They had not only to identify the individuals, who had received money through, what Raj aptly had described as the Cuckoo's Nest operations, but also locate and apprehend them before they put into operation the mission planned by the ISI. He asked his staff officer to send for Raj who was waiting in the library.

Raj and Saxena were closeted in the office well past 9 pm. They had gone over the information collected in the B.K. Dossier case and were convinced that the sums disbursed were very large and more than usually required to sustain the operations of the sleeper cells. The money was definitely being provided to procure equipment and build up inventories for some major strike and long drawn operations. More than thirty crores had been transferred through the havala channels into B.K.Enterprises and almost the entire amount had been disbursed till the date on which the diskette had been recovered in the ED raid. The money was paid to six individuals who were either the key conspirators or merely doing a postman's job without having much information on the end use. It was very necessary to get these six for leading the investigations to the next stage.

Saxena found a striking similarity of these preparations with those of the 1993 bomb blasts. The ISI and the mafia had smuggled besides the RDX, caches of arms to simultaneously carry out assassinations of important community leaders in the city to trigger off communal riots in Mumbai and across the country. The arms cache had included the deadly AK 47 automatic rifles, hand grenades and automatic pistols. These weapons had also been distributed to a group of criminals who formed the hit squad for striking pre-determined targets and individuals for triggering a wave of communal violence across the city and the country. The plan had failed as the vehicle carrying the main group of terrorists broke down at the city centre, moments after the blasts were triggered. The hit squad had panicked at the sight of police road blocks and fled leaving their vehicles and weapons behind. The main objective of the ISI had been to alienate the two communities and disturb the secular character of the society.

Secondly, a nexus appeared to be emerging` between a senior nuclear scientist working with the AECP and his daughter involved in the conspiracy. Raj's investigations so far indicated that Vijaya was perhaps coerced into the conspiracy of the havala transactions for the scheme cleverly drafted to maintain high degree of concealment. The whole operation appeared to have been masterminded by the ISI to carry out major strikes in the country, possibly involving small nuclear devices, by the non state players. The scenario was frightening but was in the realms of possibility. Similar plans in the past had alerted the IAEA to issue advisories to various countries where strikes were expected. The recent smuggling of nuclear material from the dismantled missiles in Kazakhstan and the abduction of Collins from Majuli to secure release of an incarcerated Sri Lankan Tamil engineer from a prison in Britain were indication of efforts at team building to fabricate some nuclear device. There had been some more developments reported from Dadyal in the POK; aerial photos taken by the Bombardier air reconnaissance unit of the R&AW and the MI's satellite images had only confirmed suspicious activities being undertaken by the AECP.

The possibility of a device in a knocked down condition being smuggled into the country and reassembled by trained terrorists was never ruled out. The arming of such a devise, however, required special skills. Was the Dadyal project taking care of this operation? It was a very audacious plan of the ISI and Saxena was determined to stop it. He would definitely sound the Mossad of these developments and if need be, they could jointly thwart ISI's plans to provide nuclear teeth to the terrorist organisations.

He was glad that Venkat had the PM convinced on pro active policy towards the Pashtuns and the Baloch tribes. The Pashtuns were already stirred and giving sleepless time to the Pakistan army brass. They could easily be won over to create trouble and harass the local army units. But Saxena was not interested in engaging the might of the Pakistani army and their air force against these brave fighters. He wanted their help in covert operations and his mind was already planning one such operation. He would speak to Venkat in the next few days and seek his approval for this operation after assessing further intelligence gathered by the Kabul agents and the aerial surveillance.

# NEW DELHI

The Prime Minister returned to New Delhi late Monday evening and Venkat postponed his meeting with him to Tuesday afternoon. He was awaiting some more inputs from Saxena on the Dadyal developments. He wanted to apprise the PM on important security issues and obtain his consent for the covert operation planned by Saxena. The week's aerial surveillance undertaken by the RA&W had only confirmed his early fears. The news from Kabul station officer Vikram Singh had also confirmed the presence of AECP scientists at Dadyal and a positive identification of Dr. Humanyun Kabir. The photos taken by his agent at Dadyal had matched with the photos available in Dr. Kabir's dossier at the R&AW headquarters. Vikram also confirmed a daring plan hatched by the Pashtun counter insurgency agent in Dadyal to abduct Dr. Kabir and deliver him to Kabul. Dr. Kabir could then approach the Indian Embassy for political asylum which would be granted to him. He could stay on at the Embassy and later evacuated to New Delhi for investigations relating to the ISI's project of arming state sponsored terror outfits with nuclear devices.

Saxena had in the past week come to believe that Dr. Kabir was alive. Information gathered by Raj in Dhaka and Kolkata had been very valuable and had almost solved the Vijaya murder and the B.K. Dossier puzzles. He was however very surprised at the pace at which events had moved in the past ten days and the fresh inputs received from Vikram Singh in Kabul. There is always an element of luck in intelligence gathering when the pieces of a jig-saw puzzle start falling in place and bring out the image in stark perspective. It rarely happens in counter espionage operations, except in story books, that information start falling into your lap as happened in the case of Dr. Kabir. The resurrection of Dr. Humayun Kabir, long declared missing and possibly dead, would be a major coup in the annals of counter espionage for any agency in the world. Dr. Kabir could expose the nefarious plans of the ISI and the dangerous agenda of a rogue state. Dr. Kabir could appear before the International press, the IAEA, the UN, the Interpol and representatives of the Human Rights Watch and tell his side of the story. He could make a statement on his thirty three years of involuntary stay in Islamabad as a captive of the ISI and coerced to work on clandestine projects of designing weapons of mass destruction. The Pakistanis would disown him as they had already announced his disappearance from Dhaka in 1971 and therefore cannot accuse anybody of abducting him. The AECP had also written him off their records after his 'disappearance' from Dhaka in 1971. The ISI would call him a fraud and declare it as another plot of R&AW to denounce their country.

Saxena had to be cautious before he gave his clearance to this mission. Dr. Kabir was still in Islamabad and the whole daring plan of the Pashtun agent, Gul Mohammed was yet to receive the nod from the Prime Minister. The plan must work was his main concern now, and Dr. Kabir should reach the safe house in Kabul, alive. There were too many risks involved and it was totally out of their hands. In a way it was also an advantage, as in case of any failure the Pakistanis could not pin it on the R&AW. The spin offs from a successful evacuation of Dr. Kabir from Pakistan to Kabul and then onwards to New Delhi and Dhaka would be enormous. Saxena had weighed the pros and cons and was willing to risk the mission.

While Venkat waited for the Prime Minister's call, the British High Commissioner called on the hotline to say that the British Government had difficulty in agreeing to the conditions being put by the abductors for Collin's release and the cabinet had voted for the Indians mounting the rescue mission through their Special Forces. He said that he had been given the authority to give the go-ahead and the British Prime Minister would speak to the Indian PM within the hour. Venkat called Saxena and conveyed the message of the British High Commissioner.

Shortly afterwards Pratap Sharma called and asked him to come over to the PM's residence as he was busy with his party secretary's meeting and was attending to all his work from there. Venkat picked up the file folder for the PM and walked down to his car. There was a big crowed of visitors at the PM's residence, most of them party functionaries from various states waiting outside on the lawns of the sprawling bungalow. Venkat was familiar with these political jamborees. He had seen many such rallies in his career of thirty six years and had come to despise these selfish, corrupt and venal political animals.

Venkat walked into Pratap's room through a milling crowed of political who's who. He recognized many heavy weights and a few ex-chief ministers; there were a couple of money bags and wheeler dealers too who had become indispensable to the country's political system. Pratap looked pretty fatigued after the twenty hours flight home from Washington. He had had many sleepless nights during the weeks visit to the US and was looking forward to some rest when he got summoned to take care of the developing political crisis in Uttar Pradesh. Pratap knew most of the political notables well as he had served in that state for more than twenty five years till he came away to the center, disgusted by the murky politics and degradation in public life. Pratap was on first name terms with most of the senior politicians and the PM trusted him fully for his advice on UP matters.

"Come Venkat, the PM is waiting for you in the garden behind his bedroom. I will ask somebody to escort you. I am a little tied up with the bad boys and will join you if I get free."

Venkat found a very pensive PM pacing up and down in the garden.

"Ah Venkat Sahib, I got the news from the British PM about the breakdown in their hostage negotiations; they want us to send in the Special Forces to rescue Collins. In fact I was sleeping when he called. I can never get enough sleep while flying. I spoke to Saxena and he said he had heard from you and had given the go ahead to the Commander of the Special Forces."

"Sir I must first of all congratulate you on the successful visit to the US. All the papers and the media are commenting on the very adroit handling of the new foreign policy issues. The US media has given the most positive coverage to an Indian Prime Minister for the first time, perhaps in decades."

"Thank you Venkat I have an excellent team of advisors and they worked very hard for the visit. Pronob Sen at the UN Mission is an excellent officer and deserves better assignments. He should have been the foreign secretary but the Punjab lobby in our party upset our cabinet sub committee's recommendations by lobbying for that incompetent Baijal. Remind me next week when I meet the President. I want to bring Pronob to Lucknow as the next Governor. He will sort the unruly mob there. You had something in your mind when we spoke last."

"Sir, we have some interesting developments in Kabul." Venkat said. He gave a complete briefing to PM on the Dadyal facility and the confirmation received by Saxena from the aerial surveillance and the Pashtun agents.

"The Pashtun agents not only confirmed the presence of Dr. Kabir but themselves came up with the plan to snatch him and deliver him to us at Kabul. They fear that that the Taliban will first destroy their homes and villages using the atom bomb, as they call it, before they do so in India or elsewhere. If they succeed and Dr. Kabir reaches Kabul we will give him political asylum to protect him from further harassment from the ISI. The ISI has used him and his daughter and they also murdered her when they feared their plot was exposed. We will bring him down to New Delhi after he gets to Kabul. The Pakistanis will be in a catch 22 situation; they cannot accuse us of kidnapping Dr. Kabir, as they only had declared him absconding in Dhaka after the 1971 disturbances. The AECP had closed his record and informed even the IAEA that he was missing from duty, while all the while they held him captive in Islamabad. Dr. Kabir will now be available to the world to expose the perfidy and diabolical plans of the ISI to arm the terrorists with weapons of mass destruction. He will do so before an international audience of the media, IAEA and Interpol representatives, Human Rights Watch observers and the ambassadors of the prominent missions in the capital."

The PM listened to Venkat without an expression on his face. He heard every word of what he said with rapt attention and was amazed at the simplicity of the plan which could have such far reaching consequences and ramifications. He just shook his head in agreement when Venkat asked if it was okay by him.

"Yes, yes," he said loudly. "We are mere spectators in this abduction. But we will have a lot to gain if it succeeds. We can finally hope for some lasting peace in the sub-continent and also other regions of the world."

"I will take your leave Sir; you have a very busy day before you. I will keep Pratap posted with all developments in the Myanmar operations."

# MUMBAI

The CCTV camera records from Hotel Hilltop provided valuable graphic evidence about the people who met Vijaya. There were six men other than Pradeep who met her during the four months period till the day she was murdered. The meetings were one to one and took place in the coffee shop or the business center and the persons meeting Vijaya always carried a lap top computer. The meetings lasted between half an hour to forty five minutes. At the end of the meetings Vijaya would hand over a CD to the person concerned, who would invariably verify the details and then leave. It was evident from the pictures and the video recordings that there were no discussions or arguments and the meetings were cordial. It was only at the last meeting on the afternoon of the day she was killed, that the two persons at the meeting carried no lap tops. One person was a stranger who had not appeared in the CCTV recordings earlier. They appeared to have come after a prior appointment as Vijaya had checked out from Ambay Valley Resort and come down to Khandala especially to meet them instead of returning to Mumbai with Pradeep as planned. This sudden change of programme had been recalled by Pradeep to Raj during his stay at the Nuwara Eliya plantations. He had mentioned that Vijaya had suddenly become tense that morning when she got a call on her mobile. She was very quiet at breakfast and would not tell Pradeep anything when he enquired from her if all was well. She merely said that some matter had come up and she had to arrange an emergency meeting with a party at Khandala. She asked him to return to Mumbai and said she would be back by the evening.

The CCTV recordings show these persons approaching the receptionist. She then makes a call on the house phone possibly to Vijaya to inform about the visitors and directs them to wait in the coffee shop. The new visitor is of medium height and clean shaven. When Vijaya comes down from her room, the receptionist is seen directing her to the coffee shop. The visitors get up as she enters and she joins them at the table. They are seen discussing but it's the visitors who seem to be doing all the talking. Vijay is trying to say something but the visitors continue their monologue. She appears to be denying and pleading with them. The new visitor appears to lead the discussion and is seen banging the table with his fist. He appears to be angry and Vijaya is trying to persuade them but she appears to be making no headway. Then all of a sudden she says something angrily to the visitors, shaking a finger at them and before they can respond she gets up and walks out of the coffee shop. The visitors stay at the coffee shop for some twenty minutes talking animatedly and then walk out. The images of both the suspects were clear and sharp and Bhonsle got copies made for circulation to various police stations in Mumbai.

# INDORE

Arun Bannerji had been posted as the Intelligence Bureau Chief at Indore since last two very uneventful years. Indore was a peaceful industrial town and there had been nothing subversive to report to the headquarters. He was therefore pleasantly surprised when he received the wireless message with Crash Priority from the Home Secretary's office that he put the Balak Baba Akhada and its chief Raghunath Bhide under close surveillance. The message gave information that Bhide had recently convened a camp of his disciples in Pokhra, Nepal where some Hindu activist organisations of Nepal had also participated. During this camp some associates from the Akhada were met by Colonel Adhikari and Major Virender Singh both serving officers of the Dogra Regiment of the Indian Army, when Bhide was also present. They were travelling in Nepal under assumed names Raj Tilak and Gurbachan Singh respectively. Col. Adhikari briefed the group on the ISI plans to attack Hindu pilgrimage centers using their proxies. He emphasised that the Government will not take any serious measure as in the past but only lodge protest with the Government of Pakistan. This had become the pattern for sometime past and innocent Hindus were being slaughtered by Jihadist from Pakistan. These terrorist groups were getting logistic support and shelter from the local Muslims organisations who were

246

also involved in planting of the bombs in trains and places of worship. Incidents of bomb blasts had already taken place in the holiest of holy Hindu shrines like in Varanasi, Ayodhya, Mathura, Jammu, Ahmadabad and of course the Amarnath Yatra. Besides bomb blasts had taken place in Mumbai, New Delhi, Bangalore, Pune, Hyderabad and Coimbatore. It had therefore become imperative that the Hindus themselves should get organised and motivate young men and women to come forward and prepare themselves for making sacrifices for protecting their faith. He proposed that we should attack places of worship of Muslims and destroy them as an act of revenge. He is proposing to visit Indore in August to prepare a blueprint for training of the young recruits in subversive activities including handling of explosives. The Army Officers have already been put under surveillance by the Military Intelligence, the message added. Matter was most serious and requires to be nipped in the bud. Arun was advised to prepare a dossier on Bhide and his Balak Baba Akhada and include a report on their activities in his monthly bulletin to the IB Chief in future.

Arun had seen the location of the Akhada in the old city area but had no clue about Raghunath Bhide and the activities of the Akhada. There had been no news, however benign, of Bhide or his organisation in the local vernacular dailies or the local intelligence bureau's weekly dispatches to the DG Police, State Intelligence at Bhopal. Enquiries with his contacts in the District Police Headquarters revealed that Raghunath Bhide's family had long association with the Maratha Royal family of Indore and his grandfather had been a minister in the court till Indore State was merged with the Union of India in 1947. Raghunath had been to the Doon School in Dehradun and graduated from the London School of Economics. He had on return to India joined a multi national company in Mumbai but had later resigned after six years and returned to his family home in Indore. It was reported that he had turned deeply religious and even left home in the mid nineties and wandered off to Hardwar and lived for years in the company of sadhus. He had returned to Indore sometimes in the year 2000 and set up the Balak Baba Akhada. The local police had nothing adverse to report against Bhide or his Akhada.

# CHIANG MAI

**R**avi Karan's agents managed to infiltrate the Karen rebels group holding Peter Collins when they ran into the headman of the village where the camp was located at a trading post near Myitkyina. He was trying to procure mineral water which was a rare commodity in the region. The agents cornered him on the jungle road and on an assurance to get him a case of mineral water he informed them that it was required for an Englishman in the Karen rebel's camp. They reconnoitered the village the same day and got a close look at the camp area. After confirming the coordinates of the location on their GPS, they passed on the information to Ravi who promptly informed Major Bisht, head of the Special Forces group via the satellite phone. They also managed to locate the World War II air strip identified by the R&AW for the rescue mission. The agents confirmed that the airstrip was in good order and just 10 kilometers from the Karen rebel's camp where Peter was held hostage.

The long wait for Ravi and Gopal finally got over when they got a signal from the Delhi office that the Special Forces were moving in to rescue Collins. Anand was out swimming at the hotel pool when the news came through. Ravi got busy trying to contact Rahim and Siva, who were coordinating arrangements to assist the Special Forces in the operation code named 'Flying Fox'. Siva and

Rahim had gathered a force of ten mercenaries comprising of five local Karens, three Ahom's supporting the NDLF and two rebel Naga gun runners. They were to rendezvous at a place two kilometers south-west of Myitkyina where the airstrip was located. The air strip had been up-graded by the Myanmar government in the past but was practically lying unused after they lost control of the area to the rebel forces. The drug overlord Kuhn SA had used the old airstrip during his heydays for smuggling and now it was a dry stretch of clearing with weeds and small bushes. The Special Forces had deployed the Air Force Hercules C 130 transport aircraft with the call sign Delta Tango One for the operation 'Flying Fox'.

Ravi managed to alert his agents when he got Siva on the satellite phone. The local support team organised by Siva was already in Myitkyina and would be at the airstrip when the Special Forces arrived. Ravi signaled to the Special Forces that all local arrangements were in place and reception was arranged at Myitkyina. The Special Forces contacted Siva and set their watches; ETA for Delta Tango One for Myitkyina was set at 0100 hrs. Delta Tango One carried a crew of five and the Special Forces team comprising of the leader Major Ranbir Singh Bisht and his group of ten commandos. They had two Stryker Combat Vehicles each mounted with a 105mm canon and 7.62mm machine gun. The men carried their standard Heckler& Koch MP5 sub machine guns and Glock 9mm pistols. According to the plan the Stryker's would drive Major Bisht and his team along with the local mercenary force to three kilometers from the camp where Collins was held captive. The commandoes would then walk up to the target area while the mercenaries would enter the camp undetected and neutralize any guards on duty. They would then lead the commandos to the hut where Collins was held captive. According to the latest reports given by the R&AW agents there was only a small group of Karen's present at the camp as the chances of the captive making a bid for escape were considered remote in this thick jungle hide out. The commandos would rescue Collins and the team would retreat by the same route it entered the camp. The expectation was that the entire operation would be carried out without firing a single bullet. Once they reach the Stryker's they would speed back to the C-130 and take off before sunrise.

Ravi who had travelled in the jungles of Myanmar had worked out the entire operation minutely. He knew that the rebels would have gone to sleep after feasting on a hearty meal of the goat and two small pigs and the case of XXX Rum that Siva had procured and delivered to the camp through his compatriots, a day before operation 'Flying Fox'. The Myanmar army had stopped all operations against the rebels almost a year ago and the rebels were the overlords in the region. They collected taxes and were available for transporting contraband for whoever demanded their services. They would trek through the jungles of southern Mizoram into the Chittagong Hill tracts of Bangladesh and deliver cargo to the long unpatrolled sea coast south of the Chittagong harbor and Cox's Bazar. They were no longer a fighting force and were not expected to defend the camp against a trained force.

Operation 'Flying Fox' went off smoothly almost as Ravi had planned it.

Major Bisht and his commandos left the Stryker Combat Vehicles two kilometers from the rebel camp. Then along with the ten local mercenaries they proceeded towards the rebel camp in small groups of five each.

Maintaining a distance of five meters between them, the first raiding party stealthily walked into the camp. As expected the guards on duty were found asleep and were quickly disarmed. The second and the third groups moved into the camp and searched the huts to locate Collins. One of the Karen mercenaries managed to locate the hut where Collins was held captive and brought him out to where Major Bisht was holding his position and directing his troops. Peter looked most surprised and was for a moment not quite sure what was happening.

"Peter Collins I presume, I am Major Bisht from the Special Forces," he said.

"Thank you sir," was all he could say as Bisht clutched him by the elbow and pushed him towards the jungle tract to exit the camp. He gave a low whistle which was responded after a short interval by others in the group and as if on signal the commandos moved out of the camp.

The mercenaries held back and covered the retreat of the commandos. No shots were fired and Operation Flying Fox was over; the commandos reached the Stryker vehicles with the mercenaries covering every step of their retreat. Once in the Stryker the party sped off towards the waiting C-130 and were soon airborne. Ravi Karan got a call minutes after take off from Siva that all was well and the hostage was on his way to Tezpur abroad the C-130. He and Gopal exchanged high fives and headed for the pool looking for Anand to give him the good news.

"I cannot for a moment believe that this is true. I was worried all the while and did not believe half of what you guys told me, but I must thank you for getting Collins out safely."

"Anand the real people to thank are the Special forces who planned the entire operation on the basis of intelligence inputs we gave and the Air Force team which flew them in that C-130 in pitch darkness and landed it on a virtual football field. In half an hour's time Delta Tango One will be landing at Tezpur and you can say hello to Collins in an hour's time when he settles down after a bath and breakfast at the local Air Force Officers Mess."

# DADYAL

The Kabul Station officer Vikram Singh was worried about his agent Gul Muhammad who was planning to kidnap a senior AECP scientist right under the nose of the ISI agents in Dadyal. The Pashtuns were seething with anger on the massacres carried out by the Pakistan Air force during the last six months in their joint operation with the army. It was the old game played by the Punjabi landlords running the country under the directions of the Generals. They wanted the Pashtuns to give up their political ambitions of representing their people in the Federal Parliament. They were considered a bunch of illiterate thugs and trouble makers. Gul Muhammad and his band of patriots never lost an opportunity of hitting the Pakistanis where it hurt them the most. In the last three years they had managed to kill an Air Vice Marshal who was visiting his family farms in Mingora. He was shot using the latest US Army M 24-42 sniper rifle procured from an Afghan army deserter. This was followed by the assassination of the Senate member representing their area in the Federal Parliament. He was a puppet and hated in the frontier area. They also managed to blow up an army jeep carrying a commander to his unit in Peshawar from Islamabad. A week earlier the same unit had used Chinese multi-barrel rocket launchers to attack some villages in Mingora district killing ten women and five children. The

Pashtuns believed in quick retribution and never spared the enemy or their tormentors. They had a long history of protecting their land and had slaughtered and savaged the British Frontier Force personnel during their campaigns in Afghanistan and in the frontier region on many occasions in the nineteenth century.

Gul Muhammad was a simple tribal who wanted to live peacefully and pursue his family occupation of farming. His extended family had farm land on both sides of the border. During the Soviet army's presence in Afghanistan his family like so many Pashtuns had crossed over to Pakistan and lived in refugee camps in Peshawar district. He tilled his family lands with his cousins and would plant winter wheat when he got some water from the village irrigation system; pruned his grapes and his apple trees. The government agriculture department had suggested that he re-plant his apple orchard with better varieties. He had agreed to take their advice and visited their office in Peshawar but the promised new variety saplings were never made available. The official wanted money for the saplings but Gul refused to oblige him. That was just one example how the Punjabis treated the Pashtuns. He had become a rebel only to uphold his honor which was so dear to all Pashtuns. He had visited the Indian Embassy in Kabul at the end of Taliban rule for a visa to go to India. When asked by the consulate officials why he wanted to visit India, he replied that he wanted to start an export business in dry fruits and import textiles from India. He was asked to meet Vikram Singh who found a good recruit in Gul. He promised to send him to India provided he did some work for him.

Gul found a friend in Vikram and agreed to travel around and collect information on the terrorist groups working against Indian interests. He was recruited and trained by Vikram and then sent across the border with other agents. Vikram found him very good in his work and soon sent him on difficult assignments to the POK region. Gul, Vikram realised was good material for being upgraded to counter insurgency tasks. Vikram wanted to put him in a group of trained counter insurgents, when the AECP project at Dadyal was discovered. Gul got so enthusiastic about destroying the center and the people involved with the project that he assembled his own group of Pashtun rebels from his area for the task. By the time Vikram realized what was happening, Gul had worked out his plans and trained his team for the operation. When Vikram tried to stop him, Gul went underground and stopped responding to calls from his office.

A week after Gul went underground; the convoy of the AECP was ambushed a few miles outside Dadyal late evening. Another agent who was operating in the Islamabad area informed Vikram how Gul's men managed to plant an explosive devices in the police escort jeep and one of the Lexus SUV's used by the three senior scientists from the AECP. This was done during the daytime when the vehicles were parked outside the AECP facility. The drivers and the police men would wander into nearby tea shops for snacks and lunch or go behind the shops to relieve themselves. Gul's men had studied their pattern of activity for few days and then decided to strike. When one of the staff vehicles was unattended, an insurgent engaged the driver of the other vehicle in a conversation while two others sneaked under the vehicle and tied an IED device to the axel. The police escort vehicle was an easy affair. Gul had noticed that the police escort vehicle invariably carried a bag or two of vegetables and fruits purchased by the policemen, who were bored sitting idle in their jeeps and would wander off into town to shop. As the visits to Dadyal became a long drawn affair their shopping lists had also grown. They found that rice and other food stuffs were cheaper in Dadyal than Islamabad; so they started making daily purchases of food items. Gul had a stroke of luck when one of the constables wanted help to carry his bags of rice to the vehicle. One of Gul's men immediately offered his services and picked up the two gunny bags.

The vehicles were parked behind the training center and the constable asked him to go around and leave the bags behind the driver's seat. While he lit up a cigarette and started chatting with the other constables, Gul's men managed to put a small IED under the driver's seat in front of the rice bags. They also placed two steel objects with nails to puncture the tires of the police escort when the vehicles moved out. The plan worked well as the police escort vehicle had both its rear tires punctured and had to stop within fifty meters of the training center. As there was only one spare tire to replace the other had to be fixed. It took around two hours to get the tire repair shop opened at this late hour and then to fix the puncture. By the time the convoy finally started for Islamabad it had become dark. Gul's men were waiting some fifty kilometers ahead on the road to Kahuta at a sharp bend on the road. They set off the IED in the rear SUV carrying the three officers of the AECP as the convoy slowed down to negotiate the curve, which immediately burst into a fire ball. The police escort jeep in the front applied its brakes to investigate when the Lexus SUV carrying Dr. Kabir with his two guards, almost crashed into it. Then all of a sudden the police jeep exploded and caught fire as Gul pressed a button on his mobile. In a panic, the driver and the guards in Dr. Kabir's

SUV jumped out and ran for cover fearing it would too explode. They were mowed down by Gul's men who fired at them from their AK 47's. Within minutes Gul and three of his team dressed as police men had taken over Dr. Kabir's vehicle, and drove off furiously towards Islamabad. They stopped on the way and switched over into two waiting Toyota pickup trucks. Abandoning the Lexus on the roadside they drove off into the night.

The SUV abandoned by Gul's hit team was picked up by two members of his group who drove it all night first towards Rawalpindi and then towards Lahore. Gul had told this diversion team to drive away from the main highways and make a lot of detours and abandon it by mid day. That gave him and his hit team enough time to get away and cross over into Afghanistan. The AECP authorities were late to react as they had expected delays in the convoys return. They alerted the police and their senior officials only late in the morning after the GPS in the hijacked Lexus gave an indication that the vehicle was moving away from its normal route and heading for Rawalpindi. They had also realised by now that the GPS in the second Lexus was not emitting any signal on its location and calls made on the wireless and the mobile phones of all the team members did not get a response. By the time the police set up barriers on the highway leading towards Rawalpindi, Gul and his boys had crossed over into Afghanistan with Dr. Kabir.

They drove more than a hundred kilometers on a dusty road and then abandoned the Toyota trucks. Dr. Kabir had by now recovered from the shock of the exploding vehicles and the ambush and was himself dressed in a salwar and long shirt like a Pashtun tribal. Gul had provided the change of clothes for Dr. Kabir and had arranged a simple meal of bread and lentils from a village near Jamrud. Here he also managed to get a lift for Dr. Kabir and his compatriots on a relative's truck ferrying supplies of grain and potatoes to Jalalabad. They dropped off two kilometers short of Jalalabad to avoid the check point set up by the Afghan and NATO forces and rested in a cave for a couple of hours. The ISI, Gul knew, would have alerted their local Taliban agents, to look out for Dr. Kabir and his men. Gul and his boys knew the terrain well but they had to be cautious. The stretch between Jalalabad and Kabul was the most treacherous and difficult to negotiate. The region was the domain of the Ghilzai tribes who for last two centuries had controlled the movement of all trade and commerce through the high mountain passes from Khyber to Kabul by levying the *rahdari* tax, for guaranteeing safe passage. The majority of the Taliban guerrilla mujahedeen belonged to this tribal group and had played a major role in driving the Soviet forces out of Afghanistan. Gul knew the Taliban and hated them for their senseless brutality. They had murdered thousands of his brethren and brutalized their womenfolk. He had been shocked by their horrific deeds during his first visit to Kabul in 1996. The extent of brutality could only have been perpetrated by Satan he imagined, and decided to oppose them as he did their masters, the ISI.

Gul and his men kept a sharp lookout as they progressed trough the rough terrain. At places they had to abandon even the mule tracks and walk cross-country. Their progress was further slowed down by Dr. Kabir who was unused to the steep mountain trails. His age and long captivity made difficult for him to take on any extended physical activity. He had been permitted to take a walk for half an hour each day in the compound of the bungalow where he was held but that was not enough. Now this mountainous landscape with some remnants of winter snow was too much for his frail body. He was however quite excited by the fact that he was free from captivity and would soon reach safe haven in Kabul. He could get no information from Gul except that he would take him to the Indian Embassy which could provide him with political asylum and evacuation to India.

# NEW DELHI

In New Delhi Saxena was excited by the success of his two missions. The Collins rescue by the Special Forces was an outstanding operation and he commended Ravi Singh in Chiang Mai for the meticulous planning and logistic support provided to the Special Forces by the mercenaries arranged by him. The Prime Minister called his British counterpart and broke the news to him as he was stirring out of his bed early morning.

Saxena had also heard from Vikram in Kabul that the Dadyal operation had been a success and that Gul and his hit team had succeeded in their mission to rescue Dr. Kabir but their whereabouts were not known. There was a major manhunt organised by the Pakistani army and Police in Punjab province where the hijacked AECP Lexus SUV was found, abandoned by Gul's diversion team. It took some time for the police and the ISI to realize that they had been sent on a wild goose chase. All the villages from Rawalpindi to Lahore had been alerted and the police, paramilitary and home guard volunteers pressed into service. The ISI had also alerted the Taliban and other terrorist cadres mentored by it to hunt down and capture alive Gul and all the members of the team. The ISI chief was worried that Dr. Kabir's flight would cause lot of embarrassment to his country; Pakistan will have lot of explaining to do now to the IAEA and the world at large if Dr. Kabir reached India or Bangladesh. He was confused and angry that the R&AW had pulled off a major mission and exposed them. His head was on the chopping block; he will never become the Army chief now. Dr. Kabir had to be captured before he reached India or crossed into Afghanistan. He was furious with the security chief of the AECP for bungling Dr. Kabir's security. He alerted his agents in Kabul to prevent Kabir from reaching the Indian Embassy. The possibility of Dr. Kabir crossing the LOC into Kashmir was also not ruled out and he called the Army commander and briefed him on the incident.

Gul had not responded to the calls made on his satellite phone by Vikram, which appeared switched off. That was sensible Saxena thought, as the ISI would locate his position within minutes the phone was activated. He advised Vikram to wait and watch. There was no need to inform the Afghanistan Government and seek its Army's help to locate and rescue Gul's team as no secret could be kept by them. Many of its men and officers had sympathy with the Taliban, and this was well known to the NATO forces training and mentoring them.

Saxena had kept Venkat posted with the progress of Operation "Flying Fox" and Gul's ambush of the AECP convoy in Dadyal. Venkat had been busy with drafting the policy papers for the Cabinet sub committee on Foreign Policy Review and the Nuclear Doctrine. The Prime Minister had been encouraged to go ahead with cabinet consultations by the excellent press he had received after his address at the UN General Assembly. He felt a bold approach was imperative to bring about a paradigm shift in our relations with our neighbours. The nation had to flex its muscles and not accept any compromise to its security. He had spoken his mind to the Foreign Secretary again on the return flight from Washington had advised him to produce the Foreign Policy Review paper urgently for the consideration of the Cabinet sub committee. The PM had his eye on the parliament elections just eleven months away. He did not want to yield any ground to his opponents and wanted to cover all his flanks well.

Venkat had been busy at home too as Suhasni had sprung a major surprise by her decision to marry Vishnu Dube. They both were in Columbia University, and Vishnu had just completed his PhD in Monetary Economics. Chitra had met him in New York a month ago. On her return she had met Vishnu's parents. Now Suhasni and Vishnu were arriving next week for a simple marriage ceremony arranged at the Balaji temple in R.K.Puram followed by a traditional lunch for the family members. In the evening a dinner reception had been arranged at the India International Center. Venkat had been very happy at the turn of events. He had felt guilty on occasions of neglecting his family and being too involved with his work to care for them. Now Suhasni's forthcoming wedding lifted a major burden of his mind.

# MUMBAI

**R**aj followed up the investigations with Satish on his return from Delhi. The Mumbai CID had managed to pick up two suspects from the Lokhandwala. One had leased a small apartment near the market and maintained contact with his group using five different SIM cards in his two mobiles. Both the mobiles and the SIM cards were recovered from him. He was one of the regulars who collected cheques from Vijaya at Khandala and was featured well in the CCTV images collected from the Hotel Hilltop. He went by the codename Salman Khan in Vijaya's pen drives. He had given the same name at the hotel reception when he met Vijaya on the last occasion to collect his cheques, a week before she was killed. The date on the hotel message records matched with the date on the CCTV images recorded on that day. He had been the only visitor on that date. The other suspect was a local property agent who had arranged the lease for the flat occupied by Salman Khan. The search of the premises led to the recovery of the lease agreement that was drawn in the name of Raju Shetty from Mangalore. A passport recovered showed that Salman Khan was the alias for P. Muhammad Kutty of Thrissur in Kerala. His occupation was shown as electrical contractor and the Visa and the immigration stampings showed that he had lived in Dubai and Sharjha for more than six years. This was a major break for the Crime Branch and they succeeded with Kutty's help in deciphering many more names in the B.K. Dossier. The mystery of the names in Vijaya's pen drives was almost solved. The Crime Branch raided a number of places in Mumbai, Thrissur, Ranchi and Hyderabad and arrested the suspects.

The special team assembled by the Commissioner worked around the clock and managed to trace many trails of money laundering in B.K. Dossier to the local builders lobby who had managed to open dollar accounts in the names of shell companies in Mauritius and then transferred money from there to the Swiss Banks in Geneva and Zurich. Some had purchased flats in Belgravia and Kensington in Central London and some others had squirreled money into the tax haven of St. Kitts. From there, money had travelled to Florida, Atlanta and New Jersey to purchase town houses and food chains. Satish had sought Pradeep's help to get information from his Mauritius Bank contacts. His help had proved invaluable in getting the local banks to part with information on the havala racket. The builders had broken no law in Mauritius in opening the dollar accounts but could not explain how their havala money had actually been transferred back to Mumbai from accounts held in Dubai and Sharjhah. The Economic Offensive Wing of the Mumbai Police, the Reserve Bank of India and the Enforcement Directorate took over this part of the investigation and arrested four major builders in the city. The city woke up one morning to see the morning newspapers carry the headlines of the arrest of these prominent builders with close connections with the Chief Minister and the Housing Minister of the state. Some of the newspapers published photographs from their archives showing the Chief Minister attending the glittering wedding reception of the daughter of one of these builders, and blessing the couple. The event had found mention in almost all the newspapers and the television news channels and was billed as the most expensive event held in the city.

Similar stories connected other builders to prominent politician of the city. Names of several police officers and civil servants who had acted as facilitators in the illegal land allotments by the Chief Minister figured prominently in the media for next few days. The opposition parties demanded a CBI enquiry against the CM and the Housing Minister and called on the Governor to act swiftly. The dissident lobbies and the Chief Minister's opponents were demanding his resignation and calling on the party high command to convene a meeting for deciding on the successor. Eminent citizens of the city including retired police officers and civil servants convened a public meeting in the gardens of Horniman Circle and condemned the scandalous behavior of the politicians and the builders joining hands with the enemies of the country. They urged the PM to dismiss the state government and arrest the traitors. The Chief Minister and most of his cabinet colleagues went underground and were not available to the press and media to clarify the allegations against them.

# MAJULI

**P**eter had stayed back at the Tezpur Air Force Mess for two weeks to undergo a health check and recover from a serious bout of dysentery contracted during his captivity. The British High Commissioner had visited him during his stay in Tezpur offering to fly him out in a RAF aircraft standing by at the air base near London. Collins had politely thanked him for the offer and said he was keen to get back to Majuli and his project. He had also refused to be interterviewed by the media on the story of his abduction and captivity and had told Venkat, when he phoned him, that he was happy to be home. Venkat had been touched by his humility and sincerity and commitment to work. Anand travelled to Tezpur after getting back from Bangkok and had a long chat with Collins. They were happy to see each other and Anand felt delighted that Collins was only waiting for the doctor to give him an okay to rush back to Majuli. Anand felt assured and promised to visit him in Majuli after he got back.

Peter Collins travelled back to Majuli from Tezpur in an Air Force chopper and was received by his entire team and the people of Majuli who gathered in the football field he had helped develop for the students. They organised a hero's welcome for him and carried him on their shoulders from the helipad to the gate of the Majuli campus.

Brig Sondhi called on Peter a few days after he got back along with the local Superintendent of Police to complete a few formalities regarding the case of his abduction. They wanted his side of the story to conclude their investigations. Collins told them that he had got a call on his mobile from the gate security that there was some problem in one of the new plants he had commissioned a couple of weeks ago. The time was around four in the morning, so he dressed and drove his Pajero out from the camp area towards Plant No. 2. He had just driven two hundred meters when a water tanker appeared suddenly behind him. Collins said he drove his vehicle to the edge of the road to let the tanker pass, but it swerved in his direction and came to a stop, blocking his way completely. Before he could find his wits, two men wearing project uniforms, jumped out of the tanker and accosted him with guns. They asked him to get off the vehicle and follow them. Once seated in the cabin of the tanker behind the driver's seat, a dark mask soaked in some strong smelling chemical was thrown over his head. That was all he remembered as he passed out. He must have slept in that drugged state for more than eight hours. When he regained consciousness, he was in a dark brick and tin sheet structure. There was a small kerosene lamp in the room and some gunny bags like the ones used in the tea gardens and a bottle of water. He finished all there was in the bottle in one go as he was very thirsty. He then got up and looked around and found the door locked from the outside. The only window was also boarded but through the cracks in the wooden planks he could see a light bulb hanging from a pole which lit up the compound. There were a group of people talking there but he could see only two of them. They looked like the local NDLF cadres and were dressed in jeans and denim jackets. One of them carried an AK 47 and the other had a web holster on his belt with a large caliber pistol. They spoke some dialect of Assamese and were arguing about something which he could not follow.

Collins added that as he had not eaten anything that day since early morning and it was now past seven in the evening, he decided to try his luck and knocked on the door. He could hear no sound as the men dropped their voices to mere whispers. He knocked several times before he heard the bolt turn and the door open a crack. Someone was shouting and then they were all trying to say something at the same time. Collins saw a silhouette on the door frame and waved his bottle. The man at the door shouted to his companion who came in a hurry carrying two more bottles of water and left them on the floor. Collins spoke to them in Assamese and asked for something to eat. They all spoke animatedly and then one of them replied in Assamese, saying that they would get him some rice and curry soon. Collins used the water to rinse his mouth and splashed some on his face to feel fresh. After a while the Assamese speaking youth came in with an enamel plate full of rice, some potato curry and lentils. There was no spoon so Peter dug into the rice and curry with his fingers. He had lived long enough in Assam and learnt to eat as the locals did. The rice was coarse and home milled and the curry full of chilies, but he relished his first meal of the day. After he had eaten his captors bolted the room again. He tried to sleep but was quite restless. After a couple of hours of tossing in fitful sleep on his makeshift bed of gunny sacking, he heard a vehicle drive up outside. The door opened and he was woken up. He was blind folded and a rope fastened to his waist. He was put on a jeep and driven off into the night.

They drove through rough hilly tracks and stopped somewhere after being on the road for hours. He was handed a glass of sweetened tea and a few biscuits. They drove off again for almost half a day without a break and reached a mountain stream. They took off his blindfold and after some discussion four of the escort team got off the jeep and ordered him to step down too. They picked up their haversacks and their weapons and marched single file towards the stream with Peter in tow. Crossing it, they took a narrow jungle trail and walked for a couple of hours before stopping by another stream. They opened their haversacks and took out bowls of rice mixed with the same lentils and vegetables of the night before and offered some to Peter. They had even carried mineral water for him.

They trekked for the next three days through undulating terrain and tropical rain forests in an easterly direction and Peter reckoned they should cross into Myanmar soon. On the forth afternoon they reached a village where they were met by an armed party of some Myanmar militia. All were dressed in olive green fatigues and carried AK 47 rifles and pistols in their holsters. They were short statured and in their mid-twenties; Peter surmised these must be the Karen rebels who along with the Kachin Rebel Army controlled the northern and eastern half of Myanmar. The group took over his custody and continued their trek through jungles for another day, till they were in a wide valley with villages scattered every five to six kilometers. They walked through the habitations camping by night and starting at dawn again after breakfast of boiled rice, curry and tea. There was no bottled water available in these villages and Collins preferred to drink black tea wherever they halted. By the sixth evening they reached a small hamlet where the rebels had set up camp.

His escort party walked up to a hut which was guarded by two armed sentries. After some wait the door opened and a middle aged person appeared smoking a cheroot. He was short but stocky and was dressed in the same olive green outfit. Collins escort party doffed their hats and bowed. He walked up to Peter and said something which was translated into crude Assamese by one of the residents of the camp. He wanted to know if he was well. Peter spoke in Assamese and replied that he was well but very tired. The commander spoke again and gave some instructions. Collins was taken to a hut nearby, which was sparsely furnished with a wooden cot, a small table and chair. There was a hurricane lantern on the table along with some chinaware plates and bowls and two glasses. He was left there alone by his guards. After a while a woman entered with a pitcher of water and left it on the table. The door of his hut was not locked, so he got up after sometime and walked out with the pitcher of water. There was no one in sight and beyond at some distance from the camp he could see the green paddy fields. He washed his face of the dust and grime of last six days and felt better. He actually wanted a soak himself in a tub of hot water to rid his body of fatigue and filth. He realized he had no change of clothes and he returned to the hut and lay back on his bed too tired to think of food and soon fell asleep.

He was wakened up by the same woman who had brought him the pitcher of water. She had brought him food and a flask of tea. Peter knew he was far away from civilization and his fate was in the hands of his captors. There was no chance of escape; he would never make his way to safety if he tried to get away. As his captivity progressed from days to weeks with no sign of any relief, his mood swung from depression to ennui. Resigned to his fate he would sit outside his hut staring at the lush greenery and admire the countless birds that settled in the fields to pick insects and worms. There were no books in the camp and the insurgents had no idea where to get what he wanted to read. They, however, gave him a Panasonic transistor radio and that was a major relief as he could pick up the BBC programmes beamed for Asian listeners. Besides he was treated well by his captors and the food was reasonably okay. They gave him a set of their olive green military fatigues for a change of clothes and he was provided with water for bathing whenever he asked for it.

The evening before his rescue he saw a major feast being prepared. He was given a lavish dinner of rice and curried mutton and some roasted pork. One insurgent got him a mug of rum which he politely declined. The carousing went on till past midnight and he was taken by surprise when at early dawn he was shaken awake by somebody calling him 'Collins Sahib' in Assamese. He was led outside his hut to Major Bisht who took him out of the camp and captivity and brought him to Tezpur.

# KABUL

Vikram Singh was waiting anxiously for news from Gul on the fourth day after the ambush of the AECP convoy on the Dadyal-Islamabad highway. There was continued silence maintained by Gul, but Vikram knew he and his party were safe as he had heard enough on the wireless traffic monitored from across the border. Dr. Kabir's ISI handlers and the army brass were bickering and the language was getting fouler by the day as the impact of Gul's caper sank in. The instructions given to the border guards by their commanding officer were to go in hot pursuit after Gul and party if they were traced in their jurisdiction. The commanding officer at Landi Kotal was getting an earful about his ancestry and competence from the area commander in Peshawar. Vikram was somewhat worried about the consequences of Gul's bold strike on the Pashtun people by the vindictive army and the ISI. The ISI had always been a vengeful lot and he feared reprisals against the Pashtuns. The only positive side was that till date the media was unaware of the incident. The rules of engagement and NATO protocols had also kept the Pakistani gunships out of Afghan airspace in their pursuit of Gul and Dr. Kabir. The army and the ISI were keeping the news secret to avoid any embarrassment. Vikram hoped it would stay that way otherwise many more innocent lives would be lost in the frontier region. Saxena had advised him to maintain total secrecy if Dr. Kabir made it safely to the Embassy. He had positioned the R&AW Bombardier Challenger 850 at Mumbai airport and it would fly to Kabul after he got the signal that Dr. Kabir was in the Embassy. Vikram was to inform the Afghan Foreign Ministry authorities that a senior diplomat was critically ill and was being flown out by a special flight. He was to keep all papers ready pending Dr. Kabir's arrival at the Embassy. The Bombardier would halt only for forty-five minutes for refueling, so he should be at the airport as soon as it landed. Dr. Kabir would travel on an Indian Diplomatic Passport issued by the Embassy at Kabul. Keeping in mind 'his grave condition' an ambulance would be allowed by the airport security to go up to the aircraft. The Bombardier would take off immediately for Mumbai once Dr. Kabir boarded it.

Vikram had made all the arrangement for Dr. Kabir's reception at the Embassy and the file relating to his request for asylum and his Passport had been processed. The Ambassador had obtained the necessary clearances from New Delhi and Venkat had kept the PM briefed on these developments. The Chiang Mai station officer had already knocked one operation of the ISI for a six by getting Collins safely back and now Vikram wanted to deliver a double whammy by putting Dr. Kabir in New Delhi. It would be a major triumph for the R&AW as Dr. Kabir would have more than a story of personal tragedy to tell the world. He had been separated for more than thirty years from his wife and daughter, held against his will, coerced and blackmailed to work on projects of death and destruction.

Unknown to Vikram, Dr. Kabir was having difficulty in coping with the conditions of travelling through the hazardous and hostile territory. Gul was worried about him and had considerably slowed down his pace. Dr. Kabir was a patient of hypertension and was on regular medication. He had travelled to Dadyal with a small vial of his prescription medicines which had got over on the third day after the ambush and his escape. He had now been without medication for two days and requested Gul to slow down. He was trying to reduce the stress on his system. He was also experiencing difficulty in breathing which was natural for a person of his age and his ailments; but the hope of meeting Vijaya and reaching home in Dhaka was empowering him to move on.

Gul had also changed his schedule; he preferred to travel late in the evening and through the night to avoid being sighted by the Taliban looking out for them. It was cold at night and strong winds slowed their progress. The fear of the lurking pariah, the Taliban was a constant worry and Gul had to send his scouts ahead every evening before moving Dr. Kabir. The open countryside made the whole journey hazardous and worrisome. Gul had never factored in the age and the physical condition of the hostage he had planned to rescue and deliver safely all the way to Kabul. He was starting to have doubts if Dr. Kabir would survive the ordeal. It was through these trying conditions they made it to the outskirts of Kabul on the evening of the seventh day, after the Dadyal ambush. They took shelter at night in a dilapidated building near a bazaar and Gul's men went out and got some hot food for all to eat. They had not eaten a hot meal since almost a week now and had survived on dry fruits and plain bread which Gul had carried with him. They thoroughly relished this virtual banquet of fresh Nan bread and spicy mutton curry. Dr. Kabir's medicine had also been procured and he had a sound and peaceful sleep that night.

Early next morning they decided to head for the Indian Embassy. Gul assigned the task of escorting Dr. Kabir to his trusted colleague Hamid, who knew the streets of Kabul well. They put Dr. Kabir in a burqa and instructed him to walk behind Hamid all the time. He was to respond to nobody if spoken to; Hamid would do all the speaking if the need arose. They were to start for the embassy at least half an hour after Gul, who would go ahead and alert Vikram that Dr. Kabir had arrived. They were also to take a slightly circuitous route through the bazaar to avoid being followed. Gul reached the Chancery and found a small group of local Afghan students waiting for the visa office to open. There was a security barrier manned by Afghan police some distance from the Chancery, which was lifted only after the visa office opened their counter on the other side of the wall. There had been two car bomb explosions at the chancery gate in the last five years, carried out by one of the Taliban factions on ISI instructions and the government was taking no chances. The Indian Chancery had been turned into a fortified camp.

Gul approached the security barrier and spoke to the guard regarding his meeting with some officer in the Embassy. He was informed all meetings were by prior appointment and his name would be called when the officer was ready to receive him. Gul now had no choice but to call Vikram on the mobile. He gave him a missed call. Vikram who was waiting for some signal from Gul alerted his security official who asked the sentry at the barrier to escort Gul inside. After the guard left, Vikram got up from his chair and embraced Gul. He congratulated him and shook his hand warmly. Gul told him that Hamid should arrive any moment with Dr. Kabir. He however warned him to have a doctor ready as Dr. Kabir was not in good shape after the long arduous journey. Vikram then called the Ambassador Ramesh Ahuja on the intercom and told him that Dr. Kabir should be with him any moment but that he was not in a good shape and he would be taking him straight to Dr. Iyengar.

Vikram did not have to wait for long. His security officer came in escorting Dr. Kabir and Gul. Gul had taken off Dr. Kabir's burqa by now and he stood there looking very fatigued and exhausted; but he had a smile on his face and extended his hand to thank Vikram for his freedom. Holding him close, Vikram led him to the sofa and offered him a glass of water. When he was composed he told Dr. Kabir that the Embassy doctor was waiting for him for a check up. He escorted him to the clinic and left him with Dr. Iyengar. Vikram then called Saxena.

# NEW DELHI

Saxena had a very satisfied look on his face and he wanted to share his joy with Venkat who was busy with Suhasni's wedding ceremony that morning at the Balaji Temple. He would be free after lunch only; so he decided not to disturb him at the important family event. He would break the news to Venkat at the reception, hosted that evening at the India International Center. The PM was also away to Mysore to attend his party's annual convention, so he called Pratap Sharma and briefed him about Dr. Kabir. According to a message received from Kabul, Dr. Kabir was diagnosed with an ischemic heart by Dr. Iyengar. His blood pressure was under control after medication and eight hours of comfortable sleep at the Chancery. Dr. Iyengar had recommended his travel to Mumbai and New Delhi but had advised immediate consultation for the need to undergo surgical intervention. Saxena was taking no chances; he called Raj and asked him to admit Dr. Kabir at the Asian Heart Institute. The Commissioner of Police was requested to provide Z class security and treat him as a foreign dignitary and guest of the Government of India.

# MUMBAI

The Bombardier Challenger 850 landed in Mumbai at 6.30 pm and taxied to a parking bay reserved for visiting dignitaries. Raj received Dr. Kabir and drove with him to the Asian Heart Institute in Bandra-Kurla Complex in the special ambulance arranged by the hospital. The Mumbai Police had arranged full escort usually provided to VVIP's. The hospital was also bristling with security personnel as the convoy made its way to the emergency gate which took Dr. Humayun Kabir to the Intensive Care Unit. Raj took leave of Dr. Kabir and promised to come back the next day. Raj had been instructed by Saxena to look after him and visit him everyday in the hospital. He was to also arrange for Dr. Kabir's stay in Mumbai after his discharge so he could be attended by the doctors of the hospital for any post operative treatment. And he was to accompany Dr. Kabir to New Delhi for the press conference planned sometime later.

Raj visited Dr. Kabir at the ICU the next morning. He looked cheerful and complimented the doctors and the nursing staff for their attention and care. Raj called on his doctor, senior surgeon Dr. Kishore Parikh and was informed that he was keeping Dr. Kabir under observation for another day. He was also waiting for a few more tests and could wheel him into the operation theatre early next morning.

Raj headed for the Police Commissioners Office to meet Satish to follow up on the investigations. He was also compiling his report on the money laundering operations and had met the Enforcement Directorate officials twice during the week. They had by now completed their enquiries against four real estate firms and frozen their overseas accounts in Mauritius, Zurich and St. Kitts. The banks had to comply as the money was tainted and had its origins in drug smuggling, and other contraband such as weapons and blood diamonds. The Pakistanis were as usual in denial mode and refusing to cooperate with the Interpol in the arrest and prosecution of the Mumbai mafia holed up in Karachi. Raj's dossier on the Cuckoo's Nest case was also ready and he was preparing the tables and the text for his power point presentation. In his busy schedule of the last four weeks he had almost forgotten that Pradeep was in town. He called him and they decided to meet at the United Services Club for dinner the next day.

"Be there by six thirty and I will find out if Ratna is free to join us." He had not met her since Bunty's party.

The teams set up by the Commissioner of Police had done commendable work. They had picked up ten more suspects in Mumbai and Aurangabad and had with the help of the Gujarat Police apprehended four key suspects from Surat and Baroda. Satish also showed him a wireless message received from the Intelligence Bureau that morning regarding the two sharpshooters engaged by the ISI to kill Dr. Kabir. Their lookouts in Mumbai had confirmed the arrival of Dr. Kabir and his present location in the Asian Heart Institute. He had already alerted the Deputy Commissioner in charge of Dr. Kabir's security and they were after the two assassins.

It was almost eight by the time Raj finished his meeting with Satish and left his office. The latest advisory from the IB about Dr. Kabir's safety was a source of anxiety. The ISI had been stung and wanted to hit back. They were desperate now and would have sought help of the D Company in Karachi. The D Company had many dedicated agents in Mumbai and they would have set the assassins to work. However, Raj was confident that the Mumbai Police would frustrate these attempts. The police informers had a good network and kept close tabs on all the mafia elements owning loyalty to the goons hiding in Karachi.

He called Dr. Parikh at the hospital to enquire about Dr. Kabir and was informed that all test reports were available and they would be performing the surgery in the morning as planned. He assured Raj that there was nothing to worry and Dr. Kabir was a good patient. He promised to contact him after the surgery was over.

# NEW DELHI

Saxena ran into a veritable who's who of the capitals officialdom as he walked into the India International Center to attend Suhasni's wedding reception. There were many friends and even more colleagues; the city's cultural glitterati, Chitra's large circle of friends-choreographers, musicians, painters, writers and poets were all there. He had recently also witnessed the rise of another species of the cultural spawn in the city, the art curators. This new species cloned from the academic and art worlds had not risen but actually morphed out of the cultural pretensions of the city's nouveau riche, willing to splurge big money on art. He had of late run into them at cocktails and clubs holding forth on art and heritage. Dressed up in ill fitting western attires, exhibiting ample bosoms, balancing a slender flute of champagne, they would glide forth majestically into gatherings of the ignoramus. They were here today, in fiery conjeevram saris, chandelier earrings and flowers in their hair, pretentious as ever.

Saxena waded his way through this flood of the powerful and cultural flotsam to the little open area decorated as a stage where Venkat and Chitra stood with Suhasni and Vishnu and the grooms parents, receiving the guests as they walked up to bless the young couple. There was a long line of well wishers so Saxena decided to enjoy the get together and catch up with his friends.

This was also an ideal occasion to snatch an update on the gossip in the corridors of power. Senior diplomats and the civil servants almost invariably carried their committee discussions to the clubs and cocktail circuits and extended lunches at the India International Center. Rumor had it that many an inter-departmental dispute was settled over a glass of scotch and soda. The Cabinet Secretary walked up to him grabbed his hand and winked.

"Well done Saxena," he whispered. "You have really hit them where it hurts. The PM spoke to me an hour ago from Mysore. He was extremely satisfied."

Saxena moved up to the stage and found he had a chance to bless Suhasni and Vishnu. Most of the guests had moved into the dining area and only handfuls were still waiting. Saxena congratulated Venkat and hugged him to whisper into his ear, "Dr. Kabir is in Mumbai." Venkat held him tighter and thanked him as he moved on to Chitra and then extended his best wishes to the newly weds. Saxena felt he had a load off his mind now. It was not his personnel triumph; it was the work of a dozen competent and patriotic colleagues who fought behind the lines and defeated a treacherous enemy. It was by no means the final battle but a continuous process of skirmishes by which the enemy was testing a nation's patience. But it was an important battle and the final outcome was still awaited. He was convinced that there was going to be a major strategic impact of the current operation when it finally gets over.

Saxena had no plans to stay back for dinner but he ran into Manoj as he was heading for the exit.

"What! Not staying for dinner?"

"No Manoj you know my eating habits, I will have a bite back home."

"Come then at least have a drink".

They walked into the bar, which was crowded with its regulars. The scotch was always good at the Center and they settled down in one corner with their whisky.

"What's the news from Kabul?" asked Manoj enquiringly. He had a good nose for news and had many a sensational scoop to his credit.

"Manoj there's a major story all right but you will have to wait just a bit. We would like you to take the honors . . . Pay back time for the good work you did for us on the nuclear doctrine paper. Venkat and I owe it to you; but not today."

"Good, I knew something was brewing as the AHQ in Islamabad is boiling with rage. Have you kidnapped some ISI official from Islamabad? They appear to be blaming you."

"Is it so? That's new to me. Come give me some more details on that Manoj."

They bantered on for some time and left after their second whisky, promising to meet soon.

# MUMBAI

**R**aj worked on his power point presentation till around noon and then sent his peon for a plate of sandwiches and cutlets from the office canteen. He was anxiously waiting for a call from the hospital to get a report on Dr. Kabir's operation. He called Ratna and told her about the dinner meet that evening. She was happy to hear that he had been to Sri Lanka and stayed with Pradeep. She was very keen to meet him too.

"Be ready round six and I will pick you up on the way to the club."

Raj was finishing his lunch when the call came from Dr. Parikh's office that the operation had just got over and Dr. Kabir had been wheeled back to the ICCU. Raj decided to visit Dr. Kabir later in the day and resumed his editing of the Cuckoo's Nest power point presentation. The last part of the presentation he left unfinished. He wanted to consult Saxena before he added the sequel to the episode.

He called for his car and reached the hospital just before 4 pm. The security was in position and the inspector in charge saluted him smartly as he got out of his car. The ICCU was busy as ever with doctors and nurses attending to the serious cases and checking their progress on CCTV monitors. He went to Dr. Parikh's room adjacent to the entrance of the ICCU. Dr. Parikh was busy eating his lunch. He asked his secretary to get some tea for Raj. Dr.

Kabir was recovering well, he said. But the operation took long as his heart was enlarged. He told Raj that he could go right in and meet him if he was not asleep.

Raj walked into the ICCU with Parikh's secretary who took him straight to the glass cabin where Dr. Kabir lay with wires connecting his chest to monitors surrounding his bed. Some intravenous tubes were also implanted on his arms transferring saline and other fluids. He was awake and smiled weakly when he saw Raj. Raj gestured and asked him if he was feeling well. Dr. Kabir looked heaven wards as if to say 'God Willing'. He told Dr. Kabir that Dr. Parikh was happy with the operation and would discharge him in a few days. He took his leave and said that he would see him the next day around noon. Dr. Kabir smiled and nodded his head. Raj had known him for barely two days but was getting to like him; he was such a humble man for all his achievements. He must have suffered so much during his long detention, but he appeared to have no grudge against his captors.

Raj asked his driver to head for town. On the way he stopped at Worli to pick up Ratna. She was as radiant as the last time he had met her at Bunty's party and she had put on a nice perfume to match the pleasant weather. He told her of his visit to Sri Lanka and his stay at Kandy and Pradeep's estate in Nuwara Eliya. He recommended her to take a holiday to Sri Lanka and visit the hills and the tea estates there. She asked him about Vijaya's case and if the culprits had been apprehended?

"According to my friend Satish Sharma we should read about the case in the newspapers soon."

"Oh come on Raj stop being so mysterious," she remarked and Raj said it was really so. They had entered the gate of the Club's annex and drove down the road that bisected the golf course. The annex was on a picturesque rocky outcrop at one end of the crescent-shaped bay from which the city had earlier derived its name. The bar and the seating area of the two restaurants were located on the promenade facing the Arabian Sea; it was the most scenic spot in the city.

Pradeep had already arrived and approached them as they entered. They found a table near the sea-side. The weather was cool and the sea-breeze ruffled Ratna's hair; she gave up after a while and dug into the succulent kebabs.

"Raj says he had a wonderful stay with you in Nuwara Eliya," remarked Ratna turning to Pradeep.

"Vikas, how many names do you have?"

Ratna looked real puzzled and turned enquiringly to Raj.

"I am Vikas Shah to Pradeep, but I am Raj to everybody else. I travelled to Sri Lanka for an important assignment and had a cover name. I will tell you the reason soon but do not press me today."

"Well Raj you did appear mysterious at times but I have to thank you for giving me company at Kandy; I was very disturbed and distressed after Vijaya's tragic death. She had inadvertently got involved with some undesirable people and their activities. Satish Sharma was very discreet and appears to be under pressure not to disclose much. He said he would reveal details only after all the issues had been resolved and they had a case to submit before the courts for prosecution."

"Raj has been very mysterious too, but I am sure he knows something, isn't it Raj?" Ratna asked accusingly.

"Come, come how can I know? These are police matters and Satish is an old friend. Coincidently I met him after a long time just when you wanted to find out more about Vijaya's case. Then it so happened I was visiting Sri Lanka on a business trip and Satish asked me to find out about Pradeep from my friends in Kandy. Then by sheer luck I ran into Pradeep at the dinner hosted by our Deputy High Commissioner in Kandy. We got talking when he found that I had met you recently in Mumbai. In fact I should thank you for introducing him and for the lovely holiday I had at his tea estate. I have very little idea about the case; in fact I haven't even met Satish since I got back from Colombo."

Raj made a brave effort to keep his identity secret from the two.

The waiter brought in the food and the conversation drifted to the latest cultural events in the city.

# NEW DELHI

The day after Suhasni's wedding Venkat got busy in the Cabinet Secretariat consulting various groups on the final draft of the Nuclear Doctrine. He had a long meeting with the National Security Adviser, Admiral Ravi Menon. Later he had a meeting with the Air, Naval and Army chiefs on their latest assessments on threat perceptions as well as amendments suggested to the draft doctrine. The major emphasis was to make the doctrine more robust to deter the enemy from first strike as opposed to the existing draft doctrine which provided for a massive punitive response to inflict unacceptable damages on the foe after his first strike. The Director General of the Strategic Nuclear Command, Lt. General Sudhir Nambiar submitted his paper on the proactive response mode of deployment of land based Strategic nuclear missiles and the tactical Brahmos; the nuclear submarine based missiles and the tactical air command nuclear strike force. The naval arm had been strengthened since the last review by the induction of the indigenously built nuclear submarine 'INS Vajra' capable of carrying twelve missiles with nuclear warheads. This was the third submarine of its kind added to the Western Naval Command and was on patrol in the Indian Ocean and the Arabian Sea. Two others were deployed with the Eastern Naval Command in the Bay of Bengal and were on patrol duty through the Malacca

Straits up to the South China Sea. The discussions got over around six-thirty after which Venkat went to his office in the North Block where Saxena was waiting for him.

Saxena had prepared his draft report on the investigations on the Collins abduction, the Cuckoos' Nest case and the clandestine project in Dadyal to train terrorists to assemble and arm nuclear devices. These three episodes were being taken together as a continuous stream of activities with the common intent to terrorize citizens and coerce governments around the world. The investigations carried out by the Russian Intelligence into the activities of the terrorists in the Central Asian region and their close nexus with Qaeda elements was also incorporated in the draft as corroborative evidence of the conspiracy bank rolled by the ISI. This report was to be presented to the IAEA and the United Nations Security Council as a threat faced by the member states from the terrorist groups in possession of Weapons of Mass Destruction. The unmasking of the ISI plot, of course, would begin with the presentation of Dr. Kabir before the world media, Human Rights Watch groups, and diplomats of selected countries including all the permanent members of the UN Security Council.

Venkat and Saxena sat till past ten at night correcting and redrafting portions of the document. This was the most comprehensive indictment of the ISI as a rogue organisation with it main agenda of assisting Qaeda and its nameless proxies in bringing death and destruction to people all over the world. For both of them this was an important act of rendition of long and fruitful years of service to the nation. Both were due to retire from service in the next five months. They were the committed civil servants of the old school who had faith in the system of governance they had inherited from the earlier generation who had seen the power pass from the colonial masters to nationalist leaders and the emergence of a new nation. They also had confidence in the next generation they had helped groom and hoped that democracy would mature with the rise of young professional leaders. They only worried about the failed state next door which had lost it democratic compass and had got trapped in the jaws of the military oligarchy.

"Come Saxena lets go home. We will send this to Foreign Secretary and the Prime Minister tomorrow. Get me some news of Dr. Kabir too. I hope he is doing well after his surgery. His testimony should go a long way in sorting out the rogues."

# MUMBAI

**D**r. Kabir was discharged from the hospital after Dr. Parikh certified that he was fine and could go home. Raj moved him to the Sayadhari State Guest House on Malabar Hill as it was well guarded and a safe sanctuary for VIPs'. Dr. Parikh had advised consultation for another week before Dr. Kabir could resume his normal activities. So for the next week, Raj was his only visitor besides a doctor from Dr. Parikh's team came every morning at nine for a routine check up. Raj would invariably drop in at five thirty in the evening and stay with him till dinner time. He found him a very erudite and humorous person. Raj asked him one day as to what happened after he was picked up in Dhaka from his family home in 1971. At first he was reluctant to talk as recollecting the events of those tumultuous days in Dhaka brought back memories of his family and friends; but soon Raj gained his confidence and Dr. Kabir opened up.

He spoke one night after persuading Raj to stay back for dinner. He talked of his days in the US and his marriage to Payal and the birth of his daughter Vijaya after he had returned home and joined the Atomic Energy Commission of Pakistan as a junior scientist. He spoke emotionally of his brief reunion with his wife and daughter in Pakistan and then losing them after the disturbances in Dhaka and his long incarceration. He spoke at length of his house arrest in Islamabad and the pressure he was under to resume his research and his work at the atomic energy plant at Kahuta. He had refused to work for them and considered himself a citizen of Bangladesh and therefore a prisoner of war. He was subjected to mental torture and was told that he had been reported missing after the night of the slaughter of intellectuals in Dhaka, and presumed dead by his family. The AECP had also officially declared him missing from Dhaka and had informed the IAEA accordingly. The Human Rights Watch too had been told by the government that his whereabouts were not known after his visit to Dhaka to attend the regional seminar. For more than five years in captivity he had no news of his family and then one day he was shown pictures of his wife Payal and daughter Vijaya in Kolkata. They had been stalking his wife and managed to take more than a dozen pictures of them on different occasions and different places in the city.

"I was happy to get some news about my family. My daughter had grown since I last saw her off at the Islamabad airport on the flight home, just before my visit to Dhaka for the Seminar. I had a premonition then that politically the situation was not good within the country and soon we Bengalis would be in difficulties. So I managed to send Payal and Vijaya to safety. The next two months proved that I had done the right thing. The country went through a major turmoil and genocide let loose on the people of East Pakistan province by the military leaders of the country. The rest is history and you are well aware of it."

He paused and took a few sips of water.

"A few weeks later they showed me more photos of Payal and Vijaya. I pleaded with them to let me go home but they insisted that I should resume my work at the Kahuta Research Center. Then one day a senior ISI officer came to persuade me and threatened to harm my family if I refused. This was too much for me. I was helpless and had no way of warning them of the dangers they might be exposed to. I did not eat for two days and refused to talk to my captors. On the third day that officer returned. This time he had come in his army uniform. From the emblems of the ranks on his shirt I could make out that he was a Brigadier and the name tag gave his name as Parvez Mahmud. He was very courteous but repeated his proposition that I cooperate with them. I had no choice, he said and I had to give in. He promised to bring me news of my family if I cooperated and said that he would also permit me to telephone Payal on condition that she would not reveal anything. If she did, he would be shot. The same evening they connected me to Payal; she was shocked beyond belief and could not speak for a few moments. She said she knew I was alive and wanted to know where I was. I said I cannot give any details but that I was in Pakistan living comfortably and well looked after. I then told her that she must not reveal my existence to any one."

"The next day I was taken in the AECP staff car to Kahuta. They gave me a room in the main research center and arranged my meetings with the Director and other scientists. Some of them I knew as they had been my colleagues. There were others, all foreigners, whom I had not met. They were from China, North Korea, Iran, Sri Lanka and Libya. They were introduced as guest scientists. I started work on my old project from that day onwards living in the hope that my family would not be harmed and that someday I would be united with them. Years passed and there were no signs of my being released from captivity.

I wanted to go back to my country which had emerged after the Pakistani Generals surrendered to the Indian Army after months of struggle and bloodshed. Whenever I enquired about my return to Bangladesh they would avoid any commitment. Brig. Mahmud even suggested that I should get married again, hinting that I should forget ever going back. I was very upset to hear this and went into a depression. I was hospitalized for almost a month and when I got back they resumed the process of coercion. I had little choice but to do their bidding. By resuming my research work I could at least provide security to Payal and Vijaya. They brought me new pictures of Payal and Vijaya every six months. Then one day the Brigadier informed me that Payal was unwell and had been hospitalized. I was very worried for her and wanted to speak to her, but they would not permit."

"It was about a month after he gave the news; Parvez came to my lab one day and informed me that Payal had expired that morning. She had died of cancer; I was devastated. I mourned Payal in my loneliness and prayed for Vijaya's safety and wellbeing. Over the next few months I reconciled to my fate and continued working at the research center. But my heart was not in my work and never gave them my best. They were now keeping watch on Vijaya and brought me her photographs every now and then. She was growing into a charming young lady. She had joined a company in Chicago after Payal expired but moved back to India just after a year and took up work in Mumbai with a large corporate house, I was told. They denied my request to speak to her, however. Then early last year they approached me and said they would let me talk to Vijaya for three minutes on the same conditions as earlier. I was very ecstatic. They connected me to her one day and she was thrilled to hear my voice. She said that Payal had told her before she died that Baba was alive and held hostage in Pakistan. She asked me if I was okay and taking care of my health.

"Baba don't worry about me. Take care of yourself. I am waiting for you," she said.

"I was happy that I had at last spoken to Vijaya. My captors were satisfied that I looked more composed and assigned me some additional project work. I did not realize at first but they were involving me gradually in the secret project of manufacturing nuclear weapons. They said that if I cooperated they would allow me to call Vijaya every week. Brig. Parvez Mahmud came and met me again. He was in good humor and enquired about my welfare and my work. He also enquired about Vijaya and hoped she was well. He made it a habit after that to drop by every now and then. Brig. Mahmud also gave me company during the Ramzan month of fasting and joined me in prayers and the rituals of breaking of the fast. On Id he visited me with gifts and sweets and embraced me warmly. He asked me if I was happy and I replied by asking him if he would be if he was held in captivity against his will. No of course not, he said but then added that as Muslims we had to come together and destroy the enemies of our faith. I asked him who these enemies of our faith were and he gave me a long lecture on Jihad and spoke like a fundamentalist preacher. I told him I was shocked to hear a high ranking military officer speak the language of the Taliban and Qaeda. He smiled and said that the lessons of Jihad have to replace the doctrine of warfare learnt by our defense forces from the colonial masters of the past. The whole country was a madarssa now and every soldier a mujahedeen. I was disgusted by his preaching and got up and said that at least on the auspicious day of the ID, we should wish everybody peace and happiness. He left saying that I should learn to be a faithful Muslim and become a true soldier of the faith."

"I spent the next few days thinking what the Brigadier had said. I felt annoyed by the very thought of working with such people. I remembered the days in Chicago where I was happy with my work. Payal was finishing her programme in the Columbia University, and was planning to join me soon. I cursed myself for coming back; we were young then and we wanted to be happy in our own country, with our own people. Look what it has done to my family."

It was late one evening when Brig. Mahmud turned up again. He said he wanted to involve Vijaya in some work. I said that she had nothing to do with us and that he should not even think of her to say the least. He was furious and raised his voice saying that I should cooperate in the name of faith and the country. I was upset and told him to get out.

"Do you think you have any choice in the matter? You will do what we want you to do. If you defy us, I will have Vijaya destroyed like this," he said snapping his fingers on my face.

It was like a bolt of lightening that hit me. I never realized the depths to which Parvez and his conspirators could sink to demean the good name of our faith. I was really dealing with the messengers of Satan and not the faithful. I was helpless and pleaded with him not to touch my daughter and that I was fully cooperating with them.

He said he wanted Vijaya to help them do something which was very simple and posed no physical danger. The entire process would be explained to her by some people in Mumbai and that she had only to follow instructions received via internet and maintain some accounts. Raj, I was very worried about Vijaya and her safety; these people were dangerous and I wanted no harm to come to her due to my mistakes and short comings. I had become a victim of their coercion and blackmail and now I was dragging Vijaya to become a part of some conspiracy. I had to agree and tell her to accept the assignment for my sake, and asked her to forgive me."

Dr. Kabir was quiet for a long while; he got up from his bed and walked over to the balcony staring at the bright lights of the 'diamond necklace', as the Marine Drive, stretching along the curved bay, appears at night.

"Dr. Kabir we were investigating the AECP's activities in Dadyal, which we had discovered by chance. Were you and your team training non state combatants to handle weapons of mass destruction?"

"The ISI had a clandestine project of arming a few terrorists with such devices. These were being developed at a secret facility managed by the ISI. It was not a project of the AECP. But ISI associated us to train some non state agents in the safe handling procedures for fissile material. The intentions of the ISI were mischievous. Their intention appears to be to arm and motivate some terrorist organisation to use these devices against selected targets to achieve their political objectives in Afghanistan or India. I am sure they will destroy Pakistan in the process."

"Tell me Raj, how I can find Vijaya in the vast concrete jungle of this city?"

Raj was happy that his investigations in The Cuckoo's Nest case were vindicated by this first hand narration of Dr. Kabir's saga of captivity, coercion and blackmail. All the pieces he had picked up on Vijaya's story from Ratna, Pradeep and his investigations in Dhaka and Kolkata had now fallen into place. He walked up to the balcony.

"Sir she will meet you very soon."

# KHANDALA

The body recovered from Vijaya's room in the Hotel Hilltop could not be identified by the forensics experts as the face had been badly mutilated by the assailants. They had to go by DNA tests carried out on the samples of Vijaya's hair and soiled clothes recovered from her flat in Lokhandwala. The DNA report was negative establishing that it was not Vijaya who got killed in the hotel. The earlier report given to Satish by the forensics department had been tampered with; confirming identification on the basis of photos was for press consumption only. It had been deliberately done to protect Vijaya from further murderous assaults

Some doubts on the identity of the corpse found in the Hotel Hilltop had arisen in the mind of Inspector Bhonsle after he had examined the CCTV recordings closely. He found that one of the receptionists in the front office answered the description of the corpse. There were many CCTV shots of her as she was invariably on duty at the front desk in the afternoons. She had not been seen in the Hotel after the body was discovered. When confronted and grilled by Bhonsle about her absence, the Resident Manager Shaqueel Mirza identified her as Madhu Kirtikar, the chief receptionist. Apparently Mirza and Madhu were carrying on an affair and would meet regularly in some vacant room of the hotel. The evening of the murder,

Mirza knew that Vijaya was not in her room. Frightened out of her wits by her two visitors earlier in the afternoon she had phoned the Resident Manager and told him that she was urgently required in Mumbai and would return the next day. She left the keys with him and hurriedly packed her bag and left with her lap top. In her hurry she left her mobile phone which she had put for charging on the bedside table. She only realized this after she drove out of the hotel in the taxi Shaqueel Mirza had arranged for her to go to Mumbai.

That evening Shaqueel Mirza and Madhu Kirtikar met in Vijaya's room and spent a few pleasant hours together. Mirza left for his apartment around midnight and Madhu decide to sleep off in the room and return home in the morning. Some time after Mirza left some persons knocked on the door. Madhu opened the door and was caught by the two assailants. They locked the door of the room and after gagging her, brutally assaulted her. As it was dark, they mistook Madhu for Vijaya. They assaulted Madhu with iron rods and bashed in her face and skull. They left in a great hurry without disturbing the room. When the housekeeping attendant entered Vijaya's room the next morning for the routine maintenance he found the horribly battered body on the floor. He looked around and found Vijaya's phone on the charger and quietly pocketed it. He informed the front desk of the body in the room who alerted the security. Mirza was so frightened of being exposed and becoming a suspect that he did not disclose to the police that the body was of Madhu and not Vijaya's.

Vijaya reached Mumbai around nine and checked into Hotel Meridian at Sahar near the International Airport. The next morning she called her travel agent and booked a ticket for Chicago by the Air India Flight leaving early the next morning. She spent the day making arrangements to fly out of the country. She had an early dinner brought in by the room service and checked into her flight by internet, boarding forty minutes before departure. Raj had been able to trace her movements from the time she left the hotel in Khandala to her departure for Chicago by Air India Flight 127. He had also traced her to The Drake hotel in Chicago and later to the service apartment she leased just off the Michigan Avenue after she secured a job with Luca and Peabody, an accounting firm. That Vijaya was safe and in Chicago was known only to Raj, Saxena and Satish Sharma.

# MUMBAI

It was just past midnight when Raj said good night to Dr. Kabir and started back for Bandra. He was glad that he was soon going to unite a family which had almost lost everything and had been saved from the brink of total disaster. Much of what had happened was fortuitous; like Vijaya's escape from Khandala that saved her life and the daring and unsponsored operation undertaken by Gul and his band of brave Pashtuns, in the most hostile environment and right under the nose of the ISI that liberated Dr. Kabir from his captivity.

He pulled out his mobile and called Pradeep. The bell rang for some time and then a sleepy Pradeep responded with a weak, "Hello Raj what's up."

"Sorry to disturb you at this late hour Pradeep, but its important. We have to meet as early as possible. I hope you have a US visa. I want you to book yourself a ticket for Chicago by the earliest flight possible. I will explain everything, but before we meet at eleven at the bar of the Jewel of India at the Nehru Center, Worli, you must have your ticket in hand."

"But can't you give me a clue . . . ," Pradeep was almost protesting.

"At eleven tomorrow and now get some rest. Good night."

# NEW DELHI

Venkat was most relaxed. The Collins rescue had been a feather in the cap of the Special Forces and the fortuitous escape of Dr. Kabir from ISI captivity was like a lottery. Its full impact would be realized soon at the press conference he had planned at Vigyan Bhawan. Venkat and his office had kept all documents ready for circulation to the press corps and the diplomats invited to attend the event; he was only waiting for a word from Saxena to fix the date. Dr. Kabir had recovered well from his surgery and his statement on his abduction and incarceration for more than thirty years had become the most important paper for circulation amongst the delegates. The statement had been recorded by the stenographers provided by Raj. He made four copies of the statement and obtained Dr. Kabir's signature on each as proof of authentication. He had sent his office assistant Ashok to Delhi with a sealed cover, containing three copies of Dr. Kabir's statement and the pen drive, to deliver to Saxena's office.

Saxena spoke with Raj the day he received the signed copies of Dr. Kabir's statement. Dr. Kabir was fine, he was informed, but Dr. Parikh his surgeon had to do a final examination. Raj said he was following it up. He also told Saxena that Vijaya Choudhry would be present in the Vigyan Bhawan when Dr. Kabir made his appearance. She was expected to be in Mumbai within the next seven days. She would also make a statement on the conspiracy of international money laundering and money transactions for terrorist operations that she was blackmailed and coerced to join to save Dr. Kabir's life. Raj said that he had already drafted a statement on her behalf on the basis of his investigations on The Cuckoo's Nest Case. He would get it authenticated from her after she arrived. This was going to be the second serious indictment of the ISI in the terrorism and nuclear blackmail agenda.

Saxena later walked across to Venkat's office for the Wednesday cabinet briefing. This was an old routine in the Home Secretary's office when all security related papers going before the Cabinet were discussed at the senior officers meeting. He got into Venkat's room before other officers assembled and briefed him on Dr. Kabir's condition. He also told him that Vijaya was coming over from the US and would accompany her father to the press conference at Vigyan Bhawan and make an independent statement on the Cuckoo's Nest case. As her statement amounted to a confession and admission of guilt attracting criminal liability, the Advocate General has been approached to get her a pardon from the court keeping in mind the circumstances of the case. The state had agreed that it would not be pressing any charges as no criminal intent had been established in her actions.

# MUMBAI

Raj found Pradeep waiting in the bar when he reached The Jewel of India. They moved on to a table in the far corner to have some privacy. It was too early for lunch and the bar was empty but Raj knew it would start filling up soon with the corporate executives from the financial district of Worli and the tourist crowd which thronged the art galleries at the Center. Raj ordered two beers and made Pradeep comfortable by asking him about his flight bookings and his visa. Pradeep had a long term business visa of the US and his travel agent had confirmed his booking by the British Airways flight via London. Pradeep looked quizzically at Raj asking why he was heading for Chicago.

"Pradeep you are going to Chicago to meet Vijaya and bring her back to Mumbai," said Raj in a matter of fact tone.

Pradeep raising his glass to sip the beer froze half way; he looked bewildered.

"Guess I have a lot of explaining to do . . . . To put it in brief, I represent an organisation of the Government of India which looks after external security and intelligence issues. We have been investigating a very serious case of money transfers by international mafia organisations for funding terror activities in the country. They were using B.K.Enterprises film financing operations as a cover for carrying out these transactions. During the course of the investigations we came across the brutal murder of one of the senior financial executives of this firm at the Hotel Hilltop in Khandala. This murder prevented us from questioning one of the king pins of this operation. As investigations progressed we got information that an Intelligence organisation in a neighboring country, with a reputation of funding and training terrorists for carrying out operations in our country, was involved. My organisation took over the case and we have now been able to reach some successful conclusions. Much of what we have discovered would be revealed to the world soon. Suffice it to say that the investigations into the murder of the financial executive by the Crime Branch have revealed that the body discovered in the Hilltop Hotel was not that of Vijaya. She had received some warning in the course of the day and had left the hotel discreetly for Mumbai in the evening. She did not go home but checked in at the Meridian at Sahar for a day and caught a flight for Chicago. She has been in Chicago since last three months. The second good news is that her father Dr. Kabir has been rescued from captivity in Pakistan and is with us. Vijaya does not know this and would be delighted to hear this news. She has not seen him for almost thirty five years. She was a child when the family got tragically separated by a civil war. You are the best person we thought who should bring her back home. I could not tell you anything till now as lives of Vijaya and her father were at stake."

"Raj this is truly amazing and almost unbelievable."

"Finish your beer and then I will take you to meet Dr. Kabir. You should be able to tell Vijaya that you met him in Mumbai."

While they drove down from Worli to Malabar Hill, Raj told Pradeep the story of Dr. Kabir's abduction and incarceration in Pakistan by the ISI. He also told him about Vijaya's childhood in Kolkata where her mother worked for The Statesman. He gave him some idea of how Dr. Kabir was rescued by Gul from Dadyal and brought to Kabul where he was granted political asylum at the Indian Embassy, and secretly flown to Mumbai.

At the Sayadhari Guest House, Dr. Kabir had just finished his lunch and was pacing up and down in the lounge. He saw Raj and raised his hand to welcome him.

"Come my friend I was waiting for you; Dr. Parikh was here and has certified me fit to travel and resume my work."

"Sir, meet Pradeep Menon a very good friend of Vijaya. He is flying to Chicago tomorrow to bring her back to Mumbai."

"Thank you Pradeep, please bring her home soon. She was this high," he gestured with his hand up to his waist, "when I last saw her off with her mother at the Islamabad airport for New Delhi."

# CHICAGO

Vijaya had now been in Chicago for three months. The memory of her providential get away from Khandala and the night of terror she spent locked in her room in the hotel in Mumbai were still fresh. She had read the screaming headlines about her death in the Times of India on the flight to Chicago.

## Vijaya Choudhry financial consultant with B. K. Enterprises, brutally murdered in Khandala Hotel

The reports had identified her by name and called the murder a possible crime of passion. Vijaya had shuddered and pitied the poor girl who had unknowingly become the target of the vengeance of her enemies.

Vijaya read the chilling account over and over again. She remembered her escape from certain death and her drive to Mumbai that night. She had checked into the Meridian Hotel at the Sahar and spent a sleepless night. She knew she could not stay here any longer. She had to get out of the country; she was up against the mafia and international terrorists who would not spare her. She called her travel agent next morning and booked herself by the first available flight for Chicago. They had copies of her passport and confirmed her booking immediately. She hired a limousine for the day and drove down to the bank and picked up her passport and five thousand dollars she had kept in the locker. Next she drove down to Lower Parel and picked up some clothes and travel bags at the Phoenix Mall. She returned to her hotel by six and spent an hour packing her clothes. She asked reception to wake her up at midnight and arranged a drop to the airport.

She had heaved a sigh of relief as the aircraft lifted off the runway just before daybreak through the smoky mist of the shanties of Santa Cruz, the swanky bungalows and apartments of Juhu and the murky grey—blue waters of the Arabian Sea. It had taken her quite a while to compose herself. Soon she drifted into drowsiness and fitful sleep; she had hardly slept since the evening she got away from Khandala, more than thirty hours ago. She had been terrified by the threats made by the two visitors who met her at the Hotel Hilltop. She was unhappy with her decision to leave the country, but there was no alternative. If her assailants found that she had got away and they had killed the wrong person they would come after her again. Her only chance was that her secret was never discovered and she was considered dead. Her sole regret was that there was no means of communicating with her Baba, and said a silent prayer for him. She was too tired to think any more and finally drifted into a drugged sleep.

At Chicago she checked in at The Drake on Michigan Avenue for two days and then moved into a studio apartment just off the main street. On the following Monday she went to the office of Luca and Peabody, an accounting firm where she had worked earlier and joined as a consultant. She settled down on her job and tried to put her past behind her. It had been three months to the day since she joined her assignment when she got a call from the reception saying she had a visitor from India who gave his name as Pradeep Menon. Vijaya was stunned. How did Pradeep find her in far away Chicago? She thought it was a prank; still worried of her assailants. There was a rush of adrenal in her veins and she found her palms sweating. She went to a spot in the hall from where the front desk and the reception lounge were visible. Her heart was throbbing in her rib cage from fear and expectation when she spotted Pradeep standing at the reception desk in nervous anticipation. She started walking towards the reception and the last few paces were definitely a slow jog. She pushed the glass door wide open and dashed towards Pradeep who saw her and also started to move in her direction. She was in his arms and he was holding her face in his hands and kissing her with great passion, to the great amusement of the receptionist and other visitors. They soon realized that they had provided much entertainment and it was better to get away and seek some privacy.

"Pradeep lets get out of here; just wait a bit while I reschedule my meetings for the day."

They headed towards the Millennium Park and found a parking slot. They walked past Anish Kapur's spectacular sculpture "The Cloud Gate" and strolled along the Lake Front. Pradeep told her about her father, how he was rescued to Kabul and then flown to Mumbai. He told her about his meeting with him and how he was impatiently waiting for her. She was crying all the while and just clung on to him. She was happy and was at peace with herself after a long time.

"I am famished Pradeep, lets have some lunch and then we will get our bookings done" said Vijaya.

They walked up to Bistro 110 near North Michigan Avenue. Vijaya suggested the meal-French onion soup, steak and crème Brule for dessert. The meal was excellent and they washed it down with a glass of white wine. They chatted about the old times and the varieties of food they had sampled together on the streets of Mumbai and Khandala. They talked about the few common friends they had and Pradeep told her about the dinner with Raj and Ratna at the United Services Club. She wanted news about Ratna and enquired about Raj.

"He is the one who told me that you were alive and in Chicago just two days ago and later had taken me to meet Dr. Kabir. He knows all about your family and the coercion and blackmail you were subjected to. He knows about the racket you got involved in because they threatened to harass Dr. Kabir or probably kill him if you did not cooperate. He and his organisation has done much to free Dr. Kabir, but they had to do this to prevent the Qaeda terrorists from acquiring weapons of mass destruction, a project in which they had involved Dr. Kabir. Apparently they had assembled a group of rogue scientists who were blacklisted by the IAEA and put them in various locations to manufacture kits for a nuclear device. One group was to operate from Myanmar. They had even managed to kidnap a British National from Majuli in Assam and taken him to Myanmar to seek release of a Sri Lankan Tamil engineer serving a long term in a British prison on charges of smuggling contraband nuclear sensitive components. The LTTE which is part of this international conspiracy had funded that part of the operation. Another group is located in Yemen and they were recently involved in the smuggling of missile and war head components from the Russian nuclear weapons dismantled under the treaty following the SALT agreements between the Soviets and the US. The money laundering racket which you had helped operate in Mumbai was the financial component of the conspiracy to assemble a nuclear device in the country. Dr. Kabir who was then working at the AECP Research Center at Kahuta was made a part of the conspirator's team training one set of terrorists at Dadyal, in the Pakistan Occupied Kashmir, to prime the device with the nuclear core and make it ready for detonation."

Vijaya heard with baited breath as Pradeep narrated the entire story of intrigue and conspiracy, the brain child of the ISI, for carrying on Qaeda's Jihad. She felt relieved that the worst was over for her father and she felt excited at the thought of meeting him. They walked over to Vijaya's car and drove over to the travel agent. They got confirmed bookings on a flight leaving Chicago for Mumbai the next day.

# MUMBAI

The meeting of the father and daughter was too poignant for Raj to witness. He therefore decided to leave Pradeep and Vijaya on the second floor lift lobby of the guest house and promised to join them after half and hour or so. Earlier in the morning he had met them at the airport when their flight arrived from Chicago. He had never met her before and had only seen her photographs. He found her very charming and vivacious. She had held his hand and thanked him profusely for getting her father back to her. She wanted to rush to the guest house but Raj advised her against it. It was two in the morning and would disturb Dr. Kabir. They had gone to Pradeep's house on the Napean Sea Road after dropping Raj at his flat in Bandra. Later Raj had picked them up and brought them to the Sayadhari Guest House.

Raj found Vijaya and Dr. Kabir seated on the sofa with Vijaya's arms around her father. He attempted to stand up as Raj entered but sat down again when Raj walked up to him and placed his hands on his shoulders. He said he was very grateful to Raj and all his colleagues and that intrepid Gul who had laid the deadly ambush near Dadyal and saved him. He had been all praises for Gul's bravery and the risks he took to make his escape possible. They sat around for some time and then Raj informed Dr. Kabir and Vijaya about the programme in New Delhi. They would leave for Delhi next Tuesday and the press conference had been arranged on Thursday morning at eleven. Before that Vijaya will meet the Joint Commissioner of Police, Satish Sharma to authenticate and sign a statement in connection with the Khandala murder case. Later in the day they would visit the office of the Enforcement Directorate where she would record a statement in the money laundering case to accept her responsibility. She would however plead her innocence in the circumstances of the case, which would be supported by an affidavit from the Home Ministry, Government of India which was pressing no charges against her.

# NEW DELHI

The legal formalities in the criminal cases involving Vijaya Choudhry were completed expeditiously and Dr. Kabir was received at Delhi Airport by the Protocol Officer from the Home Ministry and the High Commissioner of Bangladesh who welcomed him on behalf of their President and handed him his first Bangladesh Passport. Dr. Kabir and his daughter were treated as state guests and stayed at the Ashoka Hotel.

The press conference at the Vigyan Bhawan was well attended and there were more than a dozen foreign news channels present to record the event. The IAEA, The Human Rights Watch groups and the Interpol had sent their senior representatives. Diplomats representing the UN Security Council permanent members were all present. When Dr. Kabir moved into the hall with his daughter Vijaya, there was a thunderous applause. The printed version of Dr. Kabir's statement had already been circulated to all the invitees and they had all been shocked to read the contents.

The Protocol officer introduced Dr. Kabir and his daughter to the audience and requested Dr. Kabir to make a brief statement. Dr. Kabir thanked all those present and said that he was making the statement as an individual and not representing any country or any government. He remarked jocularly that he had become a citizen of

Bangladesh only twenty four hours ago and that he had not even stepped into this country as it was East Pakistan when he was there last and had been kidnapped by his own countrymen then, the Pakistanis.

Not far from there and in North Block, it was business as usual for Venkat. He had scanned through the pile of wireless signals received from various agencies and sent them down to his staff officer. He again read through the proposal he was placing before the Cabinet this week; he wanted to show it to the Cabinet Secretary at the afternoon meeting. The cabinet sub-committee on defense had on Monday approved the paper relating to the protocols for the deployment of nuclear war heads and Venkat was now placing the comprehensive manual prepared for the revised nuclear doctrine before the cabinet for ratification. The manual prescribed the standing operating procedures for the application of the doctrine from the war room to the theatre commanders as well commanders of the weapons systems deploying nuclear warheads. The pro active nuclear doctrine was a reality now and had been made operational. The manual also laid down the procedure for giving the go ahead for launching of the weapons at the predetermined strategic targets in the enemy territory. A fail safe system had been built into the standing operating procedure to avoid any mistake or misuse by the commanders in the field. The fire control computers could be operated only by a password and code which were kept in a vault of the weapons platform under double lock system. The keys of the vault were in the personal custody of the commander and his second officer. Both the keys had to be operated simultaneously to unlock the vault and reach for the sealed packets containing the password codes for initiating the firing sequence of the weapons control computer.

The approval for accessing the secret codes by the field commanders could only be given by the Prime Minister on the advice of the Crises Management Group under the chairmanship of the Cabinet Secretary. Other members of the group were the Home and Defense secretaries, the three Service Chiefs, the Director General Strategic Nuclear Command, secretary R&AW and the National Security Adviser. This had been a major achievement for the Group of Secretaries which had drafted all documents relating to the new doctrine under the convenorship of Venkat. The chiefs of staff committee along with the National security Adviser had prepared the protocols for deployment and firing of the weapons system carried by the surface ships, the nuclear powered submarines, fighter bombers and the ballistic missiles. For this purpose they had adopted the best procedures and practices currently in vogue in the USA, Russia, France and the UK. The Prime Minister had already briefed the heads of the states of the five permanent members of the UN Security Council regarding the new nuclear doctrine adopted by his government keeping in mind the threat perceptions.

Saxena called to say that there was some alert from the Americans and a Homeland Security advisory was expected within the hour. Pratap had called to request that all the members of the Crisis Management Group be on stand by.

"I will come over as soon as the signal from Washington DC is received," was Saxenas reply when called by Venkat's staff officer requesting him to come over to the Cabinet Secretary's office.

# NEW YORK

The CBS reporter Tim Murry had picked up the first signs of the emerging crises in the city when he suddenly heard the buzzing of around a dozen NYPD and Homeland Security SWAT team helicopters grow into a roar as he emerged at the East Houston Street Metro station just off Broadway.

The NYPD SWAT and Homeland Security crises management team were all converging to the Power Plant on Hudson Avenue in Brooklyn. A shipping container on a trailer truck had been abandoned there since early morning. The crew of the trailer had parked it and apparently walked away. The security at the Power Station noticed the trailer and checked with the maintenance department if they were expecting any delivery. On getting a negative reply they informed the NYPD which directed a patrol car cruising nearby to check out the trailer. The officer who responded called back and reported that the cabin of the truck was not locked and the keys were still in the ignition. There were no documents anywhere and the locks of the shipping container appeared tampered. The officer also reported unusually high radiation levels registered on the sensors placed in his patrol car. The entire precinct was placed on high alert and evacuation ordered in the radius of eight miles after the chopper borne teams confirmed dangerous levels of radiation.

Tim Murry got a spate of mails and alerts on his Blackberry. His office had been trying to reach him since the news broke out and his camera crew was already in the CBS chopper waiting to pick him up. He hailed a cab and raced to his office calling for updates on the developing story. The FBI had got the alert from the London Metropolitan Police that they had picked up a British Citizen of Asian origin, who had revealed the plot of three devices having been placed in New York, London and Mumbai. The device planted in the container discovered in Brooklyn was one of those. The Mumbai device was with the terrorist group sent across the LOC in Kashmir. Their location was not known, but New Delhi was on high alert and security teams were carrying out raids in Kashmir and other known hide outs of the ultras. The location of the device in London was also not known but Scotland Yard and MI 5 were carrying out an electronic scan of the city.

The CBS chopper was allowed to land and drop Tim Murray and his crew at the Prospect Park in Brooklyn where the NYPD had set up a crisis management and information center. All approaches to the Manhatten Bridge were blocked and all ferry services on the East River had been closed down. An area of eight kilometers radius was being evacuated and all personnel within three kilometers radius were issued special radiation containment suits.

# NEW DELHI

Saxena almost ran across from his room in the Cabinet Secretariat to the Cabinet Secretary's meeting room where the Crisis Group was to assemble. He stopped at the entrance to catch his breath and then charged up the imposing red limestone stairway with the message from Washington still in his hand. He collapsed into one of the comfortable stuffed chairs and held out the message to Venkat without uttering a word. Venkat scanned the message and stared at Saxena in disbelief and then towards the Cabinet Secretary who stretched out his hand to take the message. He called the PM on the hotline.

"Sir, we are in condition red. The Crisis Group is already in meeting and we have alerted the Tactical Nuclear Command to deploy. The Air Force Sukhoi 30's are on combat patrol over Ambala, carrying Brahmos nuclear tipped missiles and the Naval Command has reported that one submarine, the INS Vajra is already at the launch site in the Arabian Sea. The Vajra is carrying thirty nuclear missiles. We will wait for further developments before breaking the seals on the launch codes. You may use the hotline to Pakistan Prime Minister and advice him to abort the mission within six hours failing which we launch our missiles."